NEW YORK REVIEW BOOKS
CLASSICS

THE GATE

NATSUME SŌSEKI (1867–1916) was born the youngest of eight
children during the last year of the Tokugawa shogunate in Edo, the
city shortly to be renamed Tokyo, and became the defining writer of
the Meiji period (1868–1912). Raised by foster parents until he was
nine, he made a faltering start at school but soon displayed a special
aptitude for Chinese studies and later for the English language,
ultimately earning an advanced degree in English literature. As an
undergraduate at Tokyo Imperial University, he published an essay
on Walt Whitman that introduced the poet's work to Japan. After
teaching for several years, Sōseki was sent in 1900 to England for two
years by the Ministry of Education. Upon his return he succeeded
Lafcadio Hearn in the English department at Tokyo Imperial
University. Sōseki published his first work of fiction in 1905, the
opening chapter of what would become the famous satirical novel *I
Am a Cat*. In 1907, offered a position with the Asahi Newspaper
publishing company, he left teaching to become a full-time writer,
and proceeded to produce novels at the rate of one a year until his
death from a stomach ulcer in 1916. Other major works to have
appeared in English translation include *Botchan*, *Kusamakura*, *The
Miner*, and *Kokoro*.

WILLIAM F. SIBLEY (1941–2009) was a professor of East Asian
languages and civilizations at the University of Chicago. A translator
of Japanese fiction and nonfiction, Sibley was at work on Sōseki's
First Trilogy, comprising *Sanshirō*, *And Then*, and *The Gate*, at the
time of his death.

PICO IYER is the author of several books, including *Video Night in
Kathmandu*, *The Lady and the Monk*, *The Global Soul*, and, most
recently, *The Man Within My Head*. He is a frequent contributor to
The New York Review of Books and *Harper's*. He lives in Japan.

THE GATE

NATSUME SŌSEKI

Translated from the Japanese by
WILLIAM F. SIBLEY

Introduction by
PICO IYER

NEW YORK REVIEW BOOKS

New York

THIS IS A NEW YORK REVIEW BOOK
PUBLISHED BY THE NEW YORK REVIEW OF BOOKS
435 Hudson Street, New York, NY 10014
www.nyrb.com

Edward Fowler contributed to the editing of this translation.

Library of Congress Cataloging-in-Publication Data
Natsume, Sōseki, 1867–1916.
 [Mon. English]
 The gate / by Natsume Sōseki ; introduction by Pico Iyer ; translation by
William F. Sibley.
    p. cm. — (New York Review books classics)
 "Edward Fowler contributed to the editing of this translation."
 ISBN 978-1-59017-587-3 (alk. paper)
 1. Japan—Fiction. I. Sibley, William F. II. Title.
 PL812.A8M613 2012
 895.6'34—dc23

                        2012028093

ISBN 978-1-59017-587-3
Available as an electronic book; ISBN 978-1-59017-600-9

Printed in the United States of America on acid-free paper.
10 9 8 7 6 5 4 3 2 1

INTRODUCTION
Sōseki and the Art of Nothing Happening

JAPANESE literature is often about nothing happening, because Japanese life is, too. There are few emphases in spoken Japanese—the aim is to remain as level, even as neutral as possible—and in a classic work like *The Tale of Genji*, as one recent translator has it, "The more intense the emotion, the more regular the meter." As in the old-fashioned England in which I grew up—though more unforgivingly so—the individual's job in public Japan is to keep his private concerns and feelings to himself and to present a surface that gives little away. That the relation of surface to depth is uncertain is part of the point; it offers a degree of protection and makes for absolute consistency. The fewer words spoken, the easier it is to believe you're standing on common ground.

One effect of this careful evenness—a maintenance of the larger harmony, whatever is happening within—is that to live in Japan, to walk through its complex nets of unstatedness, is to receive a rigorous training in attention. You learn to read the small print of life—to notice how the flowers placed in front of the tokonoma scroll have just been changed, in response to a shift in the season, or to register how your visitor is talking about everything except the husband who's just run out on her. It's what's not expressed that sits at the heart of a haiku; a classic sumi-e brush-and-ink drawing leaves as much open space as possible at its center so that it becomes not a statement but a suggestion, an invitation to a collaboration.

The reader or viewer is asked to complete a composition, and so the no-color surfaces make for a kind of intimacy: "Kyoto is lovely, isn't it?" is one of the most important sentences in Sōseki's novel *The*

Gate, and the other protagonist's response to it, quintessence of Japan, is to think to himself, "Yes, Kyoto was lovely indeed." For the visitor who has just arrived in the country of conflict avoidance, the innocent browser who's just picked up a twentieth-century Japanese novel, it means that the first impression may be of scrupulous blandness, an evasion of all stress, self-erasure. For those who've begun to inhabit this world, it means living in a realm of constant inner explosions, under the surface and between the lines.

It's perhaps no surprise, then, that Sōseki (his family name is Natsume, but he's usually known by his pen name, derived from a Chinese term meaning "stubborn") is still, ninety-six years after his death, the Japanese novelist most honored in his nation's classrooms and until recently featured on the back of every thousand-yen note (equivalent to our ten-dollar bill). His protagonists are masters of doing nothing at all. They abhor action and decision as scrupulously as Bartleby the scrivener does with his "I prefer not to"; the drama in their stories nearly always takes place within, in secrets revealed to or by them. This creed of doing nothing is a curious one in a country that seems constantly on the move, but in Sōseki's world doing nothing should never be mistaken for feeling too little or lacking a vision or doctrine.

The Gate is a perfect example of this. On its surface, it's just the story of Sōsuke and Oyone, a determinedly self-effacing couple in a small house in Tokyo in the first decade of the twentieth century, when the book was written. Sōsuke, for reasons that furnish the gradual drama of his story, has all but stepped out of the official world, even though (and sometimes because) he feels such a rich sense of duty toward so many of its members. The book delights, more than any Sōseki book I've read, in the everyday details of the late-Meiji landscape, from gas lamps to cigarettes and men in greatcoats to the sound of a wooden fish-block from the local temple. Yet its author, unexpectedly, goes out of his way to stress that his protagonists are living in "mundane circumstances," as befits those who are "lackluster and thoroughly ordinary to begin with." In a certain light, the entire story is about what never comes to pass: a character falls ill, and then nothing much happens; a long-feared reunion fails to take place; a search for spiritual revelation seems to reveal very little.

Look closer, however, and you can see how everything is happening, between the spaces and in the silences. To take an example almost at random, chapter 5 begins with Sōsuke's aunt, much discussed but always somewhere else, finally visiting his house, and exchanging pleasantries—you could call them platitudes—with her nephew's wife. Nothing could be more ordinary or without effect. Yet notice that the aunt's first comment is about how unnaturally "chilly" the room is, and recall that the external temperature, and especially the slow cycling of the seasons, are always telling us something about mood and tone in this book. Part of the beauty of the novel comes from the way that it begins, very carefully, in autumn, takes us through the dark and cold of winter, and ends, in its final passage, with the arrival of spring.

We also learn, in the chapter's opening paragraphs, that Sōsuke's aunt (on whom his welfare seems to depend) looks strikingly young for her age; we've already been told that Sōsuke—as his aunt likes to stress—looks unreasonably old for his. We read that Sōsuke ascribes his aunt's healthy appearance to her having only one child, yet even that thought underlines the fact that he and Oyone have none. As the laughter of kids drifts down from the landlord's house up the embankment—the location itself is no coincidence and sounds coming in from outside are at least as important here as the words that are never exchanged—Sōsuke's wife can't help feeling "empty and wistful." The aunt then says that she owes the couple an apology—which conspicuously prevents her from actually offering one—and refers pointedly to her son's graduation from university (since Sōsuke, we've already been told, owes much of his present predicament to having dropped out).

The whole scene might be taking place around me, every hour, in the modern Western suburb of the eighth-century Japanese capital, Nara, where I've been living for twenty years. "Oh, you look so well," a woman says to another, outside the post office, emphasizing, with a craft worthy of a Jane Austen character, that she didn't before, and might not be expected to now. "It's only because I have so little to worry about," the other will respond, to put the first one in her place. "It's hot, isn't it?" the first will now say, perhaps to suggest that nothing lasts forever. "Isn't it?" says the second, and no observer could find any evidence for the combat that's just been concluded.

As Sōsuke's aunt, in *The Gate*, goes on about how her son is getting into "com-buschon engines," and on his way to profits so "huge" they could ruin his health, she's drawing attention to the money she's not giving to Sōsuke, the success of her son by comparison, and, in Meiji Japan, the fact that her progeny is eagerly taking on the Western and the modern world, and is not stuck in his Japanese ways and the past, as Sōsuke seems to be. Sōsuke himself, meanwhile, is characteristically absent, at the dentist's office, taking care of a problem that his wife ascribes to age.

One magazine he picks up in the dentist's waiting room is called *Success*, and in its pages he reads of the furious forward movement that is exactly what seems closed to him. He also reads therein a Chinese poem, about drifting clouds and the moon, and finds himself at once moved by the realm of changeless acceptance and natural calm it describes, yet excluded from its quietude, too. When the dentist appears—he also has a "youthful-looking face" despite his thinning hair—he tells Sōsuke that his teeth are rotting and his condition is "incurable." He then removes a "thin strand" of nerve. Back home, Sōsuke picks up a copy of Confucius's *Analects* before going to sleep, but they have "not a thing" to offer him.

Nothing much has happened, you might say, if you consider the seven pages that have just passed. But we've learned more about Sōsuke, his anxiety, his relations with his aunt, his premature sense of decay, and his (and his culture's) inability to commit themselves either to Success or to old China than any amount of drama could provide. Everything is there, if only you can savor the ellipses.

Literary critics will tell you that Sōseki was almost unique among the writers of his day because he was sent on a Japanese Ministry of Education program to live in England at the age of thirty-three, and brought back from his two years there an even more pronounced taste for the nineteenth-century European fiction he'd already mastered at home. They will remind you that he was born in 1867, a year before the Meiji Restoration changed the face of Japan, releasing it from more than two hundred years of self-imposed isolation (since 1635 or so, it had been illegal for any Japanese to leave the nation). They will note that he became the defining novelist of the Meiji period in part because he embraced in his life the central question of the day, which was how his country could combine "Japanese spirit, Western technology," as it called it, trying to elide through slogan-making what could be whole centuries of differences. The great novelists who would follow later in the century—Yasunari Kawabata, Junichirō Tanizaki, and Yukio Mishima—would all, in their different ways, be writing about how Japan had already lost its integrity and its soul to the West.

Sōseki's time in London was famously miserable—he felt himself "a poor dog that had strayed among a pack of wolves" and almost lost his mind amongst what seemed to him cold people and strange customs—but after his return to Japan, he took over Lafcadio Hearn's position teaching English literature at Tokyo Imperial University, the country's Harvard (and Sōseki's alma mater, where he had been only the second Japanese to graduate in English literature). He left the university in 1907, after a series of nervous breakdowns, and then published nearly all his fourteen novels in nine years before dying in Tokyo, where he had been born, at forty-nine, in 1916, four years after the Meiji period ended. He dabbled in stream-of-consciousness narratives, Arthurian tales, satires, detective stories, and travel pieces, yet even the titles of his books often stress the fact of nothing happening. *Sorekara* simply means "And Then," while *Kokoro* is an enigmatic word for "Heart."

A little as his life story suggests, the man himself seems at once profoundly Japanese and something of a rebel; over and over in his books we meet a quiet maverick who, because of some moment of passion that he feels he must spend his life atoning for, has all but opted out of society, and abandoned every trace of initiative. His withdrawal from action marks him as a failure in Japanese terms, but it may also suggest his deference to "the inexorable workings of karmic retribution," as *The Gate*'s narrator puts it—and even a pride at not participating in a world of ambition and exploitation. Sōseki's wounds are never far from the surface of his books—the hovering around a gate through which his characters will never pass, figures in dire financial straits with holes in their shoes and leaky ceilings, an obscure sense that there is "guilt in loving." His characters defect from Japanese society without quite arriving anywhere else.

The Gate puts us into its prevailing mood—and theme—with its very first paragraph. A man is lying on his veranda in the autumn light of a regular Sunday, and almost immediately we are in the relaxed, undramatic world of day-to-day life, while also feeling an edge to things, allied perhaps to that character's "case of nerves." The novel seems to abound in casual descriptions of Tokyo in 1909—we hear the "clatter of wooden clogs" in the street, see the ads in a streetcar ("WE MAKE MOVING EASY"), read of posters advertising a new movie based on a Tolstoy story. But of course none of these details is casual, and all intensify the sense of restlessness and regret that seems to haunt the man on his veranda. The more Sōsuke keeps insisting on how his is a life of no consequence, the more we may wonder what all this deliberate stasis is concealing.

Thus the novel quickly establishes itself as a story of absences and withholdings, about all the things that aren't spoken about, but that keep on ticking away in the background like the couple's pendulum clock. The prematurely old and settled young partners, going through their unchanging motions, look at Sōsuke's brother, Koroku, who is ten years younger, and feel the impatience and drive they've lost. They carefully step around everything they've been thinking about—the fact that Sōsuke longs to find what you could call the courage of his non-conviction and that their lives seem already to be behind them. Sōseki builds a powerful kind of tension precisely by giving us so little (and this is conjured up with evocative grace in this new translation by the late William F. Sibley, whose text was completed just before his death in 2009).

Observant readers of Haruki Murakami may recognize something of the highly passive, though sympathetic soul in the Tokyo suburbs bewildered by everything that seems to happen to him, or that appears to have abruptly vanished from his life (Murakami has named Sōseki his personal favorite among the "Japanese national writers"). Others may recall how even Kazuo Ishiguro, though writing in English and having left Japan at the age of six, wrote his first novel, *A Pale View of Hills*, about people from Nagasaki, a few years after the atomic bomb there, going through a whole book without mentioning it. The central fact of their lives is the one they never speak about.

But perhaps the best way into this world may be to turn to some of the movies of Yasujirō Ozu, one of the defining artists of twentieth-century Japan, whose films are famously quiet, shot at tatami level, with a camera that seldom moves, in long, slow takes, about those pressures that are never explicitly addressed—and frequently draw their titles from the seasons. In Japan, as is often noted, there are separate words for the self you show the world and the one that you reveal behind closed doors; while we regard it as a sin to be reserved at home, the Japanese take it as much more cruel to be too forthcoming in the world. This reticence has little to do with trying to protect oneself and everything to do with trying to protect others from one's problems, which shouldn't be theirs; it's one reason Japan is so confounding to foreigners, as its people faultlessly sparkle and attend to one another in public, while often seeming passive and unconvinced of their ability to do anything decisive at home.

"Under the sun the couple presented smiles to the world," Sōseki writes, in one of his most beautiful sentences here; "under the moon, they were lost in thought: And so they had quietly passed the years."

At one point Oyone asks her husband, "How are things going for Koroku?"

"Not well at all," he answers, and with that they both go to sleep.

How to adjust to a world in which the climax of a scene—and sometimes the central event—is going to sleep? We're going to have to adapt, maybe even invert our sense of priority and our assumptions about what constitutes drama, as most of us foreigners have to do when traveling to Japan. Sōseki is an unusually intimate writer—the public world is only his concern by implication—and in Japan (again as in the England that I know) intimacy is shown not by all that you can say to someone else, but by all that you don't need to say.

Thus the very fact that Sōsuke and Oyone express so little to each other in the novel seems almost to intensify the depth of their shared past; their silences say plenty. While never showing the couple touching or quite baring their hearts, Sōseki evinces a sense of closeness—you could call it love—so intense that when one of them falls ill, it becomes hard to read of the other one's fears. It's everything that doesn't get externalized that knits them together in a community of two: One central scene finds Sōsuke returning to his home to discover everyone, unsettlingly, asleep; and in perhaps the novel's most magical moment, Oyone simply walks around their house, watching her husband, then her maid in sleep. Much of the novel suggests the silent, only half-shared agitation of a couple, one of whose partners falls instantly asleep, while the other tosses and turns, wide awake.

Indeed, it's typical of the predicament—and the devotion—around which the novel turns that one partner realizes that to wake up the other might be to cause suffering; yet not to do so may be to allow a worse suffering to develop. And the arrival of any outsider, whether Sōsuke's aunt or his brother, only deepens our sense of the bond between Oyone and her husband. Sōseki was suffering from acute stomach pains while he wrote *The Gate*—they would lead to his death six years later—so perhaps it's no surprise that even a wind in the novel is so strong it can "send people into depression."

The fact of nothing happening becomes a source of almost unbearable tension in nearly all of Sōseki's novels. His protagonists keep waiting to be exposed, or for something to explode (again you can see how Ishiguro might have learned to create suspense from Sōseki, just by having a character try to outrun a past that's always gaining on him). Since Sōseki's people are nearly always hard up, and bound by many conflicting obligations, they're already paralyzed in a practical sense. And since they seem terrified of dependence on others—Sōseki himself was raised by a family not his own and appears never to have outgrown the unsettledness that brought him—their only way of claiming independence is by sitting in a prison they've made themselves.

The challenge of a novel like *The Gate* is to find a way to turn inaction into a kind of higher detachment, suggestive of the sage's refusal to be swayed by the vicissitudes of the world. One of the first things that may hit a Western reader on entering the world of a Japanese novel—though of course you can find this in Edith Wharton, too—is how every character is effectively a tiny figure in a suffocating world of associations and obligations; where many an American novel might send its protagonist out into the world to make his own destiny, in Sōsuke's Japan he cannot move for all his competing (and unmeetable) responsibilities to his aunt, his younger brother, his wife, and society itself.

Free will is not an option; for Sōsuke it would be all but heresy even to reflect on his individual longings. "For some reason I have become terribly serious since arriving here," Sōseki wrote, in his "Letter from London," a year after his arrival in England. "Looking and listening to everything around me, I think incessantly of the problem of 'Japan's future.'" Its future, then as now, involves trying to make a peace, or form a synthesis, between the ancient Chinese ideal of sitting still and watching the seasons pass, tending to social harmonies, and the new American way of pushing forward individually, convinced that tomorrow will be better than today.

It's no wonder that so many of Sōseki's characters are prematurely old; this is an old man's—an old culture's—vision, in which the past has much greater vividness than the future. Yet his people don't feel nostalgia toward what's passed so much as skepticism toward the prospect of getting a new life. New Year's Day, the central festival of the Japanese calendar, features in many of Sōseki's books, as here, and it has resonance mostly because, for figures such as Sōsuke and Oyone, there seems scant possibility of starting anew or turning a fresh page.

When Sōseki traveled to England, he complained that he couldn't even "trust myself to a train or cab...their cobweb system was so complicated." He felt patronized by the cleaning women and landladies who tried to explain their culture to him (already a teacher of English literature), and both pride and insecurity arose as he felt himself superior to people who (physically) were always looking down on him. But if you read the novels, you begin to suspect that this sense of imprisonment was simply something he took with him on the boat to England. Not only is his take on standoffish and ghostly England startlingly similar to a foreigner's response—even today—to Japan; the England he evokes, of class distinctions and wraiths and people falling on hard times, is almost identical to the Japan he describes in book after book.

In his dismissals of the "lower class" barbarians he meets and the way his bleak London boardinghouses are so far from what English literature led him to expect, he sounds in fact very much like V. S. Naipaul half a century later; yet, much like Naipaul, Sōseki, for all his unease in Britain, could seem a strikingly European figure when he went back to Tokyo, affecting a frock coat, a mustache, and a love of beef and toast. It is one of the curiosities of Japan, ever since the Meiji Restoration, that its identity has been defined largely by an identity crisis; to this day, both Japanese and those foreigners who contemplate the country keep wondering if it's leaning too much toward an outdated Confucian past or toward an unsteady Californian future. Whether progress is cyclical or linear—should people honor their ancestors or their ambitions?—sometimes seems the central question in Japan. Sōseki is one of the first writers to make it the heart of his concerns, telling individual stories that seem to speak allegorically for something much larger.

Yet what a novel like *The Gate* only slowly discloses is that all the talk of nothing happening and all the meticulous avoidance of conflict and feeling speaks only for too much feeling in the past. Sōseki had an uncommonly acute sense of the power of passion—"It is the force of blood that drives the body," he writes in his late novel, *Kokoro*—even if he chooses to concentrate on those moments when people live with the embers of what was once a devouring blaze. The problem is not that a character like Sōsuke "hated socializing"; it is that, once upon a time, he was "exquisitely socialized," a flamboyant "bright young man of the modern age," whose prospects seemed "boundless." It's only his acting too strongly that has condemned him to a life of inaction.

It takes awhile for a Western reader, perhaps, to realize that in Sōseki's novels, as in Japan, external details are not just decoration; they're the main event. It's as if foreground and background are reversed, so that it's the ads in the streetcars, the sound of laughter from a neighbor's house, the talk about the price of fish that are in fact the emotional heart of the story. A man is robbed in *The Gate* and we read on excitedly to see what has happened. But when the victim is revealed, he "did not appear in the least ruffled" and sits at home with a palpable sense of well-being, talking about his dog who's off at the vet's.

It's easy to suspect that this is the character who's found the peace that all Sōseki's characters long for, just by sitting apart from events and not letting them affect his joie de vivre. Indeed, his confidence is rewarded by his receiving back the item that was stolen from him. By the end of the novel, though unmoved by Confucius and all talk of Buddhism, Sōseki's protagonist suddenly takes off on a ten-day retreat to a Zen temple in the mountains, and there discovers a world in which the fact of nothing happening can be a kind of blessing.

Nothing can be known or controlled, Zen training teaches; the only thing you can do is scrub floors and do your rounds and perhaps clear your head in the process. Enlightenment comes nowhere but in the everyday; self-realization arrives only when you throw self—and any idea of realization—out the window. Accept life and what it gives you and then you become a part of it.

It may seem strange that Japan's favorite novelist was an anxious, passive, haunted character writing about nervous disorders and falling asleep and paralysis (even the dog at the vet's is suffering from a "nervous ailment"). But it speaks for an inner world—and again this is evident in Murakami—that sits in a different dimension from the smooth-running, flawlessly attentive, and all but anonymous machine that keeps public order moving forward so efficiently in Japan. Perhaps the novel has always been one way in which the individual can get his own back at the world; perhaps this is even one of the more useful souvenirs Sōseki brought back from his life-changing stay in England. One of his most celebrated essays, the text of a lecture delivered two years before his death, was called "My Individualism," and in it he spoke out about a "nationalism" that, only a generation later, would indeed become poisonous.

Nothing is happening on the surface of his characters' lives even as so much around them seems a whirlwind of movement and perpetual self-reinvention. But each of these may be as deceiving as the other, as evidenced by the fact that, after a century of turmoil and convulsive change, Japan seems not so different, in its questions, from where it was in Sōseki's time. In Sōseki, as in Japan, it's the fact of nothing happening that makes for a tingle of expectation, a sense of imminent passion, and, in the end, the kind of privacy that stings.

—PICO IYER

THE GATE

I

SŌSUKE had been relaxing for some time on the veranda, legs comfortably crossed on a cushion he had set down in a warm, sunny spot. After a while, however, he let drop the magazine he had been holding and lay down on his side. It was a truly fine autumn day, the sun bright, the air crisp, and the clatter of wooden clogs passing through the quiet neighborhood echoed in his ears with a heightened clarity. Tucking one arm under his head, he cast his gaze past the eaves at the expanse of clear blue sky above. Compared to the tiny space he occupied here on the veranda, this patch of sky appeared extremely vast. Thinking what a difference it made, simply to take in the sky in the rare, leisurely fashion afforded by a Sunday, he squinted directly at the blazing sun for a few moments, then, averting his eyes, rolled over to his other side and faced the shoji. Beyond its panels his wife was seated, busy with her needlework.

"Beautiful day, isn't it," he called out to her.

She murmured in acknowledgment. Sōsuke, apparently not eager to strike up a conversation himself, lapsed back into silence. Presently his wife spoke up.

"Why don't you take a stroll?"

This time it was Sōsuke who answered noncommittally.

Two, three minutes later, she brought her face up close to the glass panels in the shoji and peered out at her husband lying on the veranda. She saw that at some inner prompting he had brought his knees up to his chest, prawn-like, as if he were occupying a cramped space. His head of black hair was cradled between his arms, and his face was totally obscured by his elbows and clasped hands.

"Sleeping in such a place—why, you'll catch cold," she cautioned. She spoke in a manner characteristic of contemporary schoolgirls, in which overtones of Tokyo speech mingled with undertones from somewhere else. Peering up from between his elbows and blinking exaggeratedly, Sōsuke mumbled, "Don't worry, I'm not asleep."

Once again they fell silent. Sōsuke heard two or three rings of a bell announcing the passage of a rickshaw gliding along on rubber wheels, followed by the distant crowing of a rooster. Basking in the warm sun's rays that readily penetrated to the shirt beneath his newly tailored kimono, made from machine-spun cloth, Sōsuke passively registered the sounds. Then, as if suddenly reminded of something, he called out to his wife through the shoji.

"Oyone," he asked, "what's the character for '*kin*' in '*kinrai*'?"

"It's the same as the one for 'Ō' in 'Ōmi,' isn't it?"[1] His wife's reply contained no hint of condescension, nor was it accompanied by the sort of shrill laughter peculiar to young women.

"But that's the character I can't remember—the one for 'Ō.'"

Sliding the shoji open halfway, his wife thrust her ruler out beyond the track and with its edge traced for him the character 近 on the veranda. "Like this, you see." She said no more. The tip of the ruler rested where she had ended her tracing, and for a moment her gaze lingered intently on the pellucid sky.

"Oh, so that's it," said Sōsuke, not looking at his wife and without the faintest smile that might indicate this had all been a little joke.

Oyone, for her part, appeared to make nothing of their exchange. "Oh yes, a really fine day," she remarked, more or less to herself, and resumed her needlework, leaving the shoji half open behind her.

Sōsuke raised his head slightly from between his elbows and now looked directly at his wife for the first time. "You know, there's something amazing about Chinese characters."

"What do you mean?"

"Well, no matter how simple the character, once you get to thinking about it, it starts looking a bit odd, and suddenly you can't be sure anymore. The other day I got all mixed up over the '*kon*' in '*konnichi*.'[2] I'd put it down correctly on paper, but when I scrutinized it I got the feeling it was wrong somehow. After that, the closer I looked at what I'd written the less it looked like *kon* . . . Hasn't that ever happened to you, Oyone?"

"Certainly not."

"It's just me, then?" Sōsuke asked, bringing a hand to his head.

"Just you. There's obviously something wrong."

"I wonder if it's my nerves again."

"Yes, that must be it!" Oyone said, eyeing her husband.

At this Sōsuke got to his feet. He traversed the sitting room, stepping gingerly over Oyone's sewing basket and scattered threads, and opened the sliding panels to the parlor. Its southern exposure was blocked by the vestibule, with the result that the shoji at the other end of the room presented a distinctly chilly appearance to the gaze of someone just coming in out of the sunlight. He opened these as well. Yet even here on the eastern veranda, where one might expect the sun's rays to strike in the morning, at least, they scarcely penetrated at all because of a cliff-like embankment that loomed over this side of the house, sloping down so steeply that it all but brushed the eaves. The embankment was covered with vegetation. Lacking so much as a single row of stone revetment, it looked precariously close to crumbling down. Astonishingly, however, it seemed as though nothing of the sort had ever happened, and the landlord went along year after year simply leaving things as they had always been. An elderly produce dealer, a resident of the quarter for two decades, had offered a ready explanation for this phenomenon as he stood with his vegetables outside the kitchen door one day. According to him, this plot of land had originally been covered by a sprawling thicket of bamboo; when it was cleared, the roots had not been dug up but left buried. The earth here, the peddler had said, was in fact more stable than one might think. Sōsuke had raised some doubts: If the roots were just left there, wouldn't the bamboo grow back into a new thicket? Well, the old man had said, it seems that once it had been cut down to the ground like that it couldn't easily grow back, but there was no need to worry about the cliff; no matter what, it would not crumble down. After this spirited defense, delivered as if he had a personal stake in the matter, the old man had departed.

The face of the embankment was largely colorless. Even in autumn the green vegetation merely faded into a pale, patchy tangle. There was no touch of the elegant such as would have been provided by plumes of *susuki* grass or ivy vines. In a kind of compensation several tall, slender *mōsō* bamboo trees,[3] a vestige of the former grove, rose cleanly out of the soil, two of them halfway up the steep slope, three more near the top. The bamboo had recently taken on a yellowish hue, and whenever Sōsuke stuck his head out beyond the eaves and saw the sun's rays strike their trunks, he felt as though he were observing the warmth of autumn there atop the embankment. Sōsuke was one of those men who left home for work every morning and returned after four o'clock; normally he was far too pressed for time to take in the scenery towering above him. After exiting the unlit toilet and washing his hands in the basin, however, he happened to glance up beyond the eaves and noticed the bamboo. Leaves gathered densely atop the bamboo stalks, like the stubble on a monk's close-cropped head. As the leaves luxuriated in the autumn sunlight they drooped down heavily in silent clusters, not a single one stirring.

Sōsuke returned to the parlor, closing the shoji behind him, and kneeled down at his desk. Although the couple had designated this room the parlor, as it was the one to which guests were conducted, it might more aptly have been called a study or a living room. In the alcove in the north wall hung a token scroll, a rather peculiar one, and in front of it was displayed a misshapen, murky crimson flower vase. In the space between the alcove's lintel and the ceiling glinted two shiny brass S-hooks. No plaques hung from them. The only other item on the wall was a cabinet of shelves with glass doors that contained, however, nothing worthy of note.

Opening the desk drawer, which was trimmed with silver hardware, Sōsuke rummaged around vigorously but to no avail, and finally snapped the drawer shut. He then removed the cover from an ink stone and began writing a letter. Finished, he pondered a moment and then called to his wife in the next room.

"Oyone, what's my aunt's address in Naka Roku-Banchō?"

"Number twenty-five, isn't it?" she answered, and then, after pausing long enough for him to write it down, added, "But a letter won't do the trick. You have to go over there and have a real talk."

"First let's see if a letter won't actually work," he declared, as if to have done with it. "If it doesn't, then I'll go." His wife did not reply. "Well, what do you think?" he persisted. "Won't that do?"

Oyone, seemingly loath to disagree, protested no further.

Letter in hand, Sōsuke stepped directly from the parlor into the vestibule. When she heard his footsteps Oyone got up from the sitting room and proceeded to the vestibule by way of the veranda.

"I'm going out for a stroll," said Sōsuke.

"Enjoy yourself," his wife replied with a smile.

Half an hour later, at a rattling of the door being opened, Oyone left off with her needlework and again proceeded by way of the veranda to the vestibule, where instead of Sōsuke she found his younger brother, Koroku, wearing the cap of the secondary school[4] he attended.

"It's hot!" he said as he undid the buttons of his black woolen cloak, so long that only about six inches of his *hakama*[5] showed below the hem.

"But just look at you," said Oyone, "wearing that bulky thing on a day like this!"

"Well, I was thinking it might turn cold when the sun went down," Koroku explained hastily, before following his sister-in-law along the veranda to the sitting room. "I see you're hard at work as usual," he said, glancing at a partly stitched kimono, and sat down cross-legged in front of the long brazier. After sweeping her sewing into the corner, Oyone moved opposite Koroku, took down the tea kettle, and began putting coals in the brazier.

"If it's tea you're serving, don't make any for me," said Koroku.

"None at all?" Oyone asked in a cajoling, schoolgirlish tone. "Well, what about some sweets, then?" she said with a smile.

"You have some?" asked Koroku.

"Actually, I don't," she replied truthfully, but then, as if remembering something—"Wait a minute, there just might be..."—she rose, pushed the coal scuttle out of the way, and opened a small storage compartment attached to the wall.

Koroku stared idly at Oyone from behind, focusing on the swelling above the hips where her jacket covered her obi. Whatever she was looking for seemed to take forever to find, and so he said, "Let's skip the sweets, too—but tell me, where's my brother?"

"He went out for a while," she replied, her back still turned toward him. She was intent on her search. Eventually she clapped the compartment door shut. "Nothing! Your brother must have gobbled them up when I wasn't looking," she said as she returned to her place opposite Koroku.

"Well, then, won't you treat me to supper this evening?"

"Why, of course!" said Oyone, looking at the clock on the wall. It was nearly four o'clock. Oyone made a mental note of the two hours left before mealtime. Koroku silently studied her face. He was, in fact, not especially interested in being treated by his sister-in-law.

"Nee-san,[6] do you suppose my brother's gone to see the Saekis on my account?" he asked Oyone.

"Well, he has been saying over and over that he's going to see them, but he hasn't done so yet. But then, you know, your brother goes off in the morning and doesn't come home till evening, and when he gets home he's exhausted—even the walk to the bathhouse is a chore. So you shouldn't keep pressing him, it isn't fair."

"Yes, of course he's busy, but as long as this matter is unsettled I feel too anxious to concentrate on my studies." As he spoke, Koroku picked up the brass fire tongs and, wielding them energetically, scrawled something in the ashes in the brazier. Oyone watched the tips of the tongs move this way and that.

"But he did just send a letter to the Saekis," she said by way of consolation.

"What'd it say?"

"Well, I didn't actually see it. But I'm sure it had to do with the matter in question. When your brother comes home you should ask him yourself. I'm sure that was it."

"If he did send a letter I suppose that was probably it."

"Yes, he really did send a letter. When he left awhile ago he had it in his hand and was going to mail it."

Koroku did not wish to hear another word on the subject from his sister-in-law, whether of justification or consolation. He thought to himself with annoyance that if his brother had time to go out for a stroll, he might as well have strolled right on over to the Saekis instead of sending a letter. Entering the parlor, he took out a foreign book with a red cover from the cabinet and restlessly flipped through its pages.

2

MEANWHILE, Sōsuke, unaware of his brother's visit, had arrived at a corner shop in his neighborhood. There he purchased stamps, along with a pack of Shikishima, and wasted no time in mailing the letter. That small thing done, simply to retrace his steps homeward somehow did not suffice, so he walked on, puffing out cigarette smoke into the autumn sunlight, the urge in him to wander afar, to someplace where he could etch vividly on his mind the sensation that the very essence of Tokyo was to be found here in this spot, then take it home as a souvenir of this day, his Sunday, before he lay down to sleep. To be sure, he was a man who had for years not only lived in and breathed the air of Tokyo but who also commuted by streetcar to the office and back every day, passing twice, to and fro, through the city's bustling quarters. Neither physically relaxed nor mentally at ease, he was in the habit of simply passing through these places in a daze and had not recently experienced even a moment's awareness that he lived in a thriving metropolis. Normally, caught up as he was in the busyness of his daily routine, this did not bother him; but come Sunday, when granted the opportunity for relaxation, his workaday life would suddenly strike him as restless and superficial. He was driven to the conclusion that while living in Tokyo he had never in fact seen Tokyo, and whenever he reached this point in his thoughts he would feel overwhelmed by the bleakness, the dreariness of it all.

At times like this he would set out into the busier quarters as if suddenly remembering some errand. If he happened to have a bit extra in his pocket, he went so far as to think, Why not splurge a little on a good time? Yet his sense of dreariness was not so acute as to drive him to self-abandon; before he could rush to such an extreme, he would decide that this was all quite ridiculous and give it up. Besides, as is the rule with men like him, the limited thickness of his wallet was such as to prohibit any rash indulgence, and rather than racking his brains over timid half measures, it was easier just to keep his hands tucked in his kimono sleeves and turn toward home. And so it came about that a simple walk, or a leisurely look around an exhibition of useful products, would console his forlorn spirit enough to sustain him until the next Sunday.

Today as well, Sōsuke boarded a streetcar in a characteristic oh-well-why-not frame of mind. Once on board, however, he found things uncommonly pleasant, for in spite of the fine Sunday weather, there were fewer passengers than usual. Moreover, the expressions on these passengers' faces were peaceful; each and every one of them looked thoroughly at ease. As Sōsuke sat down he reflected on his customary weekday lot: the commute to Marunouchi[7] at a fixed hour every morning, when he would hurl himself into the no-holds-barred struggle for a seat. There could be nothing more depressing than the spectacle of his fellow riders on the streetcar at rush hour. Whether he was hanging on to a leather strap or sitting on a cushioned seat, he had never once received any impression of human warmth from this daily routine. Very well then, he would say to himself, and just sit there brushing shoulders and knees with his robotic seatmates, riding along to his destination, where he would hop up and get off. Today, however, as he watched an old woman seated opposite him murmuring into the ear of her granddaughter, who looked to be about seven years old, and then a thirtyish woman with the air of a tradesman's wife showing a friendly interest in the little girl, asking her age, her name, and the like, he felt even more keenly as though transported to another world.

Overhead hung several framed advertising posters. On his weekday rides these went completely unnoticed by Sōsuke, but now he casually glanced up at the first poster, for a moving company, and read the caption: WE MAKE MOVING EASY. The next one had three parallel lines: People Who Are Economical / People Who Care About Hygiene / People Concerned About Fire Safety; below which came the culminating message: THEY ALL USE GAS—this complemented by a picture of a gas stove with flames coming out. The third poster announced in bold white characters against a red background: ETERNAL SNOWS, by the Russian Master, Count Tolstoy[8]; and: ANYTHING-GOES FARCES by the Kotatsu Troupe.

Sōsuke took a good ten minutes perusing all the posters three times over. Not that he had any desire to buy the items or attend the events advertised; rather, he derived considerable satisfaction simply from having found time for the advertisements to impress themselves on his consciousness, and beyond that, the mental leisure to read through each of them with complete comprehension. So devoid of composure were his daily comings and goings that even this one calm, collected moment was to be savored.

Sōsuke got off the streetcar at Surugadai-shita in Kanda. The instant he alighted, his eyes fixed on a row of foreign books beautifully arrayed in a store window to his right. For a while he just stood in front of the window gazing at the brilliant gilt letters embossed on red or blue or striped or otherwise patterned book covers. He could, of course, understand the titles, but they aroused in him not the slightest curiosity about what was contained inside. That time in his life when he could not pass a bookstore without wanting to go in, and once inside to buy something, now belonged to the distant past. True, one English-language volume in the center of the window with a particularly fine binding and entitled *History of Gambling* fairly leaped out at him with its distinctiveness, but that was all.

Smiling to himself, he hurried across the street, where he stopped for a second time, to peek inside a watchmaker's. On display were numerous gold watches, watch chains, and the like, which again he regarded as so many pretty-colored, well-formed objects without experiencing the slightest desire to make any purchase. Nevertheless he examined all the price tags dangling there from silk threads, comparing this item and that, and came away surprised at how cheap the gold watches were.

He even paused for a moment in front of an umbrella shop, and then a Western-style haberdashery; a necktie hanging next to a silk hat attracted his attention. It was of a much higher quality than the one he wore every day, and he thought perhaps he might ask the price. He started to enter the store, only to retreat at the image conjured up of the ridiculous figure he would cut if he were to appear at work the next day in a new tie. The impulse to reach for his wallet vanished on the spot, and he moved on. Next, at a draper's, he window-shopped leisurely and committed to memory the names of various weaves, such as "quail's crepe," "twill weave," and "summer sash weave," all previously unfamiliar to him. At the branch of a Kyoto shop called Eri-shin, for the longest time he gazed in through the window at some intricately embroidered half collars for kimonos, standing so close that the brim of his hat touched the glass. Among them was a particularly elegant one that looked well suited to his wife. He had a fleeting impulse to buy it for her. But I should have done this five or six years ago, he thought immediately thereafter, whereupon he squelched the notion and the moment's pleasure it had brought him. Detaching himself from the window with a resigned smile, Sōsuke moved on, and before he had walked half a block he lost interest and ceased to pay much attention to either the storefronts or the passersby.

But then his eye was caught by boldly printed advertisements for the latest publications, hanging from the eaves of a large newsstand on the corner. Some posters were enclosed in an elongated ladder-like frame, others pasted to strips of wood decorated with bright patterns. Sōsuke read each title and author's name, among them certain ones vaguely familiar from newspaper advertisements, others with an air of novelty about them.

Just around the corner from the newsstand, a man of about thirty wearing a black bowler was sitting cross-legged right on the ground and blowing up large rubber balloons, all the while calling out "A nice treat for your children!" Sōsuke marveled at how the balloons inflated automatically into the shape of a Daruma doll,[9] complete with eyes and mouth in black ink that had been applied to just the right spots. Once blown up, the doll stayed that way indefinitely, and rested easily on the palm of the man's hand or even on a fingertip. Then, when the man stuck a thin piece of wood like a toothpick into a hollow in the Daruma balloon's rump, it deflated with a whoosh.

Pedestrians thronged the busy street, but not a single person paused to look at the balloons. The man in the bowler, sitting nonchalantly on the street corner in the midst of the bustle and seemingly oblivious to his surroundings, alternated between calling out "A nice treat for your children" and blowing up another Daruma balloon. Taking out one and a half sen, Sōsuke bought one, had it deflated, and stuck it in the deep part of his kimono sleeve. He toyed with the idea of going to a nice, clean barbershop and having his hair cut. Not knowing where such a shop might be, he looked around for a while but to no avail. In the meantime the sun had gotten low on the horizon, and so he got back on the streetcar, homeward bound.

By the time Sōsuke reached the end of the line and handed his ticket to the conductor, the sky was losing its color and dark shadows were stretching across the damp pavement. The steel pole he grasped as he stepped down felt cold in his hand. All the other alighting passengers scattered hastily this way and that with an air of preoccupation. Surveying the neighborhood here at the city's edge, he noticed clouds of pale white smoke drifting over the roofs and eaves of houses on both sides of the street and seemingly right into the earth's atmosphere. Sōsuke quickened his pace like the others and headed in the direction of a well-wooded area. Realizing that both this Sunday and the fine weather that had accompanied it had drawn to a close, a certain mood came over him: a sense that such things did not last for long, and that this was a great pity. From tomorrow he would again, as always, be busy at work—the thought brought on pangs of regret for the good life he had tasted for this one afternoon. The mindless activity that filled the other six days of the week seemed utterly dreary. Even now, as he walked along, he could see before his eyes nothing but the outlines of the large, all but windowless office that the sun scarcely penetrated, the faces of his colleagues sitting beside him, the figure of his superior summoning him with a "Nonaka-san, over here, please..."

To reach his house, Sōsuke passed Uokatsu, the fishmonger, turned the corner at the fifth or sixth house farther on, and entered a byway—something between a side street and an alley—that dead-ended at the cliff-like embankment and was flanked on both sides by four or five rental houses with identical façades. Until recently, in the midst of this tract, well inside a tall, if sparse, hedge of cryptomeria, there had stood a weathered residence that looked as if it might have housed the descendants of a shogunal retainer. But then a man named Sakai, who now lived on top of the cliff, had bought this land and immediately remodeled the old house in the same up-to-date style as the others, doing away with the reed thatching and uprooting the hedge. Sōsuke's house, tucked in on the left at the very end of the byway, stood directly below the embankment; hence the general gloominess. But as he and his wife had agreed before settling on this particular house, it was bound to be quiet at least, being at the farthest remove from the thoroughfare.

Now that twilight had fallen on this week's one Sunday, Sōsuke's thoughts, as he hurriedly opened the latticework door in front, turned to a quick bath, perhaps a haircut, time permitting, then a leisurely dinner. From the kitchen came the sound of bowls and dishes being handled. Stepping over the threshold, he inadvertently trod on the clogs that Koroku had cast aside there. As he bent over to rearrange them, Koroku appeared. From the kitchen Oyone called out, "Who is it, your brother?"

"Well, look who's here," said Sōsuke, making his way into the parlor. Once he had mailed the letter not a single thought of Koroku had crossed his mind all the while he was strolling around Kanda and riding home on the streetcar. At the sight of his brother's face he felt embarrassed, as if he had somehow wronged him.

"Oyone! Oyone!" he called, summoning his wife from the kitchen. "You'd better fix a good meal for our brother here."

Hurrying out of the kitchen, leaving the shoji open behind her, Oyone came as far as the parlor. "Yes, right away," she said in response to this superfluous command and started back to the kitchen, only to turn around and address her brother-in-law. "I'm sorry to trouble you, Koroku, but would you please close the shutters and light the lamp? Kiyo and I have our hands full at the moment."

"Yes . . . of course," Koroku replied, a bit flustered, and got to his feet.

From the kitchen came the sounds of Kiyo chopping things up, of hot or cold water flowing down the drain, and of voices: "Where should I put this, ma'am?" "Nee-san, where are the scissors to trim the wick with?" Then came a hissing sound, as of water boiling over into the flames on the portable charcoal stove.

Sōsuke rubbed his hands silently over a small charcoal burner in the darkened parlor. A reddish tongue of flame rising from the ashes was the only spot of color in the room. Just then, in the landlord's house atop the embankment, one of the young girls in the family began playing the piano. As if prompted by the music, Sōsuke stood up and went out to the veranda in order to close the shutters. One or two stars twinkled high above the *mōsō* bamboo, their leaves grayish smudges against the clear sky. From beyond the bamboo the piano's notes reverberated in the night.

3

BY THE time Sōsuke and Koroku returned from the neighborhood bathhouse, towels in hand, the various dishes Oyone had prepared were arranged with care on a perfectly square table placed in the middle of the parlor. The flames in the charcoal brazier burned with a deeper hue than before, and the lamp shone brightly. When Sōsuke had seated himself comfortably on his cushion, which he had moved closer to his desk, Oyone, having collected the soap and towels, asked, "Did you enjoy your baths?"

"Uh-huh."

Sōsuke's reply was not so much brusque as simply indicative of post-bath languor.

"Yes, very much!" said Koroku in an agreeable tone as he turned to face Oyone.

"The place was mobbed, though—simply unbearable," added Sōsuke wearily, his elbow propped on the edge of the desk. Usually he went to the baths after his return from work, at twilight, just before the dinner hour, when other customers came pouring in. For two or three months now he had not enjoyed even a glimpse of clear bathwater shimmering in the sunlight. Still worse, it had reached the point where three or four days would go by without his setting foot in a bathhouse. He had it constantly in mind to wait for Sunday, when he would get up early and waste no time going off to steep himself up to the neck in pristine hot water. Come Sunday, however, he would awake with the thought that this was after all the only day he could stay in bed as long as he liked, and as he lay there indolently the hours would mercilessly slip away, until at length he would change his mind: No, it was too much trouble; he'd skip it today and go next Sunday—a pattern that repeated itself again and again through force of inertia.

"I really do want to take an early-morning bath, you know," he announced.

"So you keep saying," his wife replied teasingly, "but on the days when you could go early you always sleep late—it never fails."

Koroku was privately of the opinion that all this dithering stemmed from an inborn flaw in his brother's character. Being a student, he could not comprehend how precious his brother's Sundays were to him, how many hopes and wishes had been vested in these twenty-four hours out of a need to counteract six days of dark musings with the balm of a single day. There was always too much that Sōsuke wanted to do on this one day, and he could never accomplish even two or three out of the ten things he had proposed for himself. On the contrary, whenever he set out to follow through on just those two or three, he quickly came to begrudge the expenditure of time required and, hesitating to act, would just sit there until before he knew it the day drew to a close. With circumstances thus dictating that he deprive himself of his peace of mind, well-being, and various pleasures, Sōsuke's failure to tend to Koroku's needs had nothing to do with any disinclination but rather with a sheer lack of mental energy—such was Sōsuke's argument, anyway. Yet this was something Koroku could not fathom. He viewed his brother as a man who simply did as he pleased without regard for others, who chose to spend what leisure time he had in strolling about alone or just sitting around with his wife, who was utterly unreliable and unhelpful and fundamentally lacking in empathy.

Yet it was only quite recently that Koroku had come to this view of his brother—indeed, only since the issue of negotiating with the Saeki household had arisen. With his youthful impatience in all things, Koroku, when he needed a favor from his brother, fully expected that it would be done, if not this very day, then by tomorrow. That his brother had been unable to bring the matter in question to a resolution, indeed, had not so much as paid a visit to the Saekis, was a source of no small discontent.

Nevertheless, today, as soon as Sōsuke and the waiting Koroku were reunited they became two brothers again, behaving toward each other with a certain warmth that was evident in their complete lack of affectation, and refraining for the moment from blurting out what was uppermost in their minds. And so they had headed off together to the bathhouse and soon settled into a relaxed, casual conversation.

The brothers continued to be at ease as they sat down to dinner. Oyone did not hesitate to join them, occupying her own side of the table.[10] Sōsuke and Koroku each drained two or three cups of saké.

"Oh, yes, I came across something interesting!" Sōsuke announced before the rice was served, whereupon he produced from his kimono sleeve the Daruma balloon he had bought and blew it up to its full size. After placing it on his covered soup bowl he lectured them on its properties. Oyone and Koroku, their curiosity piqued, watched the fluttery balloon. After a while Koroku took a deep breath and blew at the Daruma figure; it fell from the table to the floor, nonetheless returning to sit upright on the tatami.

"Just look at that," said Sōsuke.

In typical womanly fashion, Oyone obliged by laughing out loud; but then, removing the lid from the rice container and filling her husband's bowl, she turned to Koroku and said somewhat protectively, "You see what a free spirit your brother is." Without a word in his own defense, Sōsuke took the bowl from his wife and began to eat. At this, Koroku ceremoniously picked up his chopsticks.

There was no more talk of the Daruma balloon, but it set the tone for the innocuous conversation that flowed smoothly for the duration of the meal. After his last bite, however, Koroku departed from this tenor.

"By the way, wasn't that shocking about Mr. Itō!"[11]

Five or six days earlier, Sōsuke, after having looked over the extra devoted to Lord Itō's assassination, took it into the kitchen and laid it on top of Oyone's apron. "Terrible news—Mr. Itō has been killed," he said, then went to his desk. His tone of voice, however, was so perfectly calm that Oyone made a point of remarking, half teasingly, "'Terrible,' you say, but you don't sound the least bit terrified." Every day after that, the paper unfailingly devoted five or six columns to Itō's assassination, but Sōsuke appeared so indifferent on the subject that it was unclear whether he even glanced at them. When she asked her husband, home from work, in the midst of her dinner preparations, "Was there anything more about Mr. Itō in the paper today?" he would merely reply, "Uh-huh, quite a lot..." And so unless she later extracted the folded paper from his coat pocket, she had no way of learning the latest news. Yet her main concern had been to have a topic to discuss with her husband when he came home, and she no longer saw any reason to go to such lengths in order to drag him into a discussion of matters that held no interest for him. From the day when the extra was published up until Koroku's remark at dinner, this public event that had sent shock waves throughout the nation created scarcely a ripple in the couple's life together.

"But how did he...well, get himself killed?" Oyone asked, turning toward Koroku and repeating the same question she had put to Sōsuke when the news first broke.

"It was a couple of quick pistol shots—bang, bang!" Koroku answered in all seriousness.

"Yes, but I mean, well, how could he have gotten himself killed?"

Utter incomprehension was written on Koroku's face.

"That was surely his destiny," Sōsuke offered, his voice calm, sipping his tea with relish.

Clearly still not satisfied, Oyone asked, "But why did he go to Manchuria?"

"Yes, why *did* he..." Sōsuke mused, looking sated and complacent.

"I hear that he was on a secret mission to the Russians," Koroku ventured, an earnest look on his face.

"Oh, but still, it's awful, his being killed," said Oyone.

"When an ordinary drudge like me gets killed, yes, it's awful," said Sōsuke, at last warming to the topic. "A man like Mr. Itō, though—it's much better for him to go off to Harbin and be killed."

"Gracious, what do you mean?"

"What I mean is, it's precisely because Mr. Itō was assassinated that he can become a great figure in history. If he'd simply died on his own it would never have turned out that way."

"Well yes, I suppose there's some truth to that," said Koroku, who appeared only partially convinced. After a pause, he added, "At any rate, Manchuria, Harbin—these places seem to be pretty rough-and-tumble. To me, they just spell danger, somehow."

"That's because all sorts of people are thrown together there."

Oyone registered her husband's remark with a look of dismay. Her expression was not lost on Sōsuke, who then prompted her: "Well, I guess it's time to clear the table." Scooping up the balloon from the tatami, he let it rest on his index finger. "Marvelous, isn't it," he said. "To think someone could make a thing like this, so that it works just right."

After Kiyo had come in from the kitchen and taken away the dirty dishes, along with the table itself, and with Oyone over in the next room preparing fresh tea, only the brothers remained in the parlor, sitting face-to-face.

"That's better, all the clutter's gone," said Sōsuke, clearly relieved to be rid of the table. "There's something nasty about the dregs of a meal." In the kitchen Kiyo kept laughing to herself. Then Oyone could be heard through the shoji asking her what was so funny, to which Kiyo murmured noncommittally and burst out laughing again. The two brothers sat in silence, their ears half inclined to the maid's laughter. Presently Oyone reappeared carrying a plate of cakes in one hand, a tea tray in the other. From a large pot with a wisteria-vine pattern she poured the tea, of a coarse-leaf variety unlikely to overstimulate, into bowl-size cups and placed them in front of the two men.

"What's she laughing about?" asked Sōsuke. Not looking up at his wife, he trained his eyes on the cakes.

"Well, here you are with that balloon you went and bought, balanced on your fingertip," she said. "It's not as if there were any children in the house . . ."

Sōsuke appeared unfazed. "I see," he replied. Then, rather deliberately, and with an air of ruminating his words, he finally glanced up at his wife and added, "That may be so, but there were children here once upon a time, weren't there?" His eyes were not without warmth. Oyone immediately fell silent.

Presently she turned to Koroku and asked him if he would be having a second cake, but when he said yes she paid no attention and quickly withdrew to the sitting room.

The brothers found themselves alone again.

The evening was still young, yet here in the recesses of the hilly neighborhoods that ring the city's west side, some twenty minutes on foot from the end of the streetcar line, the streets were quiet. From time to time the clatter of worn-down clogs sounded sharply out front; the night air grew steadily colder. His folded arms tucked in his sleeves, Sōsuke said, "The days are warm enough but it cools down quickly at night. Have they turned on the steam heat in your dormitory yet?"

"No, not yet. The school won't turn it on till it gets seriously cold."

"Really? Then it must be freezing."

"Yes. But the cold—well, that's something I can put up with," said Koroku, who, momentarily at a loss for words, finally found the resolve to continue. "But tell me, please, whatever has become of the business with the Saekis? I heard from Nee-san that you sent them a letter . . . ?"

"Oh yes, I mailed it. I expect they'll answer in the next couple of days. Depending on how they respond, I'll go over there, or do whatever else is necessary."

Koroku silently took in his brother's nonchalant reply. He found it wanting, and yet he could detect nothing in Sōsuke's manner meant to give offense, much less a defensive tone that smacked of some base motive, and so he was not moved to go on the attack. Instead, he simply sought confirmation of the true state of things when he asked, "Then up until today nothing else got done?"

"No, I'm sorry, nothing. It was all I could do to get that letter off today," Sōsuke said, now sounding serious. "Lately I've been plagued by a case of nerves."

Koroku smiled mirthlessly. "Well, if this doesn't work out, I could quit school. In fact, I've been thinking about going abroad, to Manchuria or Korea, and the sooner the better."

"Manchuria? Korea? Now that would be a drastic move, to burn your bridges like that. But didn't you just say awhile ago that you didn't care for the rough-and-tumble of Manchuria?"

Their discussion of the business with the Saekis twisted this way and that without finding any resolution. Sōsuke had the final word. "All right, don't worry so much—things will work out somehow. At any rate, I'll let you know as soon as I've received a reply. Then we can talk it over some more." With that, the conversation came to a close.

Peeking into the sitting room on his way out, Koroku found Oyone leaning idly against the long charcoal brazier. Only when he called out to say good night to her did she get to her feet, with a murmur of surprise, to see him off.

4

THE REPLY from the Saekis, the focus of so much agitation on Koroku's part, arrived as hoped a couple of days later. Exceedingly simple though it was—a mere note in their aunt's hand that could have been sent as a postcard—it came fastidiously encased in an envelope complete with a three-sen stamp. On returning home from work Sōsuke had removed the close-fitting jacket he wore to the office and sat down by the brazier when the envelope, placed in a drawer so as to stick out an inch or so, caught his eye. After a single sip of the tea Oyone had poured out for him, he cut it open.

"Hmm . . . It seems that Yasu-san has gone to Kobe," he said while reading along in the letter.

"When?" asked Oyone, who had not stirred since serving the tea.

"It doesn't say exactly, but she writes here, 'Inasmuch as he is expected to return to the capital in the not distant future,' so I suppose he'll be back any day now."

"'In the not distant future,' et cetera—yes, that is your aunt's style."

Sōsuke expressed neither agreement nor disagreement with his wife's critique. He rolled the letter up and tossed it aside; then, with a look of foreboding, he stroked the four or five days' growth on his chin.

Oyone quickly picked up the letter but showed no impulse to read it. Leaving it on her lap, she studied her husband's expression and asked, "'Inasmuch as he is expected . . . in the not distant future'—what's that all about?"

"'I shall confer with Yasunosuke upon his return, and we will undertake to pay our respects then'—that's what she says."

"But this 'not distant future' is so vague! Doesn't she say *when* he is coming back?"

"That's enough about that."

Wanting to see for herself, Oyone now opened the letter in her lap and scanned it. Then, after rolling it up again, she stretched out her hand. "The envelope, please." Sōsuke picked up the blue envelope that lay at his side by the brazier and handed it to his wife. Oyone opened it with a puff of air and reinserted the letter. She then went out to the kitchen.

Sōsuke gave no further thought to the letter after that. He recalled the remarks of a colleague that day at the office about a sighting, just outside Shimbashi terminal, of Field Marshal Kitchener,[12] who was visiting from England. Yes, here was a man who created a great stir wherever he went the world over—indeed, someone quite possibly born to create such a stir. When Sōsuke compared his own life—the dreary lot he dragged along with him from the past and the destiny likely to unfold before him in the years to come—to the life of Kitchener, the two hardly seemed to belong to members of the same human race.

Lost in these thoughts, Sōsuke incessantly puffed smoke into the air. Outside, the wind that had come up earlier in the evening now sounded as though, taking aim from afar, it were determined to descend upon them with real force. From time to time it would die down for a while, and these lulls, in their utter stillness, were more desolating than the stormy gusts. Sōsuke folded his arms against his chest. It's almost here, he thought, the season when fire bells would clang, announcing outbreaks throughout the city.

He went over by the kitchen and looked in at Oyone standing over a red-hot stove, grilling fish fillets. Kiyo was bent over the sink rinsing pickled vegetables. Each performed the task at hand without speaking to the other. For a while Sōsuke stood at the open shoji listening to the hiss of oil dripping from the fish, then closed the shoji without a word and returned to his seat. His wife had not taken her eyes off the fish for a moment.

When dinner was over and the couple sat facing each other over the brazier, Oyone started in again. "This business with the Saekis is getting nowhere."

"Well, there's nothing to be done about it. We have no choice but to wait until Yasu-san is back from Kobe."

"Wouldn't it be better if you met with your aunt before that and had a chat with her first?"

"No, it wouldn't. They'll get in touch soon enough, one way or another. In the meantime we'll just leave well enough alone."

"Koroku is upset. That doesn't bother you?" Oyone smiled even as she made her point. Eyes lowered, Sōsuke stuck the toothpick he had in his hand into the collar of his kimono.

Two days later Sōsuke got around to informing Koroku by letter of their aunt's reply, adding a characteristic postscript to the effect that everything would turn out all right sooner or later. This done, he felt that for the time being he was off the hook where this business was concerned. He acted as though the best approach, which also happened to be the least bother, was just to forget about it—at least until, in the natural course of things, the matter was once again shoved under his nose—and so he let nothing disturb his daily routine of commuting between home and office. It was generally late when he got home, and once there he hardly ever went to the trouble of going out again. The couple almost never received guests. If Kiyo was finished with her chores, they even sent her off to bed before ten o'clock. Every night after dinner the couple sat in the same place, facing each other across the brazier, and talked for about an hour. The topics of their conversation were tailored to the mundane circumstances of their lives. If no issue so pressing as how to pay this month's rice bill ever passed their lips, neither was there to be heard the high-spirited banter that often bubbles up, like will-o'-the-wisps, in a conversation between a man and a woman, let alone a discussion of literary matters. Young though they were, they appeared to have gone beyond this stage and become the sort of couple who naturally grows more retiring with each passing day. One might even assume them to have been the sort who, lackluster and thoroughly ordinary to begin with, had gravitated toward each other simply for the sake of conforming to the custom of marriage.

On the surface neither husband nor wife showed signs of being the worrying kind. That in fact they were not could be inferred from their attitude toward Koroku's situation. Predictably, it was Oyone who suggested once or twice: "Isn't Yasu-san back yet? Why don't you go over to Banchō next Sunday and see"; to which Sōsuke replied: "Sure, why not." But when the designated Sunday came around he appeared to have blithely forgotten all about it. While noticing this dereliction, Oyone made no attempt to admonish him. If the weather was fair she would say, "Why don't you take a stroll?"; if it was raining, "Well, it's a good thing it's Sunday."

Fortunately Koroku had not descended on them again. A young man of a compulsive and excitable temperament, he would pursue unremittingly whatever was uppermost in his mind, a trait that had been apparent in the Sōsuke of distant schooldays. On the other hand, when Koroku's mood changed he became a different person, with a good-natured look on his face, as if the cares of yesterday were totally forgotten. Here too the brothers' common blood showed: Sōsuke had been just like this long ago. Koroku had a relatively lucid mind and, while it was not clear whether it was a case of pouring passion onto his reason or cloaking his emotions in rational trappings, he was at any rate never satisfied with a proposition until he could discern its underlying logic; once he had done so, he would zealously push it to its conclusion. His will, moreover, was far stronger than his physical constitution might suggest, and his youthful impetuosity made him capable of almost anything.

Whenever Sōsuke saw Koroku he was struck by a sensation of watching his old self resurrected and in motion. At times this made him nervous. On other occasions it even made him feel bitter—a bitterness caused by the thought that fate may have deliberately thrust Koroku before his eyes in order to summon up as often as possible harsh memories of how obsessively he himself had behaved before. This thought in turn became terrifying; he would tremble at the prospect that by virtue of his birth his brother was bound to succumb to the same fate that had befallen himself. Depending on the moment, however, this prospect created not so much concern as irritation.

And yet to this day Sōsuke had never criticized Koroku for his behavior, nor for that matter had he offered him any advice for the future. His treatment of his brother was thoroughly conventional and unexceptionable. The life he now led appeared so subdued as to be completely at odds with his previous existence. Thus in his dealings with Koroku it was hard to detect anything of the experienced elder brother that suggested he even had what might be called "a past."

Two other boys had been born between the brothers but had died in infancy; Sōsuke and Koroku themselves were ten years apart. While still in his first year as a university student Sōsuke had for certain reasons transferred to Kyoto;[13] his daily life under the same roof with his brother thus came to an end when Koroku was only about twelve. Koroku's defiant, mischievous ways at that age were fresh in Sōsuke's memory. Their father was still alive then, and the family's circumstances were comfortable enough to afford a full-time rickshaw man, who had been provided with a modest dwelling on the property. The rickshaw man had a son, younger by three years than Koroku, who was the latter's constant playmate. One midsummer day Sōsuke found the two of them under a large persimmon tree, rigging up a cicada trap with a bag of sweets dangling from a long pole. "Kenbō, out in this heat bareheaded you'll get sunstroke," he had said and produced an old summer hat of Koroku's for the boy to wear. Koroku flew into a rage at his brother for having given away something that belonged to him without permission. Swiping the hat from Kenbō's hand, he threw it to the ground and with the motion of one bounding uphill repeatedly stomped on it until the straw hat was pulverized. Sōsuke jumped down from the veranda in his bare feet and smacked Koroku on the head. From that time on he retained in his mind's eye an image of Koroku as a spiteful brat.

In his second year at university Sōsuke had had to withdraw; his situation also made it impossible for him to return to Tokyo. Soon after that he moved from Kyoto to Hiroshima, where he had been living for about six months when his father died. His mother had died six years earlier. The only immediate family ties left to him consisted of his father's twenty-five-year-old mistress and Koroku, who was then fifteen.

On receiving news of his father's death in a telegram from the Saekis, Sōsuke had returned to Tokyo after his long absence. Once the funeral was over and he had begun looking into his family's finances in order to settle the estate, he not only found the assets on hand to be less than expected but was shocked to discover extensive debts he had known nothing about. After consulting with his uncle he was persuaded that he really had no choice but to sell the family house. He decided to hand over an appropriate sum to the mistress and let her go without further ado. And for the time being he entrusted the care and lodging of Koroku to his uncle. The pressing matter of the real estate sale could not, however, be resolved on the spot. To get it off his hands right away, his only recourse was to rely, at least temporarily, on his uncle's good offices. Saeki was an entrepreneur and something of a speculator who had tried his hand at assorted ventures, all of them inevitably failures. When Sōsuke was still living in Tokyo, his uncle often extracted money from his father with proposals couched in glowing terms. The total amount poured into his uncle's ventures on the basis of these blandishments, doubtless abetted by a measure of greed on his father's part, was no small sum.

At the time of his father's death his uncle's circumstances seemed to be more or less as they had always been. Nevertheless, in addition to a sense of duty toward the deceased, as is the way with such men when the chips are down, he showed himself to be of a generous spirit and did not hesitate to assume responsibility for what were Sōsuke's affairs. As part of the arrangement, however, Sōsuke gave his uncle total control over the sale of the real estate. In short, in return for a quick solution to his need for ready cash, he in effect presented his uncle with the house and grounds.

"Anyway, with a property like this, if you don't deal directly with the buyer, you'll take a beating," his uncle had said.

In a similar vein, Sōsuke simply accepted an estimated valuation of the furniture, with those items of no appreciable value to be disposed of as a wholesale lot. When it came to half a dozen scroll paintings and a dozen or so antiques, he again deferred to his uncle's view that they should wait for particularly eager buyers, in the meantime entrusting everything to his care. Excluding these various set-asides, the legacy Sōsuke was left with came to a total of approximately two thousand yen, some portion of which, he recognized, had to be spent on Koroku's tuition. But he also realized that in his present, far from stable position, it would be risky for him to take charge of the monthly tuition payments, and so, gritting his teeth, he handed over half of the legacy to his uncle, with the request that he kindly assume this responsibility, too. Having stumbled badly along the way himself, it was Sōsuke's primary concern here to support Koroku on the path to success. As for what would happen when the thousand yen ran out, he could worry about that later; and there was always the lingering prospect, by no means certain, that his uncle might come up with something more—so he had told himself as he left Tokyo to return to Hiroshima.

Half a year later a letter arrived from his uncle, written in his own hand, stating that the house had been sold, and now he could set his mind to rest on that score. But as no mention was made of how much it had sold for, Sōsuke wrote by return mail asking for clarification. Two weeks later his uncle wrote to the effect that inasmuch as the proceeds had fortunately been sufficient to cover expenses already incurred, Sōsuke need have no further worries about the matter. Sōsuke was far from satisfied with this response, in which his uncle had added that a discussion of further particulars could be deferred to such a time as he might have the pleasure of a visit from his nephew, et cetera, et cetera.

When he had read this Sōsuke felt like leaving for Tokyo immediately, and he explained things to his wife, tacitly seeking her advice. Oyone looked pained as she listened, but answered with her characteristic smile, "But you can't go, so there's really nothing to be done about it." Looking very much like a man who had for the first time had a sentence pronounced on him by his wife, he pondered awhile, arms folded against his chest. No matter how he looked at it, his hands were tied; he was a prisoner of circumstances he could not control. Thus things had reached an impasse.

With no other recourse, Sōsuke continued his correspondence, exchanging three or four more letters with his uncle. But the answer was always the same, as though etched in stone: "When I have the pleasure of a visit..."

"This is a total waste of time," he said to Oyone, the anger written on his face.

Three months later he finally had an opportunity to travel to To-kyo with Oyone and was all set to leave when he caught a cold and took to his bed, after which his cold developed into intestinal ty-phus. He was bedridden for more than two months, and for still another month he was too weak to do much work.

Not long after his recovery, new developments necessitated a move farther west, from Hiroshima to Fukuoka. Sōsuke was search-ing for a good opportunity to make a quick trip to Tokyo before the move when another set of constraints cropped up, so that in the end he had to cancel his plans yet again and instead entrust his fate to a train bound in the opposite direction. It was around this time that the money he had pocketed upon vacating the property in Tokyo ran out. During the ensuing two years, roughly corresponding to their stay in Fukuoka, it was a struggle living from day to day. Sōsuke often thought back to his student days in Kyoto, to those distant times when he would find various pretexts, for instance "special supplemental tuition fees," for extracting from his father large sums that he would then spend freely on whatever he wanted. Comparing that life to his present predicament, he trembled at the inexorable workings of karmic retribution. On occasion he reminisced about the springtime that had stealthily passed him by, and he acknowl-edged to himself, as if opening his eyes for the first time to gaze back into those far-off mists, that it had been his one moment of glory.

Things went from bad to worse for them, and Sōsuke now said to his wife, "I've let it go for a long time, but I think it's time to go to Tokyo and have a talk with him."

Oyone did not argue with him, of course. She simply looked down and responded forlornly, "It won't do any good. Your uncle has absolutely no trust in us."

"Well, maybe not, but we have no trust in him, either," Sōsuke retorted defiantly, but he had only to look at Oyone's downcast eyes and his pluck would evaporate. After the matter had first been broached, it came up in discussions of this sort once or twice a month, then once every other month, and eventually once in three, until finally Sōsuke broke down and said to his wife, "All right, then, just so long as he manages to do something for Koroku. As for the other business, I guess it can wait till I get to Tokyo and meet with him face-to-face. What do you think, Oyone, isn't that the best way to handle it?"

"Yes, that is definitely the best approach," Oyone replied.

With that, Sōsuke at last dropped the subject of the Saekis. Given his past conduct toward his father, he realized that he could not simply ask his uncle for a handout, and had never so much as hinted at such a request in their correspondence. Letters arrived intermittently from Koroku, but most of them were short and stilted. Picturing only the Koroku he had last seen shortly after their father's death, Sōsuke still saw him as a guileless boy whom he would not dream of using as an intermediary in negotiations with their uncle.

The couple lived in seclusion, each utterly dependent on the other in their daily life, clinging together for warmth in a cold, sunless world. Whenever things turned especially harsh Oyone would say only, "Oh well, it can't be helped." And Sōsuke would respond, "That's right, we'll get by somehow."

They kept on together by force of a steadfast mixture of resignation and forbearance, seemingly without the balm of hope or any prospect for a better future. As for the past, they rarely spoke of it. Indeed at times they appeared to shun even the mere mention of bygone days, as if by tacit agreement.

Occasionally Oyone would offer her husband words of encouragement: "Things are bound to get better soon," or "Bad times like this can't last forever." To Sōsuke, however, those words sounded like the spiteful tongue of fate—a fate that had so twisted him around its finger—conveyed through the mouth of his pure-hearted wife. He could only grimace, offer a forced smile, and say nothing in reply. If on these occasions Oyone unwittingly went on in the same optimistic vein, he would cut her short and declare, "But then, people like us don't have the right to expect very much, do they?" At which she would finally get the point and fall silent. As they continued to sit facing each other in mutual silence, they would eventually slide back into the dark hole of the past they had dug for themselves.

In accordance with the principle of As Ye Sow, So Shall Ye Reap, the couple had erased any prospects for the future. That no resplendent vistas would open up on the path that lay ahead for them was something to which they were simply reconciled, and they contented themselves instead with making their way together hand in hand. As for the land and various rental properties that the uncle had sold off, from the outset they had not expected any huge profit. "But still," Sōsuke would say after it had all been settled, as though the thought had just occurred to him, "with prices at the level they've reached lately, he must have gotten twice the amount he raised back then to cover debts, even if he just dumped it on the market. I mean, it's outrageous!"

"Back to the property sale, are we?" Oyone would answer with a wan smile. "You just can't get it off your mind, can you? But weren't you the one who said to your uncle, 'Please, sir, be so kind as to take care of everything'?"

"Yes, but I had no choice. At the time there was nothing else I could do about it."

"Well then, don't you think it's possible that in your uncle's mind, instead of any money he'd at least inherited property from his brother?" said Oyone.

Listening to Oyone, Sōsuke could see that there might be some basis for his uncle to have taken such a view of things, but he launched a spirited defense. "Maybe that was his intention, but it doesn't mean he's right."

And yet, after each revisiting of the issue it receded further and further into the background.

For two years the couple continued their life of warm intimacy surrounded by desolation, at the end of which Sōsuke had an unexpected meeting with a former classmate named Sugihara, who had been a close friend during his university days. After graduation, Sugihara, who already held a post at a certain ministry, passed the advanced civil service examination, which led to his being dispatched from Tokyo to Fukuoka and then to Saga on special assignment. From an announcement in the local newspaper Sōsuke was well aware of the time of Sugihara's arrival and where he was to stay. But aside from the pitiful figure he imagined himself cutting—a complete failure groveling before a highly successful colleague—he had good reason to avoid meeting any friend from those days and would not in any event have dreamed of visiting him at his inn.

In the meantime, however, through a chance connection, Sugihara had found out for himself that Sōsuke was languishing hereabouts and insisted on a meeting. Sōsuke felt obliged to assent. It was entirely thanks to this Sugihara that it then became possible for him to move back to Tokyo. The day the letter arrived from Sugihara confirming the final arrangements, Sōsuke had set down his chopsticks and said, "Oyone. At last we can go to Tokyo."

"My, what good news!" she replied, gazing at her husband's face.

For the first two or three weeks after their arrival in Tokyo the days went by in a dizzying blur. Along with the predictably hectic business of setting up a new household and settling into a new job, they were nearly overwhelmed by the concussive stimuli that, day and night, filled the air of the bustling metropolis. They lacked the time to think about anything at leisure and the composure to weigh their options with any care.

The long-deferred reunion with his aunt and uncle finally occurred when their train arrived at Shimbashi terminal. It may have been simply the effect of the weak light in the station, but in Sōsuke's eyes neither of the two radiated much good cheer. An accident along the way had resulted in a rare thirty-minute delay, and there was in the weary impatience betrayed by the couple a suggestion that this had somehow been Sōsuke's fault.

The only thing his aunt had said to him on this occasion was, "Gracious, Sō-san, it hasn't been that long since I last saw you, but how you've aged!" Not having met Oyone before, she glanced at her nephew and said somewhat hesitantly, "And this is, uh . . . ?" Oyone, at a loss for a proper greeting, merely bowed her head in silence.

Koroku had of course accompanied his uncle and aunt to greet the couple. Sōsuke took one look at him and was astonished to see that in his absence his brother had grown to a height that rivaled his own. He had just finished middle school and was preparing to enter secondary school. On coming face-to-face with Sōsuke, Koroku barely managed an awkward greeting to his brother. He did not say "Welcome home!" nor did he address him as "Nii-san."[14]

After just one week's stay at an inn, Sōsuke and Oyone had moved into the house they now occupied. While they settled in, Sōsuke's aunt and uncle helped them out in various ways. There was no need to buy all those little things for the kitchen if secondhand would do, they insisted, and sent over a complete set of utensils adequate to the needs of a small household. "With the move and all you must have had considerable expenses," his uncle said, and followed his words up with a gift of sixty yen.

What with all the distractions, half a month went by without a word to the uncle about the property sale that had exercised the couple so greatly when they were living in the provinces.

"Have you spoken to your uncle?" asked Oyone.

"No," said Sōsuke, "not yet."

"How strange—when the matter was so much on your mind," said Oyone with a faint smile.

"Well, it's not as if I've had the occasion to bring it up," he said in his defense.

Ten days later it was Sōsuke who raised the subject. "You know," he said, "I still haven't brought it up. Doing so now is such a bother that I've lost interest."

"If it's that much of a bother you needn't force yourself to speak to him."

"You don't mind, then?" Sōsuke asked.

"But why should I mind," said Oyone. "Hasn't it always been something for you to decide for yourself? It's never mattered to me one way or the other."

At which Sōsuke said, "Well then, since it would look odd for me to launch into some formal inquiry all of a sudden, I'll just wait for the chance to ask him in a natural way. Some kind of opening is bound to come up." And so he put the matter off.

Koroku was comfortably lodged at his uncle's house. If he passed the examination and was admitted to the secondary school, he would have to move into a dormitory, an eventuality about which he and his uncle appeared to have already reached an understanding. Having received little help with his tuition from Sōsuke, so recently relocated to the capital, Koroku seemed disinclined to confide in his brother the kind of personal matters he discussed with their uncle. As for his relations with their cousin, so far he and Yasunosuke had been getting along very well. Indeed, the two seemed more like brothers than did Koroku and Sōsuke.

In the natural course of things Sōsuke's visits to his uncle's house became less and less frequent, and as even these occasional visits came to seem like a mere formality, they left him feeling quite empty on the way home. In time this tendency reached the point where he barely got through the obligatory comments on the weather before he was itching to leave. It had become a trial to sit still for half an hour and string together enough banal remarks to pass the time. His hosts, too, appeared constrained and somehow ill at ease.

"What's the hurry? Stay awhile!" his aunt would invariably say, but her effort to detain him only made him all the more eager to leave. All the same, when he had absented himself for a stretch he felt uneasy, as if from a twinge of conscience, and he would resume his visits. From time to time he would go so far as to say, with a nod of apology, that Koroku must be quite a burden for them. But to go beyond this and broach the subject of his brother's future tuition, or the issue of the property sale executed on his behalf in his absence, was still too great a hurdle. Yet clearly it was not just out of a sense of duty, or the need to meet the world's expectations where ties of blood are concerned, that, however reluctantly, Sōsuke continued to call on this uncle who held no attractions for him. Rather, his visits were attributable to nothing but an urge to be rid of a kind of knot still lodged in his breast.

"My goodness," Mrs. Saeki remarked to her husband at one point, "Sō-san is a different person, isn't he."

"Yes, he certainly is," replied her husband. "But when you get right down to it, the kind of business he got himself mixed up with was bound to take its toll, sooner or later." He made as if to cringe at the iron laws of karma.

"Yes, it's truly frightening," she said. "He wasn't always this subdued. He used to be so full of life—too lively, in fact, for his own good. And now, over the past few years since we last saw him, he's aged so much I hardly know him. Why, he looks more like an old man now than you do."

"I wouldn't go that far," he said.

"No, I mean it," she insisted. "Maybe not his hair or his face, but, you know, just the way he looks in general."

Since their nephew's return to Tokyo the old couple had engaged in not a few conversations along these lines. And it was true that whenever Sōsuke showed up at their house he looked very much the old man in their eyes.

Oyone, meanwhile, after being introduced to Sōsuke's uncle and aunt upon arriving at Shimbashi, had for this reason or that never ventured to cross the threshold of their house. When they showed up for an occasional visit, she was the polite hostess, addressing them cordially as "Uncle" and "Aunt." Yet despite their parting invitation to "come over sometime," she would merely bow her head with a word of thanks and never get around to paying them a call.

Even Sōsuke had once urged her to follow through.

"Now, why not pay them just one visit?"

"Oh, but I..."

Noting the look of distress on her face, he resolutely avoided any further suggestions of this kind.

Relations between the two households continued thus for about a year. Then Mr. Saeki, whom his wife had declared to be more youthful in spirit than Sōsuke, suddenly died. His death was attended by virulent symptoms of meningitis or some such disease: After a few days in bed with what had appeared to be influenza, he fainted in the midst of washing his hands after a visit to the toilet; hardly a day later, he was a cold corpse.

"Well, my uncle's dead and gone," Sōsuke said to Oyone, "without my ever having had that talk with him."

"You were still thinking of bringing that up? My, you do know how to nurse a grudge!" she said.

A year after the uncle's death, Yasunosuke had graduated from the university and Koroku was about to begin his second year of secondary school. Yasunosuke and his mother moved to Naka Roku-Banchō.

A year after that, during summer vacation, Koroku went on a swimming holiday to the Bōsō Peninsula. Having spent more than a month there, with September upon him he set out from Hota across the peninsula to the Kazusa coast, traveling by way of Kujūkuri to Chōshi, from where, as if it had just occurred to him, he reversed direction and headed back to Tokyo. He turned up at his brother's just a few days later, on an afternoon still heavy with summer's lingering heat, and stretched out in the parlor, the room most protected from the sun; his eyes were the only two bright spots on a deeply tanned face that might as well have belonged to someone from the South Seas. The moment Sōsuke appeared Koroku sprang to his feet. "Nii-san, I have something to consult with you about," he announced, in such solemn tones that, without pausing to change from his office attire, the mildly astonished Sōsuke heard him out.

According to Koroku, on the evening he had returned from Kazusa he was put on notice by their aunt that, regrettably, she would no longer be paying his tuition after year's end. Having been immediately taken in by his uncle after his father's death, Koroku had been lulled into a passive sense of security; he had been able to get on with his life much as he had while his father was alive, with no worries about school fees, clothes, even pocket money, all of which had simply been taken care of, such that until that evening the very thought of tuition as a problem had never crossed his mind. When his aunt issued her decree, then, he had been too dazed to offer even a polite response.

With a look full of apology, she proceeded for the next hour, woman that she was, to detail the reasons why she could no longer help him out. There was the death of her husband and the ensuing financial adjustments, then Yasunosuke's graduation, and on the heels of that, the question of his marriage.

"I'd hoped at least to see you through your graduation from secondary school, and I made a lot of sacrifices…" Koroku repeated this remark by his aunt twice over. At that point in the conversation he suddenly remembered how Sōsuke, when he had come up to Tokyo for their father's funeral and to make the necessary arrangements, had told him before returning to Hiroshima that funds for his education had been entrusted to their uncle. But when Koroku had asked the aunt about this for the first time, she seemed taken unawares. "Well, yes, at the time Sō-san did leave some small amount with us," she said, "but that's long gone. Even when your uncle was still alive we were paying your tuition out of our own pockets, you see." Since Koroku had never been told by Sōsuke how much had been provided for his schooling, or how many years it was supposed to cover, he was unable to say a word in rebuttal to his aunt's account.

Then she had added: "But it's not as if you're all alone in the world. You have a brother, and you should have a serious talk with him. Come to think of it, I might just meet with him myself and make sure he fully understands the situation… Sō-san hasn't come by much lately, and I've been neglecting him myself, so there really hasn't been any chance for us to discuss things."

When Koroku had finished recounting the incident, Sōsuke looked his brother in the eye and said simply, "What a mess." He showed no sign of erupting into a rage and racing off to give his aunt a talking-to, as he might formerly have done; nor did he appear to take offense at the sudden change in attitude on the part of his brother who, up to a moment ago, had kept his distance, as if to make it clear that he could get along perfectly well without any help from this quarter.

Having seen off Koroku, who as he retreated was clearly shaken by what he no doubt saw as the havoc wreaked by mere bystanders on the brilliant future he had projected for himself, Sōsuke stood in the doorway and gazed for a while through the latticework at the patches of fading sunlight.

That evening he snipped two large leaves from the *bashō* plant[15] behind the house and spread them out on the veranda for Oyone and himself to sit on as they enjoyed the cool air. They talked about Koroku's situation.

"Evidently your aunt has made up her mind that Koroku is our responsibility now..." said Oyone.

"Until I've seen her and talked things over," said Sōsuke, "I really couldn't say what she has in mind."

"You can be sure it's as I just told you," Oyone replied, vigorously waving her fan amidst the shadows.

Sōsuke made no reply. He craned his neck and studied the narrow band of sky visible between the eaves and the embankment. They sat there in silence for a while until, at length, Oyone said, "Still, this just isn't possible for us."

"To see someone through university is way beyond me," her husband agreed, leaving no doubt about his own limited capacity.

The couple's conversation shifted to another topic and touched no further on either Koroku or his aunt. A few days later, when Saturday came around, Sōsuke ventured a visit to his aunt's in Banchō on his way home from the office. His aunt declared herself to be pleasantly surprised and treated him with an extra measure of affability. Overcoming his distaste, Sōsuke broached for the first time the question he had stifled these four or five years. Not surprisingly, his aunt mounted the strongest defense possible.

According to her, the money his uncle had realized from the sale of the house and grounds—well, she could not be sure, but over and above the amount owed on the loan he'd hastily taken out to cover debts, it had come to 4,500 yen, or was it 4,300? Be that as it may, it was his uncle's opinion that inasmuch as Sōsuke had given him the real estate outright before he went away, no matter how much over the advance the property sold for, it could reasonably be considered his personal gain. Still, it would make him uncomfortable to have it said that he had profited from selling his nephew's property, and so he would keep it in trust for Koroku and leave it to him as his patrimony. As for Sōsuke, seeing that he'd been all but formally disinherited by his own father over that business he got himself involved in, he really didn't deserve a single penny.

"Now don't be angry," his aunt quickly added. "I'm only repeating exactly what your uncle said." Sōsuke held his tongue and heard her out.

Thanks to his uncle's shrewdness, though in this case there was a later, unfortunate turn of events, the money set aside for Koroku's "patrimony" had then been invested in a building on a busy street in Kanda. But before he could take out insurance on it, there was a fire and the building burned to the ground. Since Koroku had never been told about the "trust" arrangement, his uncle thought it better not to inform him of this mishap.

"So there you have it. Believe me, Sō-san, I can understand how upsetting this must be for you, but nothing can be done about it now, it's beyond our control. You might as well accept it as your fate and just resign yourself to it. Of course, if your uncle were still alive he'd work something out, I'm sure. Even now that he's gone, if I were in better straits I'd somehow be able to repay Koroku the amount that went up in smoke with that building, or at any rate see him through to graduation."

Having said this much, his aunt proceeded to launch into another tale of domestic woe. This one had to do with Yasunosuke's business affairs.

Yasunosuke, an only child, had just graduated from the university this summer. He'd had a cosseted upbringing and no social exposure beyond his circle of classmates, and could be described as obtuse about the ways of the world. Along with this obtuseness, however, was a generous spirit that he brought to his first venture into the arena of practical affairs. Being a graduate of the mechanical engineering program, there were of course suitable openings for him at some of the many well-established companies around the country, even with the recent decline in entrepreneurial fervor. However, showing a speculative tendency he seemed to have inherited from his father, he instead resolved to go into business for himself. Just then an opportunity materialized thanks to a chance encounter with a fellow engineering-department graduate a few years his senior, who had built a modest factory on Tsukijima[16] that he owned outright. In the course of their discussions they hit on the idea of a joint venture, with Yasunosuke investing some capital of his own. Herein lay the new source of woe for the family.

"You see, I sunk the few stocks I owned into this venture," said his aunt, "and that's left me as good as penniless. Naturally I know people will look at me and think, Her family's very small, she owns her own house and the land—she's got it easy! Just the other day Mrs. Hara was here visiting and she said to me, 'My, what a nice life you've got. Every time I drop by you're busy washing each and every leaf on your lily plants.' Well, if she only knew!"

Sōsuke listened to his aunt's explanation in a daze and was hard-pressed to offer even a token response—further proof, it struck him, of his nervous disorder having robbed him of the capacity he once had to think on his feet and come to quick, clear conclusions. For her part, his aunt seemed worried that he had not taken her at her word and blurted out the amount of funds diverted to Yasunosuke:

5,000 yen. For the time being Yasunosuke had to live on his meager salary plus whatever dividends he received on this investment.

"And who knows what will happen with these dividend payments," she added. "If he's lucky it might come to somewhere around ten to fifteen percent, but there's always the possibility that if some little thing goes wrong, it'll all go up in smoke."

In the absence of any glaring evidence of greedy behavior on his aunt's part, Sōsuke felt at a distinct disadvantage; yet the thought of ending his visit without some sally on behalf of Koroku's future struck him as absurd. Setting aside the issue of the property sale, he interrogated his aunt on the question of the thousand yen he had entrusted to his uncle for Koroku's education.

"That's all gone, every penny of it spent on Koroku," she replied. "And that's the honest truth, Sō-san. Seven hundred yen have gone into his secondary-school expenses alone."

While he was at it Sōsuke thought he might as well try to find out what had become of the paintings and antiques he had asked his uncle to dispose of for him.

"Oh, those! Well, the most ridiculous thing happened..." she began, and then paused to gauge Sōsuke's reaction. "But really, weren't you told about all that earlier?" He replied that he had not been. "Oh, my goodness! Your uncle must have completely forgotten about it," she said, and proceeded to recount the incident in full.

Shortly after Sōsuke returned to Hiroshima, his uncle had sought advice from an acquaintance—Sanada, she thought his name was— on how best to sell such objects. The man was said to be quite the connoisseur of paintings, antiques, and all, and as a regular broker was evidently well known in the trade. Anyway, this Sanada had accepted his uncle's assignment on the spot, and after that he would carry off one object or another, saying that so-and-so is interested in this, so-and-so wants to see that, but then he'd never bring anything back. Whenever his uncle pressed him, he made excuses—the prospective buyer still had it and what not—and never produced the item, until finally things must have got too hot for him to handle and he simply disappeared.

"But you know, there's still one folding screen left. We noticed it when we last moved. I remember Yasu saying, 'This belongs to Sō-san. When you have a chance, why not send it over to him?'"

She spoke about the objects that Sōsuke had entrusted to her husband's care as though she attached no importance to them whatsoever. Yet Sōsuke himself, in having simply let the matter go up to now, could scarcely be said to have shown much interest in them, either, and he refrained from expressing anger, even faced with someone who seemed unruffled by any twinge of conscience. But then she went on to say, "Listen, we have no use for the screen here, so if you like, why not take it home with you? They say that these things have gone through the roof lately." For all his diffidence Sōsuke had a mind to accept her offer.

When the two-panel screen was taken out of a closet and Sōsuke viewed it in the light, he was sure it was something he recognized. Toward the bottom of the screen were depicted in dense profusion bush clover, bellflowers, *susuki*, kudzu vines, and *ominaeshi*;[17] above them, a perfectly round silver moon; and off to one side of the moon, the verse: "A country lane, the sky above / amidst the moonlight / *ominaeshi*," which was signed by Ki'ichi.[18] As Sōsuke knelt in front of the screen and his eyes lingered now on a dark discoloration on the silver disk, now on the underside of the wind-tossed kudzu leaves, looking positively desiccated, and now on the signature, "Hōitsu,"[19] written in semi-cursive style in the middle of a crimson circle the size of a rice cake, he was transported back to the time when his father was still alive.

During the New Year's holidays his father would without fail bring this screen out from the dark storehouse and set it up in the vestibule, then place in front of it a square box made of rosewood in which to collect New Year's greeting cards. At the same time he would hang in the parlor a pair of scrolls depicting a tiger—auspicious on this occasion, he always said. To this day Sōsuke recalled his father having informed him once that these scrolls were the work of Gantai, not Ganku.[20] There was an ink spot on the figure of the tiger. It was no more than a small splotch on the muzzle of the beast, depicted here with its tongue out, drinking from a valley stream, yet it was still conspicuous enough to have irritated his father no end. Whenever his father caught sight of Sōsuke near these scrolls, he would look at him with a peculiar mixture of amusement and resentment and say, "Do you remember splashing that ink there? You could be very naughty when you were a little boy."

Now, as he knelt in obeisance to the screen and thought of the life he used to lead in Tokyo, he told his aunt, "Thank you, I'll accept your offer."

"Oh yes! You certainly should take it," she said, adding in an abundance of goodwill, "If you like I'll have a courier deliver it for you."

Once the necessary details had been worked out, Sōsuke decided that that was enough for one day and went home. After dinner he went out on the veranda with Oyone. As they refreshed themselves in the cool air, two white yukata side by side in the darkness, he reported on the events of the day.

"Didn't you see Yasu-san?" Oyone asked.

"No, evidently he's at the factory all day long, even on Saturdays."

"It must be hard work." Such was Oyone's comment about Yasunosuke's situation; about the uncle and aunt's past conduct, she had nothing to say.

When Sōsuke expressed his concern about Koroku's future—what ever could be done about it?—she said only, "Yes, I wonder."

"If she keeps making excuses, there are a lot of things I could say to her," Sōsuke said, letting his imagination run wild. "But if I start down that road, it's bound to end in a lawsuit, and since there's no proof of anything, we could never win."

"No one expects you to win some judge's ruling."

Sōsuke smiled wryly at Oyone's quick response and ceased to pursue this scenario.

"This all happened because I couldn't come to Tokyo then."

"And when you were able to come to Tokyo, it didn't make a difference anyway."

The couple continued for a while in this vein, then, again peering up at the ribbon of sky beyond the eaves, spoke about tomorrow's weather and retired beneath their canopy of mosquito netting.

The following Sunday Sōsuke sent for Koroku and told him what their aunt had said, sparing no details.

"I have no idea why she chose not to tell you all of this herself," he said. "Maybe it's because she knows you're a hothead, or maybe it's because she still thinks of you as a child who can only be fed a simplified version of things. But in any case, what I've just told you is the truth of the matter."

But Koroku's craving to know was not to be satisfied by even this highly detailed account. He replied only with a curt "I see," and cast at his brother the peevish look of someone who had been wronged.

"There's nothing to be done about it now. Anyway, your aunt and Yasu-san meant well enough, I suppose."

"Yes, I know that!" Koroku's tone was bitter.

"Well, then, maybe you think it's my fault. And it is, of course. I've been full of faults my whole life!" Stretched out on the tatami, puffing a cigarette, Sōsuke had nothing further to say about the matter.

Koroku, too, fell silent, and fixed his gaze on the Hōitsu screen that had been set up in a corner of the parlor. "Do you remember this screen?" his brother asked. Yes, Koroku murmured, he did. "It was delivered from our aunt's the day before yesterday. It's the only thing of Father's I have left. If it could be sold for enough to cover your tuition, I'd give it to you here and now. But a single, peeling screen is hardly going to get you through university," said Sōsuke. Then, with a self-deprecating smile, he muttered, "And what insanity to leave such an object standing here in this heat. But I don't even have a place to store it."

In spite of his chronic exasperation with this nonchalant, dithering brother of his and the yawning gulf between them, Koroku could never bring himself to quarrel over anything serious. This time, too, he appeared to wither. "I don't care about the screen," he ventured, "but what would you suggest I do from now on?"

"Well, it is a problem," said Sōsuke. "But we don't have to decide anything before the end of the year. So in the meantime you should think things over carefully. And I'll do the same."

By nature Koroku could not stand having things left up in the air. He began to complain bitterly about his intolerable situation. Even if he were to attend his classes, how could he concentrate? How could he even prepare his lessons? But his complaints had no effect on his brother's detached attitude. When his litany became too shrill to ignore, Sōsuke cut him short.

"To be able to muster so many complaints about one little thing—yes, you'll get ahead, that's for sure. Well, if you want to quit school, there's really nothing to stop you from dropping out right now. You're made of a lot stronger stuff than I am." Their conversation thus stalled, Koroku returned to his dormitory in Hongō.[21]

That evening, after a bath and dinner, Sōsuke went out with Oyone to a festival at a local tutelary shrine. There they bought two inexpensive plants and took them home, Sōsuke carrying one pot, Oyone the other. To give the plants the benefit of the night dew they opened up the shutters that faced the embankment and set them down side by side in the garden.

"How are things going for Koroku?" Oyone asked her husband as they crawled into bed under the mosquito net.

"Not well at all," Sōsuke answered. In about ten minutes they were fast asleep.

Sōsuke awoke the next day to another week at the office, where he had no time to think about Koroku. Even while relaxing back at home he took care not to expose the problem directly to the light of his mind's eye. The brain beneath his thatch of hair could not withstand such perturbation. When he recalled how, with his penchant for mathematics, he once had the stamina to sketch out the most complicated geometric figures in his head, he couldn't help shuddering at the drastic decline in his faculties, which seemed to have set in over an incredibly short time.

All the same, once every day or so, the figure of Koroku hovered indistinctly at the back of his mind and triggered the reaction, for that moment at least, that he must give serious consideration to his brother's future. The next moment, however, he invariably stifled the thought on the grounds that there really was no cause for haste. Thus Sōsuke passed the days, unable to dispel the nagging sense of indecision lodged in his breast.

Early one evening at the end of September, when dense clusters of stars were visible in the Milky Way, Yasunosuke showed up at their door as though fallen from the sky. His visits were so rare that Sōsuke and Oyone were taken by surprise, and they suspected that he had come with some definite purpose in mind. And in fact he had come to discuss matters related to Koroku.

Recently Koroku had turned up at Yasunosuke's factory and unburdened himself. Yes, he'd heard from his brother all about the money meant for his tuition, but then he'd made it this far as a serious student and was not at all happy at the thought of being unable to attend university, and so whatever it might take—borrowing money or whatever else—he really wanted to go as far as he could . . . Now couldn't Yasunosuke come up with some solution? Yasunosuke had answered, "I really need to discuss these things with Sō-san," but Koroku stopped him in his tracks, saying that his brother was not the sort to listen to anybody, and since he himself had dropped out of university he thought it was perfectly all right for others to give up on their education, too. If you wanted to pinpoint the cause of all this, well, basically Sōsuke was to blame, in spite of which he wasn't fazed a bit and paid no heed to anything others might say. This being the case, Yasunosuke was the only one he could turn to. It might seem strange to rely on him now that his own mother had formally refused any further assistance, but he hoped Yasunosuke would be more understanding than she was. Koroku persisted in his queries and showed no sign of letting up.

Yasunosuke did his best, he said, to mollify Koroku before sending him home, telling him he was mistaken about his brother, who was actually quite concerned about him and due to come over soon for another discussion. As Koroku was about to leave he had taken out of his pocket several blank sheets of paper and asked his cousin to affix his seal: He would need them, he explained, to complete the requisite absence reports for school.[22] Until it was resolved whether he was to continue his education or drop out, he could not possibly study, and so there was no point in his attending classes every day.

Yasunosuke left after chatting for less than an hour, saying that he was busy, without reaching any concrete agreement with Sōsuke about Koroku's future. His parting words were that in any case they should all have a leisurely get-together sometime and come to a decision, preferably with Koroku present if that would be all right.

When the couple was alone Oyone addressed her husband: "May I ask what you're thinking?"

Striking a pose with hands thrust under his sash and shoulders slightly raised, Sōsuke said, "I'm thinking how much I wish I could be like Koroku again. Here I am constantly worrying that he might meet up with the same fate that I did, while for him his brother doesn't even exist. Can you beat that?"

Oyone took the tea things out to the kitchen. Their conversation over, husband and wife spread out the bedding on the tatami. The cool, silvery river of the Milky Way hung suspended high above their dreams.

The following week having passed with no visit by Koroku or any further communication from the Saekis, Sōsuke's household reverted to its normal uneventfulness. Every day the couple rose at an hour when the dew still glistened and witnessed a beautiful sun shining above the eaves. After nightfall they would sit together, a lamp with a base of dark red bamboo between them, casting elongated shadows in its light. When their conversation stalled, as it did with some frequency, the only sound to break the silence was the tick-tock of the pendulum clock.

Even with this return to their weekly routine they did discuss certain issues concerning Koroku. It was a foregone conclusion that if he was determined to continue his education, or for that matter even if he was not, he would soon have to vacate his current boardinghouse and either move back to the Saekis or stay with Sōsuke and Oyone; there really was no other choice. Nonetheless, while it might seem as though Sōsuke's aunt had addressed this issue once and for all, it was likely that if appealed to she would not refuse to take Koroku in again for the time being, as a gesture of goodwill. Yet it would then be ethically remiss of Sōsuke not to assume responsibility for everything beyond his brother's lodging, that is, tuition, spending money, and all other expenses necessary for Koroku to continue his education. Sōsuke simply could not afford to do this, however, given their current household budget. Sōsuke and Oyone calculated in minute detail their present income and expenses.

"No, it can't be done," he said.

"Any way you look at it, it would be impossible," she agreed.

Next to the sitting room they occupied at the moment was the kitchen, which was flanked by the maid's room, on the right, and on the left, a six-mat room. There being only three of them in the house, including the maid, Oyone had deemed the six-mat room of no particular use and placed there, by the east window, her small vanity with a mirror attached. It was here that, once Sōsuke was done with his ablutions and his breakfast, she retired in the morning to change her clothes.

"Instead of Koroku staying at the Saekis, couldn't we clear out the six-mat room and have him live with us?" Oyone proposed. Her idea was that if they took charge of room and board and the Saekis contributed something each month toward the remaining expenses, then Koroku would be able to realize his wish and finish his schooling. "As for his clothes," she added, "he could make do with hand-me-downs from you and Yasu-san that I redid to fit him."

The idea had in fact already occurred to Sōsuke, who had not, however, been keen to ask so much of Oyone, and had therefore not even mentioned it. Now that his wife had suggested this arrangement herself, though, he naturally lacked the conviction to reject it. He wrote to Koroku. As long as his brother had no objections, he said, he would visit the Saekis once again and discuss the matter. The very same evening Koroku received the letter he dashed right on over, the rain pelting down on his oilpaper umbrella. He was in high spirits, as if the deal were already done.

Oyone gave Koroku cause for such assurance. "After all," she said, "your aunt only said what she said because back then, we just foisted everything to do with you on them and did nothing about it for the longest time. Say what you will, if only it had been possible, your brother would somehow have made things right a long time ago, but they just didn't work out, as you know. Anyway, if we present them with this plan for you to live here, neither your aunt nor Yasu-san could say no. It will all surely turn out well, so you can stop worrying. I promise you."

Thus reassured by Oyone, Koroku returned to Hongō in the driving rain. Two days later he was back to ask if his brother had talked with the Saekis. Three days after that he appeared again, saying that he'd been over to their aunt's and learned that she still hadn't had any visit from Sōsuke, and urging that his brother move on this matter as soon as possible.

For his part Sōsuke passed the days telling himself that he would go over soon; in the meantime, autumn settled in with the visit still unpaid. And so it had come about that one splendid Sunday afternoon, deciding he could delay no longer, he addressed the issue in a letter that he mailed to Banchō. And in response he had received a reply from his aunt to the effect that Yasunosuke was presently unavailable, having gone to Kobe.

5

MRS. SAEKI paid a visit on a Saturday afternoon after two o'clock. It had been unusually cold and cloudy since morning, now that the wind had suddenly shifted to the north, and the guest warmed her hands over a cylindrical brazier encased in bamboo.

"My goodness, Oyone-san, this room must be nice and cool in the summer, but it does get chilly this time of year, doesn't it!"

Mrs. Saeki's naturally curly hair was piled neatly on top of her head, and her kimono jacket was tied in front with an old-fashioned braided cord. The woman was fond of her drink at the dinner table, and it was perhaps to this that she owed her lustrous complexion and plump figure, both of which contributed to a remarkably youthful appearance for someone her age. Whenever she stopped by, Oyone would comment to Sōsuke afterward on how young she looked, and he would invariably reply that so she should, having in all these years borne only one child, as though this fact alone accounted for her appearance. Oyone thought that he might have a point. But after listening to Sōsuke's remarks she would often retreat to the six-mat room and glance at her face in the mirror. Each glance gave her the impression that her cheeks had grown still more hollow than the last time she had looked. Nothing was quite so painful for Oyone as thinking of herself in relation to children. In the household of their landlord, on top of the embankment behind their house, there was a whole flock of children whose clamorous voices, which could be heard clearly as they played on the swing or at hide-and-seek in the garden up above, always made Oyone feel empty and wistful. And here, in front of her, sat the aunt who, precisely because she had borne a single son and seen him grow up without incident into an educated gentleman, wore this look of complacency—and also of sufficient prosperity to have conferred on her a double chin. Yasuno-suke seemed to worry constantly about his mother's weight and the risk of a stroke; but to Oyone, the worried son and the mother who was the object of his concern appeared equally fortunate.

"And how about Yasu-san?"

"Well yes, my dear, finally he's back. He got home the night be-fore last. Of course his being away is why we've taken such a terribly long time to respond—I mean, it seems I really owe you an apology." Without expanding on this gesture, however, she returned to the subject of her son's affairs. "Well, the boy did manage to graduate from the university—and thank you for all your warm encourage-ment!—but it's what happens from now on that's absolutely crucial, and I do worry. Still, he's had that job at the Tsukijima factory since September, and so long as he sticks to it the way he's been doing, I'm pretty sure things will work out all right in the end ... But then, where young people are concerned, you can never tell what kind of turnabout they might make somewhere down the road."

Oyone could only get in edgewise a "how nice" here and a "con-gratulations!" there.

"The trip he just made to Kobe," she went on, "was all bound up with this new business of his, you see. Something about a com-buschon engine or con-bustion engine that gets attached to a bonito boat somehow ..."

Not understanding a word of this, Oyone nevertheless mur-mured politely inquisitive monosyllables, which were enough to en-courage her visitor.

"Well, I don't have the faintest idea myself what it is. The first time Yasu tried to explain it to me, all I could say was 'My, my!' and 'Oh really?' and even now I don't have a clue about the com-buschon engine." The repetition of the unfamiliar term was accompanied by a raucous laugh. "Anyhow, the general idea seems to be some sort of machine that you fire up with gasoline in order to make the boat move on its own, which as far as I can gather is the big advantage to it. Evidently, when one of these machines is attached, nobody has to bother much with rowing the boat anymore—a dozen miles, two dozen miles out to sea, it doesn't matter; it still just keeps going like the wind. Do you have any idea how many bonito boats there are in this country? Well, my dear, it's truly staggering. And if you could fit out every one of them with this machine, why, Yasu says you could make a killing. Lately he's been in a perfect frenzy, working constantly on it with no time left for anything else. Just the other day I told him, 'Huge profits are all well and good, but if you keep on at this rate and ruin your health, what's the point?,' and even he had to laugh."

The aunt went on and on about Yasunosuke and the bonito boats. Bursting with pride and, for all her protestations, supremely confident in her son's venture, she never brought up Koroku's predicament. There was still no sign of Sōsuke, who should have been home long since, leaving Oyone to wonder what possibly could have happened to him.

On his way home that day Sōsuke got off the streetcar at Surugadai-shita and from there, with his cheeks puffed out and his mouth puckered as if with something vinegary, made his way on foot a couple of blocks farther to the gate of a dentist's office. At the dinner table with Oyone a few days earlier, he had taken up his chopsticks as he chatted and somehow managed to bite down hard the wrong way on a front tooth, which immediately erupted in pain. The tooth wobbled when he grasped it with his fingers, and it stung when sipping tea or exhaling. This morning as he cleaned his teeth with a toothpick, avoiding the one that was troubling him, he examined the inside of his mouth in the mirror and found two coldly glinting silver-filled molars, relics of the Hiroshima years, and an irregular row of front teeth, so worn that they might have been filed down. Changing into his office clothes he had said to Oyone, "I must have been born with bad teeth—see how this one moves," and stuck his finger in his mouth to show her the wobbly lower tooth.

"That comes with age," Oyone said with a smile as she adjusted his detachable collar and fastened it at the back of his shirt.

Thus it had come about that Sōsuke resigned himself to visiting the dentist. Entering the waiting room, he found there a large table flanked by velvet-covered benches on which three or four patients sat waiting, all hunched over, their chins tucked in. They were all women. Nearby stood a handsome brown gas stove, as yet unlit. Waiting his turn, Sōsuke cast his gaze at the white wall reflected from where he was sitting in a full-length mirror; then, out of boredom, he turned his attention to the magazines piled up on the table. He leafed through one, then another. They were all women's magazines. He looked repeatedly at the images of women adorning the photogravure sections in front. Then he picked up a magazine with the title *Success*. On the first page appeared a list of "secrets to success," among which he noted one directive exhorting readers to charge full speed ahead in any undertaking, and another cautioning them that it wouldn't do simply to charge ahead in one's endeavors—a firm foundation must first be laid. He put the magazine down. "Success" and Sōsuke were poles apart. Indeed, he had been unaware up to this moment that a magazine of this name even existed. Presently, his curiosity revived, he opened the magazine again. Two lines of block-printed Chinese characters, uninterrupted by any Japanese script,[23] caught his eye: "The wind blows across azure skies; drifting clouds disperse / The moon climbs o'er the eastern hills: a great shining sphere." Normally Sōsuke was not one to take much interest in poetry, whether Chinese or Japanese, but somehow this couplet appealed to him deeply. It had nothing to do with the nice parallelism between the two lines or anything of that sort. Rather, he felt a mild thrill at the thought of how happy a person would be if he could feel at one with the state evoked by the landscape of the poem. His interest piqued, he read the essay to which the poem was appended but found it totally irrelevant. After he put the magazine aside, the poem alone continued to reverberate in his mind. Certainly, in his day-to-day life over the past four or five years, he had encountered no such landscape.

Just then, the door opened across from where he sat and an intern with a slip of paper in hand summoned him by name to the treatment room. The room turned out to be twice the size of the waiting room, and of a brightness that suggested it had been designed to maximize natural light. Four dental chairs were arrayed on either side of the room; at each of them stood a white-jacketed man administering treatment. Sōsuke was conducted to the farthermost chair where, as prompted, he stepped up onto a kind of footstool in order to seat himself. The intern carefully covered him from the waist down with a striped apron.

Reclining comfortably in the chair, he found the pain from the offending tooth to be not all that serious. On the contrary, he felt a delightful sensation of ease settle over his shoulders, down his back, and around his waist. He simply lay back and gazed at the gas pipe that hung from the ceiling. Then it occurred to him that given such an office, with its various appurtenances, he might be charged a good deal more on his way out than he had bargained for.

At which point there appeared a very fat man, with hair rather too thin for his youthful-looking face, who proceeded to greet him with such elaborate formality that Sōsuke, sitting in the chair as he was, hastened to nod his head slightly in response. After making a few general inquiries about his condition, the fat man examined the inside of his mouth and gently wiggled the problem tooth.

"Once it starts to wobble like this," he said, "I'm afraid there's no way to reset it firmly in the gums. We have some necrosis here, you see."

This diagnosis descended on Sōsuke like the autumn sun's weak rays. "So I've finally reached that age, have I?" is what he wanted to say but, mildly embarrassed, he responded, by way of confirming the diagnosis: "Then it can't be fixed?"

Smiling, the fat man replied, "Indeed, I fear I have no choice other than to respectfully submit that it is incurable. In the worst case we will have to resign ourselves to extracting the tooth, but at present I don't think that is necessary, and so I shall simply relieve the pain. With necrosis, you see—but then perhaps you do not comprehend the term 'necrosis'—it means that the inside of the tooth is pretty much rotten."

Murmuring abjectly, Sōsuke prepared himself to submit to whatever treatment the fat man might mete out. The man proceeded to drill a hole in the tooth's root with a whirring machine; next, he passed a long, wirelike device through the hole; finally, after sniffing at the wire's tip, he drew out a thin strand of some substance. "I've removed this much of the nerve," he said, showing it to Sōsuke. After packing the hole with a medicinal preparation, he told Sōsuke to return the following day.

When he climbed down from the chair and straightened himself up, his field of vision shifted from the ceiling overhead to the garden outside the windows, where a large potted pine, at least five feet tall, came into focus. A sandal-shod gardener was meticulously covering the pine's roots with matted straw. Yes, this was the season, he thought, when the dew at night began to stiffen into frost—a sign for people who could afford it to busy themselves with preparations of this nature.

On the way out he stopped at the pharmacy counter and received a specially prepared powder, with instructions to dilute it in warm water to a strength of 1:100 and gargle at least ten times a day. He was pleasantly surprised at the modest fee charged for treatment. Calculating that at this rate the four or five additional visits the dentist had advised would pose no hardship, he was about to put on his shoes when he noticed for the first time that the soles had holes in them.

When Sōsuke reached home he learned he had just missed his aunt.

"Oh, is that so?" Noncommittal response notwithstanding, he changed out of his office clothes with a show of annoyance, then sat down at his customary place in front of the brazier. Oyone gathered up an armful of shirt, trousers, and socks and carried them off to the six-mat room. His mind wandering, Sōsuke began to smoke; then, at the sound of clothes being brushed in the six-mat room, he asked, "Oyone, did my aunt have anything in particular to say?"

His toothache, in the natural course of things, had subsided, and the chilly, autumnal mood that had assailed him abated somewhat. In due time he had Oyone fish out the gargling medicine from his pocket and bring it to him diluted in warm water. He stepped out onto the veranda and began rinsing his mouth vigorously.

"The days have really grown short, haven't they?" he said, calling back inside to his wife.

Presently the sun set. From the early-evening hours this neighborhood, where even in the daytime the noise of rickshaw traffic was not very noticeable, fell quite still. As was their habit the couple drew near the lamplight. In the whole wide world this spot where they sat together felt like the only source of brightness. In the light that shone from the lamp Sōsuke was conscious only of Oyone, Oyone only of Sōsuke. They forgot the dark world of human affairs, which lay beyond the lamp's power to illuminate. It was through spending each evening this way that as time passed they had found their own life together.

Tranquillity having resumed, the couple leisurely discussed the reply that Mrs. Saeki had given to Sōsuke's proposal, all the while shaking a container of dried-kelp snacks—a souvenir from Kobe, courtesy of Yasunosuke, she had said—and picking out the ones seasoned with pepper.

"But can't they be expected to take care of Koroku's monthly tuition and pocket money?" asked Sōsuke.

"She said they can't manage that. She told me any way you look at it those two expenses add up to ten yen a month, and for them to come up with that amount every month would be a crushing burden at this stage."

"But for us to put up twenty yen a month through the end of the year—isn't that simply out of the question?"

"Yes, of course. And so she did say that Yasu told her they would somehow kick in a contribution for just the next couple of months, but in the meantime would we please come up with some other arrangement."

"Is it that they really can't manage this much?"

"I can't answer that. All I can tell you is what your aunt told me."

"But then, I suppose when they make their killing on those bonito boats they won't have to think twice about such a piddling sum."

"Oh, absolutely not," Oyone chimed in with a little chuckle.

Sōsuke's mouth moved at the corners as if he were about to say something else, but the conversation simply died out.

After a while he spoke up again. "In any case we've simply got to take Koroku in. Everything else depends on that. He's been attending classes lately, hasn't he?"

"I think so." Scarcely listening to Oyone's reply, Sōsuke, in a departure from his usual habits, retreated to his place of study. An hour or so later, when Oyone softly slid open the panel and peeked into the parlor, she found him at his desk reading.

"Are you working on something? It's really time for you to go to bed," she urged him.

Turning toward her, he assented and rose from his desk.

As he was changing into his sleeping robe and wrapping the wide crepe sash around his waist, he said, "Tonight I was reading the *Analects*[24] for the first time in ages."

"Did the *Analects* have something to offer?" Oyone asked in response.

"No, not a thing," he replied. Then, as he laid his black head of hair on the pillow, he said, "Oh, you were right. This trouble with my tooth does come with age. It seems that once they start to wobble like this there's no way to fix them."

6

IT WAS now settled that, whatever else, Koroku would be moving into his brother's house as soon as he was ready.

"I hadn't thought much about what a bother it would be to find another place to put these things," Oyone observed plaintively to Sōsuke, gazing with a look of mild regret at the mulberry-wood mirror stand in the six-mat room. And in fact, once deprived of this space, she would have no place to attend to her appearance. At a loss for suggestions, Sōsuke rose to his feet and cast a glance at one of the oblique panels of the mirror, which stood across the room next to the windowsill. From this angle he could see a reflection of Oyone in profile, from her cheek down to her neckline. Distressed at the sight of her poor color, he shifted his gaze from the reflection in the mirror to the actual person. Her hair was disheveled, the back of her collar faintly soiled.

"Are you feeling all right?" he said to her. "You look very pale."

"It must be the cold," she replied, and then quickly opened the door to a closet on the west wall. At the bottom of the closet there was an old, badly scarred chest of drawers and, on top of that, a Chinese-style trunk and a couple of wicker containers.

"There's absolutely no place to put these," she said.

"Then you should just leave them there."

On the level of small details like this, Koroku's impending entrance into their household posed no little trouble to them both. Therefore they did not go out of their way to urge haste on Koroku, who, after agreeing to move in with them, as yet showed no signs of doing so. They tacitly shared the view that each day's postponement was an extra day's reprieve from living at what were bound to be very close quarters. Perhaps out of the same apprehension, Koroku for his part seemed determined to stay at his lodging house as long as possible and kept putting off the move day after day. Unlike his brother and sister-in-law, however, he was not by nature one to sit quietly, merely waiting for the time to pass.

Meanwhile a thin coating of frost settled on the ground, reducing the *bashō* plant behind the house to shreds. In the mornings a bulbul[25] called out shrilly from the landlord's garden atop the embankment. In the evenings, mingling with the toots of the tofuseller's horn, the drum of the wooden fish-block[26] resounded from Emmyōji, the local temple. The days grew ever shorter. Oyone's complexion did not regain its customary color and luster but remained as Sōsuke had first noticed it in the mirror. On several occasions he came home from the office to find her asleep in the six-mat room. When he asked her what was wrong, she replied only that she was feeling out of sorts. When he suggested that she see a doctor, she would not hear of it. There was no need, she said.

Still, Sōsuke worried. Even at the office he grew preoccupied with Oyone's condition, to the extent that it was, he realized, interfering with his work. Then, one day, as he sat on the streetcar on his way home from work, he suddenly slapped his knee. Arriving at the house, he gleefully opened the door and in high spirits asked Oyone how her day had gone. As she proceeded with the usual routine of scooping up his clothes and socks and carrying them away, he followed her as far as the six-mat room and chortled, "Oyone, couldn't it be that you're pregnant?"

She did not reply, and, her head bent down, sedulously brushed the dust from her husband's suit. Later, when the sound of brushing had ceased and his wife still did not emerge, he returned to find her seated by the mirror stand, looking quite alone and cold in the dim room. She stood up and acknowledged his presence in a voice that retained a trace of tears.

That night the couple sat facing each other with hands cupped over a cast-iron kettle that had been placed on the brazier.

"So, what do you think of the goings-on in this world of ours!" Sōsuke's tone was uncharacteristically effusive, and it summoned up in Oyone's mind's eye a bright image of the two of them together before their marriage.

"Shouldn't we do something to liven things up?" he went on. "Things have been so dreary around here lately." Whereupon they launched into a discussion about whether to go out the next Sunday, and if so, where. Then the conversation shifted to what they might wear for the New Year. Sōsuke told Oyone, in a droll fashion that made her laugh at several points, about a colleague named Takagi who, pressed by his wife for a new kimono and such, refused out of hand, saying that he didn't work all day in order to satisfy her vanity. When she protested that she'd have nothing to wear in cold weather, he told her that if she felt chilly she would just have to throw some bedding around herself or put a blanket over her head—in short, simply make do for the time being. Watching her husband tell this story Oyone felt their past life reappearing before her eyes.

"Takagi's wife can make do with her bedding," he said, "but as for me, I'd really like to have a new overcoat. When I was at the dentist's the other day, I watched the gardener wrapping straw around the roots of a bonsai pine, and that was my reaction."

"That you wanted an overcoat?"

Sōsuke nodded.

Oyone looked directly at her husband as she said, her voice full of sympathy, "Well, then, have one made. We can pay on installment."

"Oh, let's just forget it." Sōsuke now sounded apologetic. "By the way," he then asked, "when do you suppose Koroku wants to move in?"

"I think he loathes the idea of moving here," Oyone replied. She had been conscious early on of Koroku's dislike for her. But, she told herself, this is my husband's younger brother, and ever since had gone out of her way to make herself agreeable in his eyes so as to win him over little by little. Perhaps it worked; recently she had come to believe that he felt toward her a degree of closeness that was at least average for a brother-in-law. In the present situation, however, she succumbed to irrational worries, imagining that she was the sole cause of Koroku's delay.

"Oh well, we really can't expect him to be thrilled at the idea of leaving his student lodgings for digs like this. He must be as put off as we are by the thought of us all living here at such close quarters. But then what do I care?—if he decides not to move in after all, I'll just go ahead and buy that overcoat for myself."

Sōsuke's response, brimming with masculine assertiveness, did not succeed in setting his wife's doubts to rest. Oyone remained silent. After a while, her slender chin still nestled in her collar, she turned her gaze toward her husband.

"Do you think Koroku hates me?" she asked.

When they had first come back to Tokyo, Sōsuke had often been questioned by his wife along these lines; each time the subject came up he went to great lengths to reassure her. Lately she had not said a word about it, however, as though all such suspicions were totally forgotten, and so he himself had ceased to worry on this score.

"Now don't go getting all worked up again," he said. "Why should it matter what Koroku thinks as long as you have me around."

"Is that what it says in the *Analects*?" At moments like this Oyone could be quite wry.

"Yes, that's what it says," Sōsuke answered. On this note the conversation came to an end.

The next morning Sōsuke awoke to a chilling sound on the tin-plated eaves.

"It's time to get up," said Oyone, appearing at his bedside, her sleeves still tied back from working in the kitchen. Listening to the constant drip-drip outside he wanted to stay just a little while longer under the covers. But at the sight of her animated figure, which so contrasted with her pallor, he leapt to his feet with a brisk word of greeting.

The landscape was obscured by the heavy downpour. Like a lion shaking its mane, the *mōsō* bamboo near the top of the embankment swayed occasionally, scattering raindrops all over. All that Sōsuke had to fortify himself with for the drenching he was about to get from this dreary sky were hot miso soup and warm rice.

"These shoes are going to leak again. But without a second pair, what can I do?" He stepped helplessly into the only pair he owned, punctured soles and all, and rolled up the cuffs of his pants a good inch.

That afternoon Sōsuke came home to find a metal basin full of soaking rags that Oyone had left out next to the mirror stand in the six-mat room. Directly over it on the ceiling was a single dark splotch from which water was dripping intermittently. "It's not just my shoes—now the house is getting soaked too!" he said with a hollow laugh.

In the evening Oyone placed some hot coals in the *kotatsu*[27] in order to dry out her husband's tweed socks and striped woolen pants. The next day it rained with equal force and the couple re- peated their routine. The day after that brought no relief. On the morning of the third day, Sōsuke furrowed his brow and clucked his tongue.

"It seems to have made up its mind to rain forever. My shoes are so sopping, I can't bear to put them on."

"And the six-mat room is a disaster from this nonstop leaking," said Oyone.

They talked about the roof and decided that as soon as the weather improved they would approach the landlord about having it patched. As for the shoes, however, there was nothing to be done. They chafed and squeaked as Sōsuke forced his feet into them, then off he went.

Mercifully, around eleven that morning, the sun burst out and it turned into an unseasonably mild day, with sparrows chirping in the hedges. When Sōsuke came home, Oyone, her face astonishingly radiant, asked him out of the blue, "Dear, would it be all right to sell the screen?"

The Hōitsu screen stood once again in a corner of the parlor, where it had first been placed upon delivery from the Saekis. Given the room's location and size, however, it had proved to be a decorative nuisance. Set up by the south wall, it half blocked the way in from the vestibule; alongside the east wall it shut out the light; in the only other remaining spot, it interfered with the view of the alcove.

"Here I've finally managed to get myself one keepsake from my father," Sōsuke had grumbled more than once, "and it turns out to clutter up the house."

Whenever the subject came up, Oyone stared at the perfectly round silver moon and its discolored rim, and at the ripe *susuki* plumes, whose color was all but indistinguishable from that of the silk it was painted on. She made it plain with her body language that she had no idea why anyone would make a fuss over such an object, yet she did not express her opinion aloud, out of deference to her husband, except on one occasion when she asked him, "I wonder, though—is this is actually a good painting?"

Sōsuke had taken this opportunity to explain to Oyone for the first time who Hōitsu was, but succeeded only in repeating random bits and pieces of what he hazily recalled his father telling him long ago. He was far from sure of his answers concerning the painting's true worth, the details of Hōitsu's career, and the like.

Still, this explanation was enough to make Oyone act with uncommon decisiveness. Making the connection between what she now knew about Hōitsu and what had been said in the course of their other conversations over the past week, she smiled quietly to herself. After the rain had stopped and the sun's rays had burst forth on the sitting-room shoji, she draped over her everyday kimono an oddly colored woven cloth, neither scarf nor shawl, and went out. After walking a couple of hundred yards she turned in the direction of the streetcar tracks and followed the road straight until she came to a rather large used-furniture store that was flanked by a bakery and a grocer's. Oyone was familiar with the store from having once bought a dining table with foldable legs there; this was also where Sōsuke had acquired the cast-iron kettle now sitting on the brazier.

Hands tucked in her sleeves, Oyone stood in front of the store and looked inside. There were plenty of the popular new iron kettles lined up in a row. The next things to catch her eye, thanks to their abundance, predictable at this season, were the small braziers. But there did not appear to be a single object that could properly be called an antique. Straight ahead of her hung a solitary tortoise shell of dubious provenance, below which, like a tail, dangled a long sacerdotal whisk[28] of yellowish horsehair. She also noted a couple of rosewood tea cabinets, but the wood looked so green it seemed likely to warp. Not that Oyone could tell for sure, but once she had satisfied herself that there were no hanging scrolls or paintings to be seen in the store, she went inside.

She had of course made her way to this place with the firm intention of realizing at least some gain from the screen her husband had received from the Saekis; having acquired considerable experience in transactions of this sort ever since their Hiroshima days, she was quite capable of initiating a sales pitch with the proprietor unhampered by all the effort and stress it would have cost the average housewife. The proprietor, a fiftyish man with a dark complexion and hollow cheeks, sat reading a newspaper through outsize tortoiseshell glasses and warming his hands over a bronze brazier, its exterior covered with knobs.

"Yes, I suppose I could come and have a look at it." The man was quick to answer, but Oyone was inwardly disappointed by his less than enthusiastic response. Still, as she herself had not set out on this venture with any high hopes, she felt obliged to take him up on his tepid offer, even if she felt as though she were asking him a favor.

"Very well," he said. "I'll be over later—the shop boy's not around just now, you see."

Their business concluded for now with these brusque words, Oyone went straight home, thinking to herself that it was far from certain the proprietor would show up. Having finished her simple, solitary lunch, she had just had Kiyo clear the table when a loud voice suddenly boomed out a "Hello!" and in came the furniture dealer from the front entrance. Oyone ushered him into the parlor and showed him the screen. He stroked the frame and the backing.

"Well, if you want to dispose of it . . ." Then, after a moment's consideration and with a great show of reluctance, he named a price: "I'll take it off your hands for six yen."

This struck Oyone as quite reasonable. But it occurred to her that it would be presumptuous of her to close the deal without at least a few words with Sōsuke; then too, the object has a certain history to it, she thought, becoming still more cautious. Telling the dealer that she would discuss it with her husband as soon as he came home, she showed him to the door. On his way out he said, "Well, madam, since you've gone to so much trouble, I suppose I could be a bit generous here and offer you one more yen."

Although trembling inside, Oyone was emboldened to reply, "But you know, sir, it is a Hōitsu!"

Unimpressed, the man said dismissively, "There's not much of a market for Hōitsu these days." After eyeing Oyone at length, he added, "Well, then, be sure to talk it over carefully," and walked away.

That evening, after describing this scene in detail, Oyone became the ingenue again as she asked, "But then, we couldn't really sell it, could we?"

Recently Sōsuke had become very preoccupied with material wants. And yet he was so used to living on a modest scale that it was now second nature for him to make do on what was in fact an inadequate budget; it simply never occurred to him to seek, through some clever maneuver, the means to provide even a small degree of extra comfort in his life. Listening to Oyone's account of the day's events, his main reaction was one of astonishment at her keen resourcefulness. At the same time he doubted that any of this was really necessary. When he prodded Oyone on this point, she said that if they ended up with a little under ten yen from the sale, not only could he order a new pair of shoes, there would be enough left over for her to buy a bolt of *meisen*[29] silk for a kimono. That may be true, thought Sōsuke, but when he weighed in his mind the Hōitsu screen handed down from his father against a pair of new shoes and a bolt of ordinary silk, the disparity seemed extreme to the point of absurdity.

"If you want to sell the screen," he said, "well, go ahead and sell it. I mean, it's only taking up space here. Still, I'll get along without the new shoes. It's only a problem when we have the kind of deluge we had a few days ago. The weather's fine now."

"But when it does rain again you'll have the same problem."

Sōsuke could hardly give Oyone a lifetime guarantee of good weather; for her part, Oyone could not bring herself to tell him they must sell the screen before it rained again. They looked at each other and laughed.

Oyone finally asked him, "Do you think the price is too low?"

"Yes, it most likely is." When confronted with this question, the furniture dealer's offer did strike him as too low. If they were to sell the screen, he wanted to get as much money for it as possible. He vaguely recalled having read something in the paper to the effect that for certain old paintings and calligraphy scrolls, the market had recently soared. If only he had an heirloom like that, he thought, but then faced up to the reality that no such thing had dropped into the microcosm he inhabited.

"They always say, 'It all depends on the buyer,' but it also depends on the seller. As great a work as it may be, it won't matter, since the fact that it's mine means it won't sell for much. Even so, seven or eight yen—that's really too cheap."

There was a defeatist ring to Sōsuke's words. Even while he was at pains to defend not only the Hōitsu screen but also the furniture dealer, he gave the impression that his involvement alone rendered the situation hopeless.

Looking somewhat depressed herself, Oyone dropped the subject.

The next day Sōsuke told all of his colleagues at the office about the screen and its prospective sale. More or less unanimously they said the offer he'd been made was ridiculously low. Not one of them offered to broker a more lucrative deal, however, nor did anyone acquaint him with certain steps he should take, channels he should explore, in order not to end up a sucker. Finally, then, he was left with no choice but to sell to the furniture dealer on the side street.

That is, the only real alternative was not to sell the screen at all but to set it up again in the parlor and live with the nuisance. He opted for this alternative, and there stood the screen once more when the furniture dealer turned up and asked them to sell it to him, this time for fifteen yen. The couple smiled at each other. Having decided between themselves to hold out awhile longer, they declined to sell. Oyone had begun to take pleasure in rejecting the dealer's offers. The dealer visited them again. They declined another offer. On his fourth visit he brought along a man they had never met; after a whispered conversation with the man, the dealer at length came up with an offer of thirty-five yen. The couple proceeded to huddle off to one side for a discussion of their own, then made up their minds finally to dispose of the screen.

7

THE CRYPTOMERIA around Emmyōji had turned reddish black, as though scorched. On clear days a jagged white line of mountains appeared along the distant rim of the wind-scoured sky. The waning year pursued the couple, each passing day driving them further into the cold. The cry of the *nattō* peddler[30] as he made his regular morning rounds was redolent of the frost that gripped the roof tiles. Listening to the cry as he lay in bed, Sōsuke realized that winter had come again. Oyone began her annual vigil, worrying over what might go wrong between year's end and the coming of spring. "Let's hope the pipes don't freeze like last year," she would mutter in the kitchen. Evenings, the couple kept close company with the *kotatsu*. They recalled wistfully the mild winters of Hiroshima and Fukuoka.

"We're just like Mr. and Mrs. Honda across the way," Oyone laughed. The Hondas were a retired couple who lived in the same tract and likewise rented from Sakai. With the assistance of one young housemaid, they lived such a quiet life that from morning till night not so much as a squeal or a scrape could be heard from their house. From time to time Oyone, alone sewing in the sitting room, could hear a voice calling out "Grandpa!," which was how old Mrs. Honda referred to her husband. When on occasion she bumped into Mrs. Honda at her gate or elsewhere outside her house, they would exchange formal greetings appropriate to the season, and Mrs. Honda would invite Oyone over for a chat. Oyone, however, had never paid a single visit, nor had Mrs. Honda ever called on her. What she knew about the old couple was, then, very sketchy. That the Hondas had one son who had an excellent post in the administration of the residency-general[31] of Korea or some such office, and who sent them enough money each month for them to live comfortably—this much she had gleaned from someone who delivered goods for one of the local shops.

"Is old Mr. Honda still fiddling around with his potted plants?" Sōsuke asked.

"It's too cold for that now. He's probably stopped. There are a lot of pots stacked up under their veranda."

The conversation then shifted from the house across the lane to their landlord's domicile. The polar opposite of the Hondas, this household struck the couple as lively in the extreme. At this season the grounds were desolate and no longer swarmed with the boisterous play of children, but the sound of the piano persisted night after night. Even the raucous laughter of scullery maids and whoever else was in the kitchen reverberated down to the couple's sitting room.

"What does this fellow do for a living?" Sōsuke asked. For some time now he had been pestering Oyone with such questions.

"I don't suppose he does anything but amuse himself," she said, repeating what had become her stock answer to questions along these lines. "What with his land holdings and rental properties..."

Sōsuke's inquisitiveness on the subject of Sakai went no further than this. In the past, after he had withdrawn from the university, whenever Sōsuke ran into someone who wore about him the boastful air of occupying an enviable position in the world, he had to stifle the impulse to say: Just you wait and see. With time this impulse turned into a more generalized sense of hatred. In the last year or two, however, he had become totally indifferent to the distinction between himself and others. The view he had come to adopt was this: Just as he had been born to lead the life that he was living, so others had come into the world bearing their own destinies; inasmuch as he and these others belonged to different subspecies to begin with, there was no connection, aside from coexisting as members of the human race, between himself and others, therefore no grounds for contending interests. Consequently, although he might occasionally ask, in idle conversation, "What does so-and-so do for a living?," he could hardly be bothered even to listen carefully to the reply.

For the most part Oyone shared this indifference toward others. But tonight she uncharacteristically responded to Sōsuke's question at length, and proceeded to mention that Mr. Sakai was a man of about forty and clean-shaven; that the daughter who was always practicing the piano was the eldest, eleven or twelve years old; and that when other children came over to play they were not allowed to use the swing.

"Why is it that the other children can't use the swing?" asked Sōsuke.

"Well, it seems that Mr. Sakai is stingy and doesn't want the swing to wear out so soon."

Sōsuke burst out laughing. The image of a skinflint evoked by such rumors was totally at odds with the landlord who, at the first mention of a leak, had in fact immediately sent a roofer over and who, apprised that their hedge had rotted out, had dispatched his own gardener to address the problem.

That night neither Honda's pots nor Sakai's swing turned up in Sōsuke's dreams. Having gone to bed around half past ten, he snored like a man exhausted by the myriad phenomena of the universe. Oyone, who had lately had trouble sleeping because of a lingering headache, opened her eyes from time to time and looked about the dimly lit room. A small lamp was sitting in the alcove. They were accustomed to keeping it burning throughout the night, and placed it there at bedtime after turning the wick down.

Oyone moved her pillow about nervously. With each change in position the shoulder on which she slept slid out a bit farther across the futon, until she ended up turned over on her stomach. She then propped herself up with her elbows and gazed for a while at her husband. Finally she stood up and, covering her nightgown with a robe that had been laid out at the foot of the bed, picked up the lamp from the alcove. Coming around to Sōsuke's side of the bed, she crouched down and called out to him. He was no longer snoring, having resumed the regular breathing of deep sleep. Straightening up, Oyone slid open the partition and, lamp in hand, entered the sitting room. In the midst of the dark room, where the lamplight shone wanly close to hand, she could make out the dull sheen of the chest's metal rings. Skirting the chest, she peered into the dark, sooty kitchen. There all she could make out were the dim white shoji panels. After standing motionless in the middle of the stone-cold kitchen, she stealthily slid open the door to the maid's room on her right and shined the lamp inside. Kiyo lay there curled up in a ball, like a mole, amid tangled bedding whose patterns and colors could not be distinguished. Next she looked left, into the six-mat room. In the emptiness that yawned before her, what immediately caught her eye was the mirror on its stand, all the eerier in the darkness.

Having made a complete tour of the house and having reassured herself that all was as it should be, Oyone went back to bed. Eventually she closed her eyes. This time she found that she could contrive not to focus on every little flutter of her eyelids, and after a while drifted off to sleep.

All of a sudden her eyes popped open again. There had been a thud—a heavy thud, she was sure—somewhere close to where she lay sleeping. Raising her head off the pillow and pricking up her ears, she pondered a moment and concluded that it had resembled nothing so much as the sound that would have been made by a very large object tumbling down the embankment behind the house and landing just beyond the veranda that bordered the room where they slept. She further concluded that it had actually happened but a moment ago, just before she opened her eyes, and not in a dream. The realization filled her with dread. She tugged at her husband's bedclothes as he lay sleeping beside her, this time determined to wake him. Sōsuke, who had been sleeping very soundly up to that moment, abruptly opened his eyes.

"Please get up right now," Oyone said as she shook him.

"All right, that's enough," he responded, still half asleep, and sat up straight on his futon. Oyone half whispered to him what she had heard.

"There was only that single thud?" he asked.

"Yes, but I heard it just now."

They both fell silent, their attention riveted on whatever might transpire outside. But all was perfectly still. No matter how long and hard they strained to hear, they could detect nothing else tumbling down their way. Complaining of the cold, Sōsuke pulled a jacket on over his unlined sleeping robe and stepped out onto the veranda, where he slid back one of the rain shutters. He peered out into the darkness and saw nothing. A wave of cold air pressed against his skin.

He quickly closed the shutter. After latching it, Sōsuke burrowed once again under the bedding.

"There's nothing out there," he said, turning over on his side. "You must have been dreaming."

Oyone insisted that she had not been dreaming. She was adamant: There most certainly had been a loud noise just overhead.

Sōsuke stuck his head partway out from under the covers and faced Oyone. "You're not yourself these days. You've worked yourself up into quite a state. You really need to calm down or you'll never have a proper sleep."

Just then the pendulum clock in the next room struck two. Momentarily deprived of speech by the chimes, they both fell silent, upon which the night grew utterly still. The couple's eyes were now wide open; neither one of them showed any sign of falling back to sleep.

"That's easy for you to say." Oyone resumed their previous conversation. "You're always so relaxed, you only have to lie down for ten minutes and you're unconscious."

"I may fall asleep fast, but it's from fatigue, not from being relaxed," Sōsuke replied.

In the midst of their conversation he nodded off again. Oyone continued to toss and turn. In front of the house a wagon passed by with a terrible clatter. Several times recently Oyone had been startled before dawn by the sound of a wagon. Thinking about these various episodes, she had come to the conclusion that since it always happened at about the same time, it must be a delivery wagon traveling the same route every morning: Someone, probably the milkman, was in a hurry to finish his rounds. Once she had settled on this explanation, she began to find the sound reassuring, simultaneous as it was with the coming of dawn and her neighbors' resumption of activity. Eventually a rooster cried out somewhere. Not long after came the high-pitched scrape of clogs in the street. Then the sound of Kiyo opening her door, going out to the privy, and on her return entering the sitting room, apparently to look at the clock. By this time the oil in the alcove lamp was too low for the short wick to reach, and Oyone was surrounded by darkness. The light from Kiyo's lamp in the next room flickered through the partition. Oyone called out to her.

Kiyo got up for good soon after this. Half an hour later it was Oyone's turn. Another half hour after that, Sōsuke, too, at last got up. On work days Oyone would come around at the proper time and say to him, "You'd better get up now." On Sundays and holidays she would say instead, "Why don't you get up?" Today, however, with the incident in the night still on his mind, he was already out of bed before Oyone came to wake him. He immediately slid open the shutters and looked out toward the foot of the embankment.

From below, Sōsuke could see the frost-melting sun filtering through the bamboo stalks, which were still in the frozen grip of early morning, and bathing the crest of the embankment in warm light. A couple of feet below the crest, where the embankment sloped most steeply, the withered grass was ripped and gouged, exposing to Sōsuke's astonished eyes patches of raw, red earth. Then, in a direct line down from this spot, just beyond where he stood at the veranda's edge, he saw that the ground had been broken up and the frost crystals smashed. Perhaps a large dog had tumbled down from the top, he surmised. But then, he decided, even a very large dog couldn't have made such a mess.

Sōsuke fetched his clogs from the front of the house and quickly stepped down from the veranda. The privy jutted out, right here, at an angle from the veranda, squeezing the already narrow yard into a very cramped defile for a few paces. Oyone fussed about this corner every time the night-soil gatherer came by. "We really do need more room here," she said, but her husband always scoffed at her worry.

Beyond this tight spot, a slender path led around to the kitchen. Formerly there had stood here a hedge of half-dead cryptomeria shrubs that served to mark their garden off from their neighbor's; but some time ago the gardener sent by the landlord to make improvements had removed the rotted-out hedge entirely, replacing this barrier with a slatted wooden fence, full of knots, that ran alongside the path to the kitchen door. In addition to receiving little sunlight, this area was where the rain poured down from the roof spout, all of which helped the begonias to thrive here in the summer. At their peak the foliage was so dense it all but choked off the path, a sight that had alarmed the couple during their first summer in the house. But when Oyone thought of how the begonia roots had survived for years beneath the only recently removed hedge, and how, long after the manor house had been razed, the plants still sent forth their seeds in the proper season, she exclaimed with joy, "They really are lovely!"

Stepping on the frost, Sōsuke reveled in memories conjured up by this out-of-the-way nook, which never saw the sun. Then his gaze was arrested by a spot on the narrow path. He stopped in his tracks. There ahead of him lay a writing box of gilded black lacquer. The contents were spread out over the frost, as if delivered to this place intentionally and then abandoned, but the cover lay a few feet away, upside down and wedged against the base of the fence, as though fastened to it, revealing the lid's brightly patterned paper lining. Among the various letters, notes, and the like strewn about at random, there was a particularly long scroll of writing; the first two feet had been unfurled, the rest crumpled into a ball like so much rubbish. Sōsuke took a closer look at the underside and smiled wryly. Human feces clung to the wad of paper.

Having gathered into a pile all the papers scattered across the ground and placed them in the lacquer box, he carried it just as it was, covered with mud and ice, as far as the kitchen door. Sliding open the shoji, he called out to Kiyo and handed her the box. Not quite believing what she saw, Kiyo made a face and took the box. Oyone was in the parlor dusting. Sōsuke, his hands folded inside his kimono, then made the rounds of the various points of entry—the front gate, the vestibule, and so on—but failed to find anything out of the ordinary.

At length he came back inside. No sooner did he sit down in his accustomed place by the sitting-room hibachi than he called for Oyone in a loud voice.

"Where have you been?" she asked, emerging from the parlor. "And so soon after getting up!"

"Listen, that noise you heard close to the bed last night—it wasn't a dream after all. It was a thief. What you heard was the sound of him tumbling down from the Sakais' place into our garden. When I went out back to look around, I found this writing box, with letters and what not scattered all over the place. To top it off, he left what you might call his personal calling card on the way out." Sōsuke removed two or three letters from the box and showed them to Oyone. They were all addressed to Sakai.

Oyone, who was still half kneeling beside him, was astonished.

"Do you suppose there were other things stolen from Sakai-san?" she asked.

"Yes, I would imagine there were," he said, folding his arms against his chest.

Having said all that could be said at this stage, the couple left the writing box where it was and turned to breakfast. But even as they wielded their chopsticks, the burglary was foremost on their minds. Oyone boasted of her keen ear and quick wits. For his part Sōsuke pronounced himself fortunate not to be so keen-eared or quick-witted.

"That's all very well for you to say," Oyone retorted, "but what if instead of the Sakais' it had been our house? With you dead to the world like that, what would've happened to us?"

Not about to let her have the last word, Sōsuke replied, "There isn't the slightest worry of anyone bothering to break into our place."

Hearing this, Kiyo poked her head in from the kitchen and, in a tone of genuine delight, said, "Just think what a fuss there'd've been if they'd gotten their hands on our Mr. Nonaka's new coat. What a blessing that the Sakais got robbed and not us!"

Sōsuke and Oyone were at a loss for a response.

Even with breakfast finished there was still time to spare before Sōsuke had to leave for work. Conscious that the Sakai household must be in great turmoil, he decided to deliver the writing box himself. Although the box was gilded, the leaf had been applied over the black lacquer in a simple tortoiseshell pattern. It did not appear to be of much monetary value. Oyone wrapped it in a *furoshiki*³² of brightly colored striped silk. The cloth proved too small to be bound up in the usual way, so she drew all four corners together and tied the opposite ends in two square knots in the middle. Clutched in Sōsuke's hand it looked like an ordinary gift of boxed sweets.

In relation to their parlor the Sakai house stood directly above them atop the embankment; yet in order to reach the landlord's front gate Sōsuke had to walk half a block down the street, climb up a steep slope, and then walk back in the direction from which he came. Approaching by way of stones set in the grass alongside a handsome hedge, he entered the gate. The house seemed submerged in a preternatural silence. Seeing that the frosted glass door to the vestibule was closed, he rang the bell several times. Perhaps it was out of order; no one appeared. He was obliged to go around to the kitchen door, where he was again confronted with a closed double-paneled shoji with frosted glass. From inside came the sound of dishes being handled. Opening the door he found a scullery maid crouched down on the wooden floor next to a gas-powered ceramic grill. Unwrapping the writing box, he addressed her.

"I believe this belongs here. I found it this morning behind my house, where it seems to have fallen, and I've come to return it."

"Oh, I see, well, thank you," the woman murmured, and carried the box over to the far edge of the kitchen floor, from where she summoned another woman, apparently a housemaid. After a whispered consultation, the box was passed to the housemaid, who cast a glance toward Sōsuke and quickly retreated inside. No sooner had she disappeared than a girl of about twelve with a round face and large eyes came running up, followed by a younger girl, evidently her sister. With matching ribbons in their hair, their faces appeared side by side at the threshold to the kitchen. Staring at Sōsuke, they whispered to each other something about a robber. Now that he had handed over the writing box, he felt he had no further business there—he did not need to speak to the Sakais—and hastened to take his leave.

"I guess the box does belong here," he said. "That's that, then." His remarks, however, only succeeded in flustering the scullery maid, who seemed to know nothing about it. Just then the house-maid reappeared.

"Please follow me," she said with a deep bow, and it was Sōsuke's turn to feel somewhat ill at ease. As she kept repeating her invitation with exquisite courtesy his discomfort finally gave way to annoyance. At this juncture the master of the house himself appeared.

The landlord's ruddy, jowly face presented the prosperous look that Sōsuke had been led to expect but, contrary to Oyone's description, did not lack for whiskers. Beneath the man's nose there was a well-trimmed mustache; his cheeks and chin, however, were shaved clean.

"My, what a lot of trouble we've caused you!" he said to Sōsuke, the corners of his eyes crinkling with goodwill.

Clad in a splash-patterned robe, he knelt on the wooden floor as he queried his visitor about various details, with a demeanor that did not appear in the least ruffled. Sōsuke gave him a condensed version of everything that had happened between the previous evening and this morning, then ventured to inquire if anything beside the writing box had been stolen. The landlord replied to the effect that a gold-covered pocket watch had been taken from his desk, in a tone as unperturbed as if it were someone else who had been robbed. Indeed, he showed much more interest in the particulars of Sōsuke's account than in the watch. Had the thief from the start intended to make his escape down the embankment or, in his haste, had he rather fallen down it accidentally? Such questions Sōsuke, of course, could not answer.

At this point the same housemaid returned bearing tea and cigarettes, which still further delayed Sōsuke's departure. His host then
produced a cushion that he insisted Sōsuke sit on, and proceeded to
describe the arrival of the detective early that morning. The detective judged that the perpetrator must have sneaked onto the property the previous evening and hid, perhaps in a storage shed. The
kitchen door had no doubt been his point of entry into the main
house. It appeared that he had then entered the sitting room, after
using a match to light a candle that he stuck into a small container
found in the kitchen, and that on noticing the mother and children
asleep in the next room, he passed along the corridor and into the
landlord's study. While the thief busied himself here the youngest in
the family, a newborn infant, woke up crying for his milk, whereupon the thief seemed to have fled out into the garden from the
study door.

"If only our dog had been on the scene," said the landlord regret-
fully. "But he took sick a few days ago and so he's been at the veterinarian's."

When Sōsuke commiserated, his host launched into a detailed
description of the dog's breed, pedigree, the occasional hunting ex-
peditions in which he'd taken part, and so on.

"You see, he likes to hunt, but he's suffered from a nervous ailment for some time and needed some rest. I suppose it has to do with
the snipe hunting I do every autumn and winter, when he has to
spend two, three hours at a time up to his hips in the wet fields—
that can't have done him any good, I'm sure."

The man, with apparently unlimited time at his disposal, went on
and on while Sōsuke, having responded only with an Oh, my! here
and an Is-that-so? there, finally had no choice but to get up in the
middle of the conversation. "I'm afraid it's off to work as usual for
me," he announced, at which his host, as if such an eventuality had
only just dawned on him, apologized for having detained him so
long. He then thanked Sōsuke in advance for any further involvement that the detective might require of him in the course of the
investigation.

"Please come over again, just for a chat," he said cordially. "And perhaps I might just drop in on you sometime—these days I seem to have a bit of time on my hands."

By the time Sōsuke passed back through the landlord's gate and hurried home, it was already half an hour past the time when he normally left for work.

"Where have you been?" asked Oyone nervously as she met him at the front door.

"I must say, that Sakai fellow is very easygoing," he said, quickly disrobing and changing into his business suit. "I suppose that kind of leisure comes with money."

8

"KOROKU-SAN, should we start with the sitting room or the parlor?" Oyone asked.

Now that Koroku had finally moved into his brother's house, some four or five days earlier, it devolved on him to help out with today's repapering of the shoji. He'd had some experience with this when still living at his uncle's, joining Yasunosuke in replacing the paper in the sliding doors to his own room. That project had commenced in more or less proper fashion with their mixing the glue in trays and applying it with trowels; but once the two repapered panels were good and dry and they went to replace them, they could not fit them back into their grooves. He and Yasunosuke's efforts had come to grief a second time: Tackling another set of shoji at the behest of his aunt, they soaked the frames in order to remove the old paper, with the result that the frames seriously warped in drying and once again they had trouble getting them back in place.

"Nee-san," said Koroku as he tore away the old paper, starting on the sitting-room panels, "you have to be extremely cautious when you repaper shoji or you'll make a mess of it. You absolutely must not soak them."

The garden just below this veranda was bordered on the right by the wall of the six-mat room that Koroku was using and by the vestibule, which jutted out on the left. These borders, along with the veranda and the outer hedge that ran parallel to it, formed what was in effect a square enclosure. On dew-laden mornings the couple would take great pleasure in this enclosed garden, which in the summer months was covered with cosmos plants and adorned with morning glories curled about the slender bamboo stakes that they had placed at the base of the hedge. Sometimes, as soon as they had gotten up, they excitedly counted the number of blossoms that had opened that day. But from the autumn through the winter all shrubs and flowers here would wither completely, leaving what resembled a small desert, so barren as to elicit pity.

With his back to this square plot, where a thick layer of frost had formed, Koroku energetically stripped the old paper off the shoji. He was assailed by sporadic gusts of cold wind that whipped about his neck and close-cropped head. With each gust he felt the urge to retreat from the exposed veranda into his six-mat room. He worked silently, his hands red, wringing out a rag in a bucket of water and wiping the shoji slats clean.

"You must be cold, you poor thing. And we certainly didn't need this chilly drizzle." Oyone was all sympathy as she poured a steady trickle of hot water from the kettle to soften up the glue prepared the night before.

Inwardly Koroku despised doing chores like this. He wielded his rag in a spirit verging on self-mortification—a spirit rooted in the position to which circumstances had recently reduced him. In the past, he recalled, when it had fallen to him to perform this very same task at his uncle's, it had been a far from unpleasant diversion. This time around, however, he felt coerced; those around him regarded him as unqualified for any other type of work. The cold out on the veranda only added insult to injury.

Koroku, then, could not manage even some simple, good-natured reply to his sister-in-law. What flashed across his mind at this moment was the time he had been out for a stroll with a law student who lived in the same boardinghouse as he did. They had stopped off at Shiseido, where the housemate proceeded to splurge close to five yen on nothing but three bars of imported soaps and some toothpaste. It had struck him then that there was no good reason in the world why he in particular should find himself in such strait-ened circumstances. He could only pity his brother and sister-in-law for being content to live out their lives in penury. From Koroku's point of view there was something terribly supine about a lifestyle in which one had to worry over something like whether to buy Mino paper[33] or settle for something less strong.

"This stuff tears easily," said Koroku as he unfurled a foot's length of the shoji paper, held it up to the light, and gave it two or three slaps, good and hard.

"Oh?" Oyone replied, gently dabbing glue on the shoji slats with her brush. "But since we don't have children it will probably hold up."

The two of them took hold of a length of paper that had been spliced together, one on each end, and tried stretching it out so as to leave no slack. But from time to time Koroku's face would register annoyance, at which Oyone would grow hesitant and, razor in hand, end up trimming her end unevenly. As a result, there were a number of conspicuous bulges in the already completed portions. Oyone mournfully surveyed one newly repapered shoji propped up against the shutter case. If only she could have worked with her husband instead of with Koroku, she thought.

"There seem to be a few wrinkles," she said.

"I'm afraid I don't have the knack for this."

"Don't be silly. Your brother is no better, and besides, he's a lot lazier than you."

Koroku did not reply. Taking a cup of water that Kiyo had brought from the kitchen, he stood in front of the propped-up shoji and blew a fine mist on the paper until the whole surface was moist. By the time they were repapering the second panel, the one he had sprayed was nearly dry and most of the wrinkles smoothed out. When they had finished a third panel, Koroku announced that his back was bothering him. Oyone, meanwhile, had had a headache since the early morning.

"Let's do one more and finish with the sitting room before we take a break," she said.

By the time they were done with the sitting room it was past noon. They sat down to lunch together. During these past several days, with Sōsuke away at the office, Oyone had not failed to keep Koroku company at the lunch table. This was the first time since she and Sōsuke joined their lives together that she'd had a companion for lunch other than her husband. All these years, whenever her husband was absent, it was her habit to eat alone. To sit here face-to-face with her brother-in-law, then, making conversation as she served the rice, was most discomfiting. It was hard enough when the maid was on duty in the kitchen, but now, with Kiyo neither to be seen nor heard, Oyone felt all the more constrained. True, Oyone was much the older of the two, and the character of their relationship in the past could hardly be expected to engender that peculiar erotic tension bound to arise when two people of the opposite sex are thrown together in a similarly novel situation; still, she wondered to herself if she would ever lose this sensation of being stifled by Koroku's presence, which was all the more perturbing for being so unexpected. All she could do was to keep up a steady conversation throughout the meal in order to avoid uneasy silences. Unfortunately, in his present state of mind, Koroku could summon neither the composure nor the discernment to engage his sister-in-law's gracious manner with any enthusiasm.

"So, Koroku-san, was the food at your boardinghouse any good?"

To such questions he could no longer respond, as he did when he was still at the boardinghouse and paying them a visit, with some ready, off-the-cuff quip. And when, at a loss for a reply, he would confine himself to something like "No, not particularly," his words struck Oyone as vague and unforthcoming, and she would worry that she was not being welcoming enough. In turn, her reaction, though unspoken, would communicate itself in some fashion to Koroku.

Today, however, with her headache, Oyone felt incapable of making the usual effort with her brother-in-law as they sat together at the table, and she was especially loath to do so only to be rebuffed. And so they finished their lunch having exchanged even fewer words than while they had been busy with the repapering.

And yet thanks, perhaps, to the experience they had acquired, the work in the afternoon progressed more smoothly than in the morning. They nevertheless felt further apart than they had before lunch. They were both much oppressed by the cold. When they first arose that morning the weather was so fine that the sky appeared to be moving away from them, carrying the sun along with it; yet just when it took on its deepest hue, clouds suddenly began to form and block out every ray, as if poised to blanket the darkening landscape with powdery snow. The two of them took turns warming their hands over the charcoal brazier.

"I gather that my brother will be getting a raise in the New Year?" Koroku suddenly asked Oyone.

Oyone, in the midst of wiping glue off her hands with some scraps of paper strewn across the tatami, looked dumbfounded.

"Whatever gave you that idea ... ?"

"Well, it said in the paper, you know, that next year there's to be an across-the-board salary increase for civil servants."

It was not until Koroku went on to explain in some detail that Oyone, who had not heard a word of this, became convinced it must be true.

"Well it's about time," she said. "We can't get by on what they're paying now—no one can. Why, since we came to Tokyo the price of a fish fillet alone has doubled."

It was Koroku's turn to be dumbfounded, not having been at all aware of the price of fish until hearing Oyone's comment. The rate of inflation simply astounded him.

Now that Koroku's curiosity had been somewhat piqued, the conversation began to flow more smoothly. Oyone repeated an account by their landlord, as related to her by Sōsuke, of how cheap things had been when he was still in his late teens. A heaping bowl of plain noodles had cost eight rin; a bowl with one topping or another, two and a half sen.[34] A full portion of ordinary beef was four sen; of choice beef, six sen. An afternoon at a vaudeville performance cost only three or four sen. An average student lifestyle then could be maintained on a seven-yen-per-month allowance from home, while a ten-yen allowance would have afforded considerable luxury.

"In those days even you could have gone through college without any worries," said Oyone.

"Yes, and you and my brother could've lived very well then, couldn't you?" replied Koroku.

By the time they had finished repapering the parlor shoji it was after three. It would not be long before Sōsuke came home, and there were preparations to be made for dinner. Having decided to call it a day, they put away the glue, razors, and other things. Koroku gave his body a single, vigorous stretch and his head a good pounding with his fist.

"Thank you so much. You must be exhausted," said Oyone solicitously. But it was not so much fatigue as dull pangs of hunger that Koroku felt. He ate some sweets that Oyone took down from a shelf after explaining that the Sakais had sent them in thanks for returning the writing box. Then she made him some tea.

"Is this Sakai a university graduate?" Koroku asked.

"Yes. Or so I gather."

Koroku sipped his tea, puffed on a cigarette, then asked, "Hasn't my brother said anything to you about his raise?"

"Not a word," said Oyone.

"It must be nice to be like him—not worrying about anything."

Oyone made no attempt at a reply.

Koroku stood up and wandered off to his room but soon came back, charcoal brazier in hand, saying that the fire had died out. Imposing on the hospitality of his brother and sister-in-law and still officially on a leave of absence from school, he put much stock in Yasunosuke's assurances that soon he would be able to help him, and viewed these arrangements as only temporary.

9

FROM THE seed of the writing box's recovery an unlikely relationship had sprouted between Sōsuke and his landlord. Previously, their dealings having been confined to the monthly dispatching of Kiyo with the rent payment and the subsequent delivery of a receipt, any semblance of neighborly friendliness had been as absent as if a family from abroad had dwelled up there.

On the afternoon of the day that Sōsuke returned the box, a detective turned up, as Sakai had predicted, to examine the area behind the couple's house, at the foot of the embankment. The detective was accompanied by Sakai, giving Oyone her first look at the man she had heard so much about. In addition to the mustache that she had originally been led not to expect, she was mildly surprised by the uncommonly polite manner in which he spoke, even when addressing her.

"Sakai-san actually does have a mustache, doesn't he," she noted to Sōsuke with some emphasis when they were alone again.

Two days later a maid descended on them, bearing a magnificent basket of treats and Sakai's calling card. She thanked them for their kindness, adding as she took her leave, "The master hopes to call on you himself in due time..."

That evening Sōsuke opened the basket and stuffed his mouth with one of the toasted sweet dumplings he found inside.

"Giving presents like this—well, he can't be all that stingy. Whoever told you he wouldn't let other children play on the swing must have been lying."

"Yes, that can't be right," Oyone agreed.

Despite this new level of cordiality in the couple's relations with their landlord since the burglary, neither Sōsuke nor Oyone entertained any notion of pursuing greater familiarity in this quarter. They were not so bold as to put themselves forward in the name of sociability or affability, and were not the sort to engage in calculations of potential self-interest arising from such a relationship. By their lights, then, it was only to be expected that in the natural course of things time would slip by quickly, with no efforts made by them to tend this new relationship, which would soon enough revert to the same footing on which the two parties had been before: the Sakais atop the embankment, Sōsuke and Oyone below, as far apart emotionally as they were topographically.

But three days later, around sundown, Sakai unexpectedly showed up at the couple's door wrapped in a warm-looking cloak with an otter-skin collar. Not used to having guests simply drop by in the evening, they at first reacted with near consternation. When Sakai had taken a seat in the parlor he proceeded to express sincere gratitude for their recent help, and, unchaining his gold-encased pocket watch from his white crepe sash for them to see, said, "Thanks to you, the stolen item was recovered."

Since it was the law, he had reported the theft to the police, but the watch was an old one, making it easier for him to accept the loss. Then suddenly yesterday a small package arrived, bearing no return address and containing the stolen watch, neatly wrapped.

"The thief must have found it too hot to handle, or not worth the risk for the money he could get for it, and so decided that he had no choice but to give it back—whatever the case, definitely unusual," said Sakai with a laugh. "But for me, at any rate, it was the writing box that was of real value." Then, by way of an explanation, he confided, "You see, it was bestowed on my grandmother when she was in attendance at court, so it's a kind of family heirloom."

Steering the conversation this way and that, Sakai stayed on that evening for almost two hours. Neither Sōsuke, who sat with him, nor Oyone, who listened in from the sitting room, could fail to be impressed by the range of topics he touched on.

"He certainly gets around," Oyone commented after he had left.

"He's got all the time in the world on his hands," Sōsuke replied.

The next day, on his way home from work, Sōsuke got off the streetcar and was walking down the side street near the furniture store when he caught a glimpse of Sakai's overcoat with the familiar otter-skin collar attached. Sakai, standing in a position that presented his profile to Sōsuke, was engaged in conversation with the proprietor, who was peering up at Sakai through large spectacles he had not paused to remove. Just as Sōsuke, not wishing to interrupt, was about to pass by in silence, Sakai shifted his gaze toward the street.

"Well, hello! Thanks for last night. On your way home now?"

Addressed by the landlord in this hail-fellow-well-met manner, Sōsuke could not simply forge ahead with a token nod; slackening his pace, he doffed his hat. At which Sakai, his business evidently concluded, advanced from the storefront.

"Out for a bit of shopping?" asked Sōsuke.

"Hardly," Sakai replied dismissively as he fell in step with Sōsuke for the walk home. After they had gone forty or fifty feet Sakai declared, "That geezer is a real crook. I was just giving him a piece of my mind for trying to pass off a fake Kazan[35] on me."

This was the first indication Sōsuke had received that Sakai shared the pastime common among the well-to-do of dabbling in rare objects. It then crossed his mind that he really should have showed the recently sold Hōitsu to someone like him before putting it on the market.

"Does that dealer know a lot about calligraphy and painting?" Sōsuke asked.

"Not really—in fact he's downright ignorant about the lot. All you have to do is take a glance around his shop: You won't find anything that smacks of an antique. As it is he's come a long way, seeing as he started off as a junkman." Sakai apparently knew a great deal about the man's background.

The Sakai family, according to the local greengrocer, had ranked sufficiently high under the Tokugawa regime to be accorded some titular governorship[36] and had the most impressive family pedigree in the area. They had not followed the last shogun to Sunpu[37] at the time of the old regime's collapse—or had they gone off only to re-emerge soon from exile? Sōsuke had been told the details, but he could no longer recollect them.

Sakai went on to dredge up tales involving the junkman from their boyhood days. "Even as a kid he was a troublemaker, you know. He was the local bully and was always picking fights."

But how on earth, Sōsuke wondered aloud, had the man imagined he could foist a fake Kazan on Sakai?

"Well, since we've given his family some business from my father's time on, once in a while he'll just turn up with some odd item," Sakai explained with a chuckle. "He more than makes up for his lack of taste with a huge capacity for greed. He's a real piece of work. On top of that, his appetite was whetted when he got me to buy a Hōitsu screen."

Sōsuke was startled but, not wanting to interrupt, held his tongue. Sakai went on about how, emboldened by this one sale, the furniture dealer had shown up regularly with scrolls and paintings that he himself made no pretense of knowing anything about, and how, under the misapprehension that it was real, he prominently displayed a "medieval Korean" ceramic bowl that had in fact been made in Osaka. "Except maybe for a dining table or, say, one of those factory-made iron kettles, I wouldn't buy anything in that shop," he cautioned.

They had reached the top of the slope. From here Sakai would be turning right, while Sōsuke had to proceed down the other side. Sōsuke wanted to accompany Sakai a little farther in order to ask him more about the screen. But going out of his way like that would appear odd, he realized, and so he took his leave.

"Would you mind if I paid you a visit sometime soon?" Sōsuke asked.

"Not at all," Sakai replied cordially.

Although the day had been perfectly calm and the sun had shone brightly, Sōsuke came home to find Oyone waiting for him in the parlor, where, claiming that the house was still piercingly cold, she had set up the portable *kotatsu* in the middle of the room and hung his change of clothes over it.

It was the first time this winter that the *kotatsu* had been put to use by day. Although they had been using it at night for some time now, they had stored it by day in the six-mat room.

"But why did you drag it out in the middle of the parlor today?" Sōsuke asked.

"Well, we're not expecting any guests, so it shouldn't matter. Koroku is using the six-mat room, after all, and it would just be in his way there."

This brought home to Sōsuke, as if for the first time, that Koroku was here to stay. He did up the sash around the warm machine-woven robe that Oyone helped him drape over his undershirt, and said, "True, this is our frigid zone here—we'll have to install a fixed *kotatsu* just to make it bearable." If the tatami in Koroku's six-mat room were less than pristine, the room itself, with its southern and eastern exposure, was the warmest spot in the house.

After a few sips of the hot tea Oyone had brought him, he asked, "Is Koroku home?"

It was of course certain that his brother was there. But not the faintest sound could be heard from the six-mat room, and it seemed impossible that there could be anyone inside. As Oyone rose to call Koroku, Sōsuke stopped her: There was no need to speak to him right now. Then, burrowing under the quilt attached to the portable *kotatsu*, he lay stretched out on his side. Twilight had already made its presence felt in this room, where the shoji all faced the steep embankment. His arm pillowed beneath his head, he simply gazed into the dark, confined space, his mind blank. The noise made by Oyone and Kiyo in the kitchen sounded as remote to him as the stirrings of faceless neighbors. Before long the room was shrouded in darkness; he could see only the pale white of the shoji. And yet he kept perfectly still. He moved not a muscle, not even to call for a lamp.

When Sōsuke emerged from the darkness to take his place at the dinner table, Koroku also appeared out of the six-mat room and sat across from his brother. Apologizing for her forgetfulness, Oyone went to close the parlor shutters. Sōsuke felt an impulse to point out to Koroku that as evenings came on it might be nice if he helped his busy sister-in-law a bit by lighting lamps, closing shutters, and the like, but then, not wishing to say anything jarring to one so recently arrived under their roof, decided to say nothing at all.

Having waited for Oyone, the brothers picked up their bowls as soon as she returned to the table. Sōsuke took this opportunity to tell them about his chance encounter with Sakai outside the furniture shop on the way home, and how Sakai had bought a Hōitsu screen from the furniture dealer with the oversize glasses.

"Well!" Oyone murmured in surprise. After scanning her husband's face for a moment, she said, "It must have been our screen, no doubt about it."

Koroku was silent at first, but once he had heard enough of the couple's exchange for the context to become clear, he asked, "So, just how much did you sell it for?"

Oyone darted a glance at her husband before answering this question.

As soon as dinner was over Koroku went straight to his room. Sōsuke returned to the *kotatsu* in the parlor. After a while Oyone came in to take the chill off her feet. In the course of their chat they agreed it would be a good idea to call on the Sakais next Saturday or Sunday and have a look at the screen.

The following Sunday, as was his habit, Sōsuke frittered away most of the morning, luxuriating in this once-a-week opportunity to sleep in. Oyone said she felt sluggish again and leaned back against the rim of the brazier, too weary, it seemed, to do anything. It crossed Sōsuke's mind that at times like this she used to retreat for the morning to the six-mat room, when it was available, and he realized with a stab of remorse that in assigning the room to Koroku he had in effect deprived her of her one place of refuge.

He urged her to pull out the bedding and lie down in the parlor if she felt poorly, but she demurred. In that case, why not set up the portable *kotatsu* again, he persisted, saying that in fact he'd like to share it with her; and in the end he had Kiyo get out the quilt and frame and set them up in the parlor.

Koroku, having gotten up slightly before Sōsuke, had gone out somewhere and was not to be seen for the rest of the morning. Sōsuke made no effort to grill Oyone about his brother's whereabouts. Lately he had been trying to spare Oyone the embarrassment of having to respond to such questions. Better that she castigated her brother-in-law's conduct openly, he sometimes thought; he could then rebuff her accusations, or commiserate, as the situation demanded.

Even at noontime, Oyone was still resting by the *kotatsu*. Thinking that she was best left in peace, Sōsuke quietly informed Kiyo in the kitchen that he was off to the landlord's, draped a sleeveless, Inverness-style cape over his everyday kimono, and went outside.

After being cooped up all morning in the gloomy parlor, Sōsuke found his spirits rising once he reached the street. The muscles beneath his bare skin taut against the cold wind, he reveled in the wintry sensation of instant bodily contraction, which led him to reflect as he walked along that it was not good for Oyone to stay indoors all the time like this; that as soon as the weather warmed up a bit, he must get her out in the fresh air before her health was seriously affected.

Passing through the Sakais' gate he noticed a bright red swatch, incongruous at this season, tucked in the hedge that separated the approaches to the main entrance and to the kitchen door. On closer inspection he discovered it to be a doll's tiny nightgown fastened to a branch of the hedge by means of a bamboo skewer inserted through the little sleeve. How resourceful, he thought, admiring the expert way in which it had been hung—and charming to boot! Sōsuke, who had no experience at all of being a father, let alone of having raised girls to the stage where they could manage such a neat trick, stood there for a while and gazed at the tiny red nightgown drying out nicely in the sun. It brought to mind the red shelves, with their array of five musician dolls, which, more than two decades ago, his parents had set up for his now deceased younger sister, along with the elegantly shaped rice cakes and the festive, cloudy cordial that looked sweet but actually tasted bitter.[38]

Sakai was at home, but Sōsuke was asked by the maid to wait in another room until the master had finished with his meal. No sooner had he been seated than there came from the next room the chattering voices of the persons responsible for the laundering of the little nightgown. When the maid slid open a panel to bring in some tea, Sōsuke could see behind her two pairs of wide-open eyes peering out in his direction. Later, when she carried in a brazier, a different face presented itself. All of this being quite new to him, it seemed that each time the panel opened there was a complete change of faces, and he could not keep track of how many children he had seen. When the maid had at last ceased her coming and going, one of the children slid the thickly papered panel open ever so slightly, no more than an inch, and in the gap revealed her shining black eyes. Beguiled, Sōsuke beckoned her silently. At this the door was slammed shut and, just behind it, a chorus of three or four voices erupted in peals of laughter.

Presently, one girl piped up, "All right, let's play house again." To which another, evidently an older sister, replied, "Okay, but today we'll play house—foreign style. Now that means," she went on to explain, "Tōsaku-san will be called 'Papa' and Yukiko-san 'Mama.'"

"That's silly—talking about your own mother like a stepmom."[39] He heard another voice giggling with delight.

Then still another voice: "But what about me? I always have to be the O-baba,[40] so you have to tell us what the word for that is, too."

"For 'O-baba,'" explained the older sister, "just 'O-baba' is fine."

There ensued a prolonged exchange of effusive greetings: "Please forgive the intrusion, but is anybody home?," "And where might you come from, sir?," interspersed with attempts to mimic a telephone ringing and the like. To Sōsuke's ear it all sounded both delightful and exotic.

Just then Sōsuke heard the sound of approaching footsteps: no doubt the master of the house. As soon as they reached the next room a voice was heard commanding, "This is no place for you to be fooling around—we have a guest. Now go back where you belong."

Immediately a little boy could be heard in protest, "No, Daddy, I won't... Buy me a nice big horsey, please... or I won't go." The boy seemed very young; his words were not well formed, and they came out in awkward spurts, rendering his protest far from forceful. Sōsuke found this particularly charming.

By the time Sakai sat down with Sōsuke and apologized for keeping him waiting so long, the children had gone off somewhere else.

"Such high spirits—it's wonderful," Sōsuke exclaimed in all sincerity, but Sakai seemed to think he was only being polite.

"No, I'm afraid their behavior is pretty wild, as you saw," he responded apologetically, then proceeded to recite the many needs of children and the endless trouble they caused. There was the time, for example, when they adorned the alcove with an elegant Chinese basket they'd stuffed full of charcoal briquettes; and another, when they filled a pair of lace-up boots he'd just had made with water and left some goldfish swimming around in them. These pranks struck Sōsuke as highly inventive. And then, Sakai continued, with most of his children being girls, there was the constant fuss about new clothes, and to make matters worse, if he went on a trip for so much as a couple of weeks, they looked as though they'd grown at least an inch when he returned. What with one thing or another, he felt he had his back against the wall even now, but then all too soon they'd be getting married, and the preparations would not only be ferociously hectic but no doubt financially ruinous. The childless Sōsuke took this all in without much sympathy. On the contrary, observing how for all Sakai's complaints about his children, his face betrayed no trace of suffering at all, he felt envious.

Having waited for an opportune moment, Sōsuke now asked his host if he might have a glimpse of the screen that had been mentioned the other day. Sakai agreed with alacrity. Clapping his hands loudly, he summoned a manservant and ordered him to bring the screen over from the storehouse. Turning toward Sōsuke, he said, "It was standing right here until just a couple of days ago, but then the children—them again!—decided it was fun to hide behind the screen and fool around, so I was worried it might get damaged and had it put away in the storehouse."

Sōsuke regretted having put Sakai to this bother and wished he had not mentioned the screen in the first place. In truth, he entertained only the mildest curiosity about the screen's fate. After all, once a thing becomes the property of someone else, establishing whether or not it had originally belonged to one was of absolutely no consequence, practically speaking. Regardless of any second thoughts about the matter, however, the screen, as he had requested, was presently brought out from the storehouse, trundled along the veranda, and set before his eyes. As expected, it proved to be the very one that had until recently stood in his own parlor. This realization did not evoke in him any strong reaction at all. Nevertheless, to view it here, surrounded as it now was by the luster of the tatami on which they were sitting, the fine grain of the wooden ceiling, the objects in the alcove, and the patterns on the sliding partitions, to which could be added the elaborate care involved in its being borne from the storehouse by two servants—all of this, Sōsuke had to concede, made the screen look ten times more precious than when still in his possession. At a total loss for words, he went through the motions of gazing intently, as though at something new and fresh, at this thoroughly familiar object.

Under the misapprehension that his guest was a connoisseur, Sakai stood with one hand on the frame, shifting his glance from the screen to Sōsuke's face and back again. When this failed to elicit the anticipated appraisal, he said, "The attribution is completely solid. Quality will out, they say."

"Yes, of course," said Sōsuke.

After another pause, the host repositioned himself just behind Sōsuke and launched into an appreciation of the screen, pointing at one detail or another with his finger and lecturing on the finer points. As one might expect of someone of his extravagance, he explained, the artist had made lavish use of the highest quality paints, which was one of the hallmarks of his works; the coloring was truly exquisite, and so on—remarks that all sounded quite original to Sōsuke, well-worn truisms though they were.

After what seemed to him a decent interval, Sōsuke thanked his host profusely and returned to his seat. Sakai likewise moved back to his cushion, where he started in on the screen's inscription about "a country lane, the sky above" and the verse's calligraphic style. Once again Sōsuke was impressed by his host's extensive interests in haiku and calligraphy. Indeed, so wide was the scope of things about which he appeared knowledgeable that Sōsuke could only wonder when the man had managed to store up all this erudition in his head. Ashamed of his own ignorance, he strained to keep his responses to a bare minimum in order to give full attention to Sakai's comments.

His guest showing scant signs of interest in haiku and calligraphy, Sakai shifted the conversation back to painting. He graciously offered to show Sōsuke any scrolls or albums among his holdings that he might wish to see, not that there was anything of great distinction, he added. Sōsuke indicated that regrettably he had no choice but to forgo the opportunity... but incidentally—and he apologized here for his bluntness—how much, he wondered, had Sakai paid for the recently acquired screen?

"Well, it was really like stumbling on a hidden treasure. I got it for just eighty yen," his host replied.

Shall I tell him the whole story or not? Sōsuke thought to himself and hesitated for a moment, but it came to him in a flash that owning up to the truth would be entertaining for both of them. At length he said, "Well, actually..." and told all, from beginning to end.

Sakai heard his guest out with a few little gasps of surprise along the way. At last he said, "So it was not out of some passion for calligraphy and painting that you asked to see the screen!" and burst out laughing, clearly much amused at his own mistaken assumptions. At the same time he expressed regret at not having dealt directly with Sōsuke nor having settled on a price that was still considerably less than what he had actually paid. He finished with a vehement denunciation of the furniture dealer: "What a scoundrel!"

After this, Sōsuke and Sakai fell into a kind of friendship.

10

SŌSUKE received no more visits from his aunt or his cousin. He, of course, had no time to visit them in their home in Kōjimachi Ward, nor, for that matter, any strong inclination to do so. The two families might be related by ties of blood, but the same sun did not shine down on both houses.

True, Koroku paid the Saekis a visit now and then for a chat, although not, it seemed, with any frequency. Upon his return from such visits, he seldom passed on to Oyone any news of his aunt and cousin. Oyone suspected that the silence might be calculated on Koroku's part. But feeling as she did that she and his aunt had very little in common, she was if anything quite relieved not to hear about the woman's sundry doings.

Still, Oyone managed to receive occasional updates on the Saekis by listening in on conversations between Koroku and Sōsuke. Just a week earlier, Koroku had told his brother how very hard Yasunosuke was working in an effort to market another invention. This one had to do with a machine that, from Koroku's sketchy account, anyway—it had something to do with producing printed matter without recourse to ink—sounded potentially very valuable. The complex nature of this process being utterly foreign to anything in her experience, Oyone simply listened in silence, as was her wont in any case. Sōsuke, being a man, found his curiosity piqued by the project and responded with spirited questions about how inkless printing might be possible.

Lacking any specialized knowledge of the subject, Koroku could hardly be expected to provide many details. He simply related all that he could recall of Yasunosuke's description. Basically, this new printing process, which had recently been invented in England, came down to still another novel application of electricity. One pole of an electric current gets attached to the type and the other to a sheet of paper. Then all you have to do is press the paper down against the type and in a flash, Koroku explained, the print is transferred to the paper surface.[41] Ordinarily the print is black, but with adjustments it can be changed easily enough to red or blue when color is needed, thus eliminating the time required for drying between applications; and when it's applied to printing newspapers, over and above the savings on ink and rotary presses, a whole printing run requires twenty-five percent less labor than what's needed for the current process—from which you can just see how incredibly promising this business will be in the future ... Once again, Koroku merely repeated what his cousin had told him.

Into Koroku's recounting there crept a suggestion that Yasunosuke already had this rosy future firmly in his grasp, and the young man's eyes seemed to gleam with the reflection of his own bright future, assured by his cousin's success. Sōsuke, meanwhile, took in Koroku's fervent report with his customary nonchalance, and even when his brother had finished, did not interject any particular criticisms. For in truth he felt that the purported invention appeared on the one hand perfectly plausible, on the other a complete fantasy; until his cousin's scheme played out one way or another in the real world, it was not for him either to support or to oppose it.

"So, he's given up on the bonito boats?" Oyone, who had listened in silence, spoke up for the first time.

"It's not that he's given them up," Koroku replied, taking on the role of promoter for Yasunosuke's enterprises. "But those would be very expensive items. No matter how useful they'd be, I gather that there just aren't enough people who could afford them."

The three of them continued this discussion for a while, but in the end Sōsuke said, "No matter what line of business you're in, success just doesn't come that easy."

"Yes, the best thing is to be rich like Sakai-san and then do whatever you like."

Oyone's comment in his ears, Koroku returned to his room.

Apart from these occasional reports gleaned from Koroku's visits to the Saekis, the couple for the most part had no idea of how they were getting along.

One day Oyone asked Sōsuke, "Do you suppose that every time Koroku stops by at Yasu-san's he comes away with a bit of money?"

"Why do you ask?" Not having paid much attention thus far to Koroku's doings, Sōsuke was startled by Oyone's sudden question.

After a moment's hesitation, Oyone said, "Yes, well, lately when he comes home, you can tell he's been drinking."

"Oh, Yasu-san's probably treating him in exchange for his listening to all that stuff about making a bundle on his inventions," he said with a laugh, at which their conversation broke off with nothing further said about the matter.

Three days later, Koroku again failed to come home by mealtime. The couple waited awhile, but Sōsuke finally declared he was hungry and, ignoring Oyone's suggestion that he take this time to go to the bathhouse, sat down to eat.

Seizing the opportunity, Oyone said, "Could you possibly have a talk with Koroku about his drinking?"

"You mean he's drinking so much that I should speak to him about it?" asked Sōsuke, looking somewhat alarmed.

Well, no, it didn't seem all that serious, Oyone replied, now feeling obliged to shield Koroku. But in truth she found it unnerving to have Koroku coming home so red in the face in broad daylight, when she was there alone. Sōsuke did not return to the subject. Inwardly, however, he began to suspect that his wife might be onto something: that his brother might in fact be borrowing, or at any rate accepting, money from someone and indulging in drink, even though he had never shown much taste for it before.

The year slipped away, and nighttime steadily encroached until it laid claim to two-thirds of their day. The wind whistled fiercely, day in and day out. The mere sound of it was enough to send people into depression. Koroku simply could not bear to stay confined all day to his six-mat room. The longer he was left to his own thoughts, the lonelier he felt, until it became intolerable for him to remain there another moment. The idea of going over to the sitting room and chatting with his sister-in-law was even less bearable. With no other alternative, he left the house and made the rounds of various friends' lodgings on foot. At first these friends treated Koroku as of old, regaling him with the sort of anecdotes that students find amusing. But then, even after they had run out of anecdotes, Koroku would turn up for more. They concluded that he came around mainly out of boredom and a desire to hone his conversational skills. There were times when his friends went out of their way to act preoccupied with research projects or class preparation. It was torture for Koroku to be treated in this fashion as a carefree idler. Yet he simply could not settle down at home for long enough to do any serious reading or thinking. In short, whether it be ascribed to insufficient motivation or external constraints, he was utterly incapable of the self-discipline and exertion that, for a young man at his stage of life, serve as indispensable stepping-stones on the path to maturity.

Despite his restlessness, when there was a driving rain or when the roads were mired in mud from melting snow, even Koroku would refrain from going out, daunted by the prospect of getting soaked and muddying the socks he wore with his clogs. At such times, clearly at his wits' end, he would occasionally venture out of his room, shuffle over to the sitting-room brazier, and pour himself a cup of tea. And if Oyone happened to be there, he even managed to bring himself to chat with her a bit about one thing or another.

Oyone would ask him questions along the lines of how many bowls of rice dumplings in broth he wanted come New Year's, and whether he was fond of saké. As these occasions multiplied the two of them gradually came to achieve a certain rapport. Eventually it reached the point where Koroku was not shy about asking some favor of his "sister," as he called her, such as mending his jacket. Then, as Oyone proceeded to repair the holes in the splash-patterned sleeves, he just sat there staring at her hands. When she did something like this for her husband she was content to sew away in silence, but it was not in her character to treat Koroku so casually. She made a special effort to keep up a conversation with him. At times like this Koroku was prone to steer the topic toward the matter so much on his mind: his uncertain future.

The first couple of times the subject came up, Oyone simply offered a few words of encouragement. "But really, Koroku-san, you're still so young, you know. There's plenty of time for you to do whatever you want. To be so gloomy about the future—you should leave that to your brother." The third time around, however, she asked him, "Didn't Yasu-san agree to help you out one way or another in the coming year?"

"Well, if everything works out just as he says it will, sure, there'd be no problem," said Koroku, with a look that was far from confident. "But the more I think about it the less likely it seems to me that things will all turn out the way he plans. I mean, he hasn't made much off those bonito boats."

Mentally juxtaposing the utterly forlorn figure now in front of her and the Koroku who had been coming home smelling of alcohol, with the ferocious look of someone wronged, though by what or by whom it was not at all clear, Oyone found herself feeling sorry for him. At the same time she couldn't help feeling amused. Yet it was out of genuine sympathy, and not out of a desire to ingratiate herself, that she said, "I know what you mean. If only your brother had the money, I'm sure he'd do anything to help."

It was that same evening, perhaps, when Koroku wrapped a cloak around his shivering frame and went out again. He came home after eight and produced a white, tubular package from his kimono sleeve and presented it to Oyone and his brother. He explained that with this cold weather a craving had come over him for buckwheat noodles and so he'd bought some on his way back from the Saekis. Oyone put the kettle on and, mentioning something about broth, threw herself into grating a chunk of dried bonito.

The couple then heard from Koroku the latest news from the Saeki household: Yasunosuke's wedding was to be postponed until the spring. Negotiations for this marriage had been entered into shortly after Yasunosuke's graduation; by the time Koroku had returned from the seashore to learn from his aunt that there would be no more money for tuition, his cousin's engagement had been all but confirmed. In the absence of any formal announcement, Sōsuke had no idea when the negotiations had in fact been concluded, and it was only through hearing this and that from Koroku after his periodic visits to the Saekis that he had come to suppose that the wedding would take place before year's end. It was likewise by way of his brother that Sōsuke came to learn that the fiancée's father was employed by a large company, that the family lived quite comfortably, and that the fiancée had attended the Tokyo Women's Academy.[42] And it was Koroku alone who'd had a glimpse of her, or at any rate had seen a photograph.

"Is she pretty?" Oyone had asked once.

"Better than average, I think," Koroku had answered.

While waiting for the noodles to be prepared, the three of them addressed together the question of why the wedding was no longer to take place before the New Year. Oyone surmised that it had been called off on astrological grounds. Sōsuke thought that it was due to lack of time.

"Actually, I'm pretty sure it's because of money," said Koroku, uncharacteristically the only one among them to voice a down-to-earth view. "I mean, the other family is pretty extravagant, so our aunt can't get away with cutting lots of corners."

11

IT WAS in late autumn, when the crimson leaves had darkened and shriveled, that Oyone began to show signs of ailing. Apart from their time in Kyoto, Oyone had seldom enjoyed extended periods of good health, whether in Hiroshima or Fukuoka, and in this respect their move back to Tokyo had not brought about any great improvement. Sōsuke had even begun to wonder if the very air here, in the place she had been born and raised, actually disagreed with her.

Of late, however, her chronic affliction had noticeably abated; episodes of the sort that caused Sōsuke alarm had dwindled to a mere handful in any given year, such that both of them gained peace of mind in equal measure, he in the course of his daily stint at the office, she in her routine at home in his absence. And so she had not concerned herself unduly when, toward the end of autumn, with the wind blowing over the frost and chilling her to the bone, she had again begun to feel unwell. At first Oyone said nothing to her husband; yet when he saw for himself that all was indeed not well with her and urged her to see a doctor, she balked.

Then the time had come for Koroku to move in. The true state of Oyone's health, in both mind and body, was clearly visible to her husband, who was reluctant to upset the household by introducing a new member. But circumstances had tied their hands, and they were forced to carry on without further debate. Still Sōsuke mouthed words of advice about her getting plenty of rest, mindful though he was about his own inconsistency. Her smiling reply that she was perfectly all right did nothing to reassure him.

Remarkably enough, Oyone experienced a heightened sense of

well-being after Koroku moved in. It appeared that this minor increase in her responsibilities had a bracing effect on her; she applied herself with unexpected vigor to looking after her husband and now his brother. If all of this was lost on Koroku, Sōsuke realized fully the extent of her extra efforts on their behalf. Even as he redoubled his appreciation for her diligence, he worried that the stress of their augmented household might deal a sudden, serious blow to her frail health.

Toward the end of the year, unfortunately, around the twentieth of December, Sōsuke's fears were in effect realized, and like tinder touched by a spark he erupted in panic. The day had dawned heavily overcast; not a single ray of sun struck the earth, and a heavy chill weighed down on people's heads. Having scarcely slept at all the night before, Oyone began the day with a headache but found, as she stoically went about her chores, that while certain motions triggered a degree of pain, these exertions, owing, perhaps, to the comparatively pleasant stimulation afforded by her surroundings, in fact made things more bearable than when she lay in bed with her mind focused on the pain alone. Up to the moment she saw Sōsuke out the door she also gained strength from the expectation that, as always, her condition would slip into a kind of equilibrium. But as soon as he had gone and she permitted herself some momentary relief after having got through the first chores of the day, her head became increasingly oppressed by the leaden skies. Outside everything looked frozen, and inside the house the cold seemed to seep through the light-starved shoji; meanwhile her head began to burn with an intense heat. She had no choice but to retrieve her futon from where it had been stored, spread it out again in the parlor, and lie down. This having brought no relief, she had Kiyo bring her a damp towel that she draped over her head. The towel quickly turned lukewarm, so she had a basin of water placed near her pillow in which to immerse it from time to time.

Oyone kept up this makeshift treatment until noontime. It brought her no relief at all, however, and she lacked the strength to join Koroku at lunch. Asking Kiyo to set out the tray and serve Koroku his meal, she remained on her sickbed. She had Kiyo bring the puffy pillow that Sōsuke normally used and exchanged it for the stiff one on which her head had been resting up to now. Even the spirit of womanly concern about her hair coming undone had fairly deserted her.

Koroku, emerging from the six-mat room, slid open the parlor door and peeked in at her for a moment, but finding her with her head turned toward the alcove, eyes shut, and assuming, perhaps, that she was asleep, he closed the door without a word. With the ample sitting-room table all to himself, he ignored proper etiquette and began his meal by pouring tea into his rice and audibly slurping it down.

Around two o'clock Oyone finally dozed off for a while. When she woke up, the damp towel she had draped over her forehead was warm and nearly dry, but at least her headache had receded some. Now, however, she was assailed by a different, crushing form of pain that spread from her shoulders down her spine. Telling herself it would make things far worse not to take some nourishment, she struggled to her feet and nibbled on a late lunch. Kiyo fussed over Oyone as she served her meal, repeatedly asking how she felt. She appeared in fact to be a good deal better and, after having the futon removed, sat down by the brazier to wait for her husband's return.

Sōsuke came home at the usual hour. He described for Oyone the sights he had seen in the streets of Kanda: the banners displayed at all the shops, where the year-end sales were in full swing; the white-and-crimson curtain that had been hung up in the bazaar,[43] providing the band that played there with a splendid backdrop. He ended by urging her, "It's very lively. You should go and see for yourself— it's easy enough to get there by streetcar." These utterances issued from a face so ruddy it appeared as though corroded by the cold.

With Sōsuke offering Oyone such thoughtful suggestions, it was all but unthinkable for her to rebuff him with protestations of poor health. And at the moment she did not in fact feel very sick. As darkness fell she helped her husband change, folding his office clothes and the like with her usual placidity.

Around nine o'clock, however, Oyone suddenly turned to Sōsuke and said that she would retire early, as she was feeling under the weather. Since she had been chatting with him until then in her normal affable fashion, Sōsuke was somewhat taken aback by this announcement. Reassured by her insistence that it was nothing serious, however, he finally sent her off to bed.

He spent the next twenty minutes looking about the room in the quiet of evening, bathed in the soft lamplight, while listening to the gurgle of the iron kettle. He called to mind the reports of a general salary increase for government workers slated for the coming year. His thoughts then turned to rumors of the administrative reform and staffing retrenchment that would ineluctably precede the pay raise; he wondered with some apprehension which category he would fall into in such a process. He regretted that Sugihara, who had arranged his transfer to Tokyo, was no longer a section chief in his department. Where attendance was concerned, Sōsuke had not been ill even once, remarkably, since the move, and he had not taken a single sick day. It was true, though, that after dropping out of Kyoto University he had scarcely read a book, and he was less learned than the average person in his position. Still, his general intelligence was not so limited as to impede him from carrying out his duties in the bureaucracy.

Having mulled over an array of factors, Sōsuke concluded that things would turn out satisfactorily for him in the end. He gently flicked a fingernail against the rim of the iron kettle. Just then Oyone called out to him in distress. Without thinking he leapt to his feet and rushed to the parlor.

There he found Oyone half out of the covers, her upper torso completely off the futon. Her brow was furrowed, and she was gripping her shoulder tightly with her right hand. Sōsuke unconsciously reached out and placed his hand on hers. He then pressed where she pressed, right on the shoulder blade.

"A little farther over," Oyone implored. It took several more tries before his hand found the right spot, just below the base of her neck and close to the ridge of her spine. Pressing down with his fingers, he felt a stonelike nodule. She begged him to bear down on the spot with all his might. Sōsuke pressed down so hard that his forehead broke out in a sweat, but even this exertion was not enough to give his wife relief.

Sōsuke was aware of a condition known by the old-fashioned term "courier's shoulder."[44] When he was just a child his grandfather had told him the story of a samurai who, suddenly stricken with a shoulder spasm during a mission, had leapt down from his horse, drew his sword, and immediately cut into the top of his shoulder, letting the blood gush out and thus managing to save his life. Now the memory of this story came flooding back. Sōsuke was of no mind to perform the remedy presented in this anecdote. Still, he couldn't help wondering whether or not cutting into the shoulder with a sharp blade would have the desired effect.

Oyone's face was uncharacteristically flushed; even her ears were tinged with red. When Sōsuke asked if she felt hot she replied, with difficulty, that she did. He called out loudly to Kiyo, directing her to fill an ice bag with cold water and bring it to him at once. Unfortunately, it seemed they had no ice bag, and Kiyo produced instead, as she had earlier in the day, a hand towel immersed in a basin of water. While she applied the damp towel to Oyone's forehead, Sōsuke immediately resumed his efforts to bear down as hard as possible on the back of her shoulder. He asked her repeatedly if she felt any relief, but all she could do was to murmur faintly that it still hurt. Sōsuke was at his wits' end. On the verge of rushing out of the house in search of a doctor, he realized that he could not possibly set foot outside the door for fear of what might happen in his absence.

"Listen, Kiyo," he said, "go out to the main road right away, buy an ice bag, and then find a doctor. It's early enough. You'll be able to find someone."

"It's a quarter past nine," said Kiyo, who had hurried over to the clock in the sitting room. She proceeded from there to the kitchen door and was rummaging around for her clogs when, fortuitously, Koroku returned to the house. As he made his way toward his room, without announcing himself to his brother, Sōsuke called out to him in a sharp tone that stopped him in his tracks. Koroku hesitated for a moment in the sitting room, but after hearing his name called twice more in rapid succession he was compelled to mutter a reply and poke his head into the parlor. His eyes were bloodshot—the lingering effect of drink. Only after a closer look around the room did he register astonishment.

"Has something happened to Nee-san?" he said. All traces of inebriation had left his face.

Sōsuke repeated to Koroku the instructions he had given Kiyo and asked him to hurry. Koroku headed straight back to the vestibule, never having had a chance to remove his cloak.

"Even if I hurry, it'll take time to find a doctor," he said. "Why don't I borrow the Sakais' telephone and call for one right away?"

"Yes, please do," said Sōsuke.

While waiting for Koroku to return from his errand, he had Kiyo constantly replenish the water in the basin as he alternated between applying pressure to the affected area and massage. He could not bear to sit idly by and watch Oyone suffer; these ministrations brought him at least some small relief.

Still, there was nothing more trying for Sōsuke than to wait for the doctor to arrive as the minutes ticked away. Even as he rubbed Oyone's shoulder he strained to hear the faintest sounds that might echo from down the street.

By the time the doctor finally arrived, Sōsuke felt for a brief moment as though the long night had come to an end. For his part, the doctor observed the normal professional decorum and showed no sign of alarm. He performed his examination with aplomb, his briefcase still tucked under his arm as though this were a short, routine visit to a patient of long standing. The thoroughly unruffled look on the doctor's face was duly noted by Sōsuke, and his racing pulse at last slowed down.

The doctor recommended three immediate if temporary treatments: applying mustard plasters to the affected area; warming the patient's feet with hot compresses; and cooling her forehead with an ice bag. He himself then prepared a mustard plaster, spreading it over Oyone's shoulder and around to the base of her neck. Kiyo and Koroku took charge of the hot compresses, while Sōsuke applied the ice bag wrapped in a hand towel to her forehead.

These ministrations continued for about an hour. Saying that he would stay and observe their effects on the patient, the doctor remained seated at her bedside. He and Sōsuke exchanged some small talk from time to time, but for the most part they silently regarded the state of their patient. Outside, night wore on amidst the customary stillness.

"My, but it's getting cold," said the doctor. Feeling sorry for the man, Sōsuke urged that he convey instructions for Oyone's further care and then linger no longer. For, compared to how she had been earlier, Oyone seemed almost in high spirits.

"I think you are out of the woods now," the doctor said to her. "I'm going to prescribe a single dose of some medicine for you that I want you to take tonight, please. I think you'll be able to sleep then."

When the doctor left, Koroku followed him out in order to fetch the medicine.

During Koroku's absence, Oyone gazed up at Sōsuke's face near her pillow and asked the time. In contrast to earlier that evening, the blood had now left her cheeks; the side of her face where the lamplight fell looked especially pale. Sōsuke thought her pallor might be exaggerated by her black hair, which was thoroughly disheveled, and he carefully brushed the locks away from her cheeks.

"You seem a little better," he said.

"Yes, I'm really quite comfortable now," she replied, displaying one of her characteristic smiles. Even when in distress, Oyone generally did not neglect to smile for Sōsuke. From the sitting room, to which Kiyo had withdrawn and simply flopped down, came the sound of snoring. Oyone asked Sōsuke to send her to bed.

By the time Koroku returned with the medicine and Oyone ingested it as prescribed, it was close to midnight. Within twenty minutes the patient was sound asleep.

"What a relief," said Sōsuke, looking at Oyone's face.

After studying his sister-in-law's appearance for a while, Koroku responded, "She'll be all right." Together they eased the ice bag away from her forehead.

Shortly after, Koroku went to his room. Sōsuke spread out his futon next to Oyone and slept his usual sleep. Five or six hours later, leaving behind sharp needles of frost, the winter night gave way to a cloudless dawn. Over the next hour, splashing light across the land, the sun rose boldly, unchallenged, into a blue sky. Oyone remained fast asleep.

Sōsuke finished breakfast and as the time for him to leave for the office approached, Oyone still showed no sign of waking from her slumber. Bending down over her pillow, he listened to her deep breathing and wondered whether he should go to work or take the day off.

12

THAT MORNING at the office Sōsuke commenced the day's tasks in his usual fashion, but his natural concern for the ailing Oyone, exacerbated by vivid recollections of scenes from the previous night by her sickbed that kept flashing before his mind's eye, prevented any satisfactory performance. He made one bungling effort after another. Then, having waited until noon, he resolved to leave the office.

On the streetcar he conjured up for himself certain encouraging developments: Oyone waking up at some point, feeling much better and no longer in danger of another attack. There being very few fellow passengers at this hour, in contrast to his regular commute, he was scarcely distracted by external stimuli, and could therefore shift his gaze inward, onto images that were spontaneously projected inside his mind. Meanwhile, the streetcar had reached the last stop.

When he came to the front gate not a sound was to be heard from inside the house, which seemed deserted. He slid open the lattice-work door, removed his shoes, and stepped across the threshold; still no one emerged to greet him. Instead of following the veranda around to the sitting room as he usually did, he went through the vestibule and directly entered the parlor, where Oyone would be resting. And there she was, still fast asleep. All was the same as it had been that morning—the red lacquer tray by her pillow with the empty medicine packet, the glass, and even the water that had been left in it. She lay facing the alcove, just as she had when he left, with her left cheek visible and the mustard plaster showing at the collar line. Even Oyone's slumber was unchanged from what he had observed in the morning, so deep that only her breathing evinced some connection with this world. Indeed, not a single detail of his wife's appearance had been altered from what had registered in his brain on his departure. Without removing his overcoat, Sōsuke bent down and listened awhile to the rhythm of her breathing. It did not seem as though she could be easily awakened. He counted on his fingers the hours she had now slept since taking the medicine the night before. For the first time his face betrayed anxiety. Sōsuke had worried when Oyone was unable to sleep the previous evening, but as he studied her now he wondered if this being lost to the world for so long was not still more alarming.

He placed his hand on Oyone's coverlet and shook her gently. Her hair billowed out over the pillow, but the rhythm of her slumberous breathing remained unchanged. Leaving his wife be, Sōsuke passed into the sitting room and from there into the kitchen. In the sink teacups and lacquer bowls were soaking in a basin, still unwashed. He peeked into Kiyo's room and found her stretched out on the floor, a small tray of food beside her, her head inclined toward the rice tub. He then slid open the door to the six-mat room and stuck his head in. Koroku was asleep, with the covers pulled up over his head.

Sōsuke changed his own clothes and, by himself, folded the articles he had shed and put them away in the closet. He then proceeded to light the charcoal brazier and put the kettle on. Leaning on the brazier, he pondered for a few minutes, then stood up and set about waking Koroku first, Kiyo next. In both cases they leaped to their feet with a start. When Sōsuke asked his brother how Oyone had fared so far today, Koroku said, actually, he'd felt so sleepy that he nodded off after eating lunch around eleven thirty; but up until then, Oyone had been sleeping peacefully.

"I want you to go to the doctor's," Sōsuke said. "Tell him that ever since taking that medicine last night she hasn't opened her eyes once, and ask him if this is normal."

With a murmur of acknowledgment, Koroku bolted from the house. Sōsuke returned to the parlor and gazed intently at Oyone's face. Arms folded, he agonized over whether to risk the possible ill effects of not rousing her immediately or to incur whatever harm might come from waking her abruptly out of this deep sleep. He could not decide.

Presently Koroku returned and reported that when he'd explained things to the doctor, who had been about to leave on his daily rounds, he said he would come by as soon as he'd seen a couple of other patients. But in the meantime, Sōsuke rejoined, was it all right simply to leave her in her present state? Koroku said only that the doctor had told him nothing beyond what he'd just reported. This put Sōsuke right back where he had been before, seated rigidly at Oyone's bedside. Both the doctor and Koroku, he felt, were lacking in concern. Recalling Koroku's flushed face upon his return to the house the previous night, while he was in the midst of caring for his ailing wife, Sōsuke's annoyance redoubled. He had not been aware of Koroku's drinking until Oyone first brought it to his attention; yet when observing his brother closely after that, he had come to the conclusion that Koroku indeed lacked a certain moral fiber and that the situation warranted a serious talk in due time. Even so, Sōsuke shrank from the prospect of exposing Oyone to sour looks on the faces of those around her, and had not yet broached the topic.

But then, he asked himself, why not come out with it now, when Oyone is fast asleep? Even if our tempers ran away with us, it wouldn't upset her now... And yet one look at his wife's utterly insensible face was enough to dislodge this train of thought and renew his anxiety. He felt impelled to wake her up this instant. Still, he hesitated. At that moment he was delivered from this agitation by the arrival of the doctor.

Briefcase tucked primly under his arm, as on the previous visit, the doctor nodded and puffed leisurely on his cigarette as he heard Sōsuke out. "Well then, if you'll excuse me, I'll examine the patient," he said, turning toward Oyone. As though conducting a routine checkup, he spent some time taking her pulse, his gaze fixed firmly on his watch. He then placed a black stethoscope over her heart, studiously edging it this way and that over her skin. Finally, he produced a reflector with a small round hole in the middle and asked

Sōsuke to light a candle. Not having a candle, he had Kiyo light an oil lamp. The doctor raised one of Oyone's closed lids and directed the ray of light from the reflector past the lashes into the recesses of her eye.

The examination over, the doctor turned to Sōsuke. "Hmm, it seems that the medicine worked a bit too well . . ." Seeing the look in Sōsuke's eyes, he hastened to explain. "But there is certainly no cause for alarm. In cases like this, any serious reaction would affect the heart or the brain, and on the basis of my examination I find nothing unusual in either department." At this, Sōsuke at last felt reassured. As the doctor was preparing to leave, he explained that this medicine was fairly new. In theory it had fewer adverse side effects than other soporifics, but its effect varied greatly according to the constitution of the individual patient.

Detaining him for a moment longer, Sōsuke asked, "There's no harm, then, in just letting her sleep on like this?"

So long as none of them had any pressing obligations, he replied, there was no need to wake her.

After the doctor's departure Sōsuke suddenly felt very hungry. The iron kettle he had put on in the sitting room was whistling away. He summoned Kiyo and told her to serve dinner. Flustered, she responded that she had not even begun preparations. Indeed, it was still some time before the dinner hour. Sōsuke sat comfortably by the brazier, legs crossed, and made do for the time being by downing four bowls of rice gruel in rapid succession, munching on pickled radishes in between. About thirty minutes later, Oyone's eyes opened of their own accord.

13

HAVING decided to have his hair cut for the New Year, Sōsuke stepped into a barbershop for the first time in a long while. With the holiday fast approaching, the shop was quite crowded, and scissors snipped in unison at several different chairs, offering a fittingly busy accompaniment to a spectacle he had just witnessed among the crowds in the streets, everyone seemingly in a rush to leap out of this frigid season into spring.

As he sat by the heating stove smoking a cigarette and waiting his turn, Sōsuke felt himself ineluctably swept forward by a force beyond his control and, along with the faceless tide of humanity, being propelled toward the New Year. Although in fact he had no fresh expectations for the year that lay ahead, he was unwittingly goaded by the surrounding populace into a certain excitement.

With time the symptoms accompanying Oyone's attack thoroughly abated. Her recovery had by now reached the point where Sōsuke was able to resume his normal routine and not worry much about being out of the house. While the couple's customary New Year's celebrations were quiet and low-key, the preparations for this season still made it the busiest time of year for Oyone. Sōsuke had been resigned to this New Year's being even more subdued than usual. Just seeing Oyone before him, however, looking as if she had been given new life, filled him with relief. He felt as though a tragic drama had receded into the background. And yet there drifted across his mind, like a dark mist, a vague premonition that this drama would someday assume another form and engulf his family.

Watching the people all around him intent on making the short winter days even busier with their frantic activity, as if driven by the ebbing year to fill every moment, Sōsuke felt all the more weighed down by this nameless dread of things to come. It even popped into his head that, were it possible, he would choose to linger amid the shadows of the nearly spent year. His turn at a chair having come at last, he caught sight of his reflection in the cold mirror, whereupon he asked himself: Who is this person staring out at me? He was draped in a white sheet from the neck down, and he could not make out the color or pattern of his suit. It was then that he noticed, in the background of the reflection, a wicker cage that housed the barber's pet bird. The tiny bird hopped lightly about on its perch.

When Sōsuke emerged onto the street, his head fragrantly anointed and his ears ringing with the barber's hearty farewell, he felt utterly refreshed. Feeling the cold air against his skin, he had to admit that, as Oyone had claimed, a haircut can go a long way toward improving one's mood.

A question having come up about their water bill, Sōsuke stopped off at the Sakais' on his way home. Ushered inside by a maid, he assumed he would be conducted to the usual place, but the maid swiftly led him through the parlor toward the sitting room. The sliding door was partly open, leaving a two-foot gap through which resounded several voices raised in laughter. The Sakai household was as usual in high spirits.

The master of the house was seated facing him on the far side of a long, low brazier of highly polished wood. His wife sat slightly off to one side, toward the shoji that opened onto the veranda, her gaze likewise fixed on him. Behind Sakai stood a tall, slender pendulum clock encased in a black frame. To the right of the clock was a plain wall; to the left, a recessed cupboard, in which hung an assortment of decorative objects such as rubbings, illustrated haiku, and painted fans with the ribs removed.

Along with Mr. and Mrs. Sakai, two of the daughters, wearing matching patterned jackets with tight sleeves and round collars, sat shoulder to shoulder. The older one looked to be about twelve years old, the younger about ten. The two pairs of eyes opened wide at the sight of Sōsuke emerging from the other side of the door, with traces of the just now subsiding merriment evident at the corners of those eyes and mouths. Sōsuke then discovered, in addition to the parents and daughters, the odd figure of a man crouched down deferentially near the threshold.

Sōsuke deduced within the first few minutes of sitting down that the outburst of laughter he had heard earlier must have erupted in the course of the family's conversation with this strange man. His reddish hair looked as gritty as sand; his face was sunburned to a hue likely to last a lifetime. He wore a white cotton shirt fastened with ceramic buttons; dangling from a cord visible around the collar of his coarse, homespun padded jacket, there was an old-fashioned traveler's purse. His appearance proclaimed him an inhabitant of some remote, mountainous locale from which he could only infrequently descend to Tokyo. In an added touch, despite the cold weather his attire managed to leave his kneecaps exposed. Every so often he would extract a towel from the back of his faded blue sash and wipe his nose with it.

"This man has come to Tokyo all the way from the province of Kai[45] with bolts of cloth strapped on his back," said Sakai by way of an introduction, whereupon the man turned to Sōsuke.

"Yes, sir. Please, won't you buy something?"

Thus prompted, Sōsuke noticed that fabric samples had been spread out all over the room: *meisen*, crepe de chine, white pongee, and the like. He marveled at the incongruity between, on the one hand, the man's ludicrous attire and style of speech, and on the other, the exquisite goods he had come bearing on his back. Mrs. Sakai related for his benefit how this peddler's village was nothing but a mass of volcanic rock where no rice or even millet would grow, so that the people had no choice but to plant mulberry bushes and raise silkworms. Even so the place was dirt-poor, it seemed: Only a single family possessed a pendulum clock, and no more than two or three children went to school beyond the elementary grades.

"I gather that our visitor here is the only person in the village who can write," she concluded with a laugh.

"You're dead right about that," the peddler chimed in, as if his confirmation had been sought. "Whether it's reading or writing, arithmetic or penmanship—there's nobody up there but me who can handle these things. You wouldn't believe that place!"

Spreading out one fabric sample after another for the Sakais' inspection, the man said repeatedly, "Please, won't you buy this?" When they told him the price was much too high, he'd better cut it way down, and so forth, he would respond with "Why, that ain't hardly nothing"..."On my knees I'm begging you, take it for this much"..."Now go on, just feel the weight of it," and other such backwoods phrases, each of them greeted by his audience with loud laughter. The master and mistress of the house, apparently at leisure today, kept egging the man on.

"But tell us now," inquired Mrs. Sakai, "when you're on the road, toting your goods and all, do you manage to eat properly?"

"I couldn't hardly go without eating, could I? I mean, if I get hungry, well..."

"And what sort of place do you eat at?"

"What sorta place? Why, I chow down at teahouses."

Laughing, Sakai asked him what he meant by "teahouse,"[46] to which he replied, a place where they feed you.

The man then amused them by recalling how, when he first came to Tokyo, the food was so good that when he settled down to serious eating, his three meals a day proved too much for most inns to handle—he had to feel sorry for them himself.

In the end the dry-goods peddler succeeded in selling Mrs. Sakai one roll of pongee made of twisted silk and another roll of white silk gauze. Witnessing this purchase of a summer fabric in the dead of winter, Sōsuke was again struck by the distinctive habits of the well-to-do. Sakai then turned to Sōsuke.

"And what about something for your wife—say, some cloth for an everyday kimono?"

Mrs. Sakai added here that there was also a good deal to be saved—such and such a percent—by buying fabric this way. She then assured him that she would take care of any payment right now: He could reimburse them whenever it was convenient. Finally Sōsuke decided to buy a single roll of *meisen* for Oyone. Sakai proceeded mercilessly to beat down the price to three yen.

"That ain't hardly nothing at all," the man said, defeated. "It's enough to make me cry!" Everyone burst out laughing.

Evidently the dry-goods peddler managed to do business with any number of customers despite his backwoods speech. As he made the rounds of his regulars all over the city, the load on his back steadily decreased, until in the end there remained only some wrapping cloths and slender "Sanada" sashes. By the time he got to this point, he explained, it was always around the old, lunar New Year, so he would return to his province for a spell and greet the spring there.[47] Then, with new bolts of cloth strapped to his back, he was off to the city again. This fresh stock would be converted into cash by the end of April or the beginning of May, which coincided with the busy season for growing silkworms, when he would again return to his small village amid the piles of volcanic rocks, below the north face of Mount Fuji.

"In the four or five years he's been coming to us, he hasn't changed a bit," Mrs. Sakai commented.

"Yes, a remarkable fellow," her husband observed.

In these times, when after a few days at home one went out to find that the streets had been widened, or, if one skipped the newspaper for a single day, missed learning about a new streetcar line, for someone who had been coming to Tokyo twice a year to have kept so thoroughly intact his mountain-man ways—it was truly remarkable. After observing the face of this dry-goods peddler, along with his attire, his language, and his way of interacting with people, Sōsuke came to feel a kind of sympathy for him.

On his way home from the Sakais', Sōsuke, switching the bundle of just-purchased *meisen* back and forth from under one flap of his cape to another, vividly retained in his mind's eye the image of the man who had just sold him this fine cloth for a paltry three yen: the stripes of his coarse homespun jacket; his desiccated, ruddy hair, which, stiff and lackluster as it was, he somehow managed to keep immaculately parted down the middle.

At home, Oyone had just finished sewing for Sōsuke a new kimono jacket to mark the New Year. For lack of a proper press, she had placed it under a cushion and was sitting on it.

"Spread it under your futon tonight and sleep on it," she said, casting a glance over her shoulder at her husband.

On hearing his account of the man from Kai who had been at the Sakais', Oyone could not help laughing out loud herself. "And so cheap," she said over and over again as she feasted her eyes on the texture and striped pattern of the *meisen* he had brought her. The material was indeed of the highest quality.

"How can he possibly make a profit at such prices?" she asked at length.

"The reason is that the middlemen are making far too much profit," answered Sōsuke, who, extrapolating from this single bolt of *meisen*, answered as if he were an expert in the trade.

The conversation then shifted to the comfortable circumstances enjoyed by the Sakais—if their wealth sometimes made them prey to swindles by the likes of the furniture dealer, it also gave them the advantage of stocking up cheaply on articles for which they had no pressing need—and from this point of departure on to the general subject of the astonishingly bright, lively lives they led.

"Of course it's not just that they have money," Sōsuke said to Oyone, his tone suddenly altered. "It also has to do with all those children they have. As long as there are children, even poor families can be very cheerful."

In Oyone's ears his tone resounded with rather harsh self-reproach over their lonely existence. Involuntarily taking her hands off the bolt of cloth in her lap, she glanced at her husband's face. So full of satisfaction at having brought some rare joy into his wife's life, in the form of this pleasing gift acquired through the Sakais, Sōsuke was unaware of how his words sounded to her. Oyone let the matter pass with only her brief glance but decided to broach it at bedtime.

Not long after they had gone to bed at their usual time of a little past ten, Oyone turned to her husband before he could doze off and said, "Earlier tonight you said not having children makes life dreary, didn't you?"

Sōsuke recalled that he had said something very general along those lines, but he had certainly not intended it as a pointed reference to Oyone herself. Grilled in this fashion, he was totally at a loss for a reply.

"Oh, I wasn't talking about us," he said.

Oyone listened in silence. Then, after a pause, she said, "But you are always thinking how dreary thing are at home, so you must have meant what you said, did you not?"

She was essentially repeating the same point she had made before. Inwardly, Sōsuke had to agree with her interpretation. But in the interest of sparing her feelings he could not bring himself to make such a blunt admission. To soothe his still-convalescent wife it would be best, he thought, to treat the matter as nothing but a joke. He shifted to the lightest tone he could manage.

"Well," he began," "I said 'dreary'... and naturally things do get dreary at times..." But here he came up against a wall, unable to think of anything novel or amusing. In the end, he was reduced to saying, "Oh, never mind. Don't worry about it." This too having met with silence from Oyone, he decided to change the subject. "I hear there was another fire last night..." Sōsuke said, venturing into current events.

"I am so very sorry for what this has done to you," Oyone suddenly broke out in a painful, heartfelt apology, then faltered and fell silent. With her back to the lamp, which was set as usual in the alcove, he could not make out her expression, but he could hear the quavering in her voice. Sōsuke, who had been lying on his back and staring at the ceiling, turned to his wife and gazed intently at her through the very dim light. She peered back at him. "For a long time I've been wanting to say how sorry I am, from the bottom of my heart," she said haltingly, "but it's been hard for me to put into words... and so I've just let it go up to now."

Sōsuke scarcely knew what to make of this. He wondered if it might be a touch of hysteria;[48] but since he could not be sure, he said nothing. He was in a daze.

Oyone spoke again, in anguish, and this time with finality: "I can never have a child." Then she burst into tears.

At a loss how to console his wife after she had made such a heart-rending confession, Sōsuke found his pity for her mounting ever higher. "Oh well, children—they're really not worth the trouble, are they? I mean, just look at that brood the Sakais have. You can't help feeling sorry for them. It's like a nursery school up there..."

"But to know that there will never be a single one—say what you will, that can't make you happy."

"Who is to say that you couldn't have one still? You might, you know."

At this Oyone only cried harder. Helpless, Sōsuke could only wait stoically until she regained some composure. Then he listened as she unburdened herself.

Although in the course of their life together the two of them had achieved a greater harmony than the average couple, where children were concerned they had been less fortunate than most. Had it been a clear-cut case of infertility it would have been easier to bear; but to lose the children they had actually conceived—this had made their misfortune all the more keenly felt.

Oyone's first pregnancy had occurred shortly after they left Kyoto, while they were just scraping by in their Hiroshima lodgings. Once she had realized her condition, Oyone went from day to day lurching between two simultaneous dreams of the future, one terrifying, the other euphoric. Sōsuke privately viewed the new development as an outward manifestation of the intangible spirit of love they shared, and was filled with joy. As he waited he took pleasure in counting on his fingers the months and weeks remaining until the lump of flesh to which he had contributed a part of himself would come to term and appear dancing before their eyes. But the couple's hopes were dashed when the fetus was cast out from the womb at only five months. This was the period when they were only barely getting by, in the most straitened circumstances. Gazing at Oyone's ashen face after the miscarriage, Sōsuke was convinced that this, too, was a result of their poverty. He lamented that such fruits of their love could be crushed by sheer material want and had now been placed out of their reach indefinitely. For her part, Oyone simply wept.

It was not long after they moved to Fukuoka, however, that once again she found herself craving sour foods. Having heard tales of how one miscarriage tends to lead to another, Oyone became cautious about the smallest things and conducted herself with the utmost restraint. Perhaps this had an effect, for the pregnancy proceeded in virtually textbook fashion until, inexplicably, she gave birth prematurely. The midwife, shaking her head, urged Oyone to have the baby seen by a doctor. After an examination, the doctor told them that since the infant was not fully developed, their room must be kept at a precise, elevated temperature, without any fluctuations between day and night—something that would of course require some mode of generating extra heat. In their current circumstances all Sōsuke could do was to provide a space-heating stove. The couple devoted all their time and meager resources in an intense effort to save the child's life. But it all came to naught. After one week this small creature, who shared their blood and bore witness to their love for each other, turned cold and lifeless.

"Whatever shall we do?" Oyone sobbed, cradling the baby's body in her arms.

Sōsuke received this new blow with manly stoicism. As the baby's cold flesh was reduced to ashes, and the ashes put to rest in the dark earth, he did not utter one word of protest. With the passage of time, the shadowy gap that had opened up between them narrowed, then vanished altogether.

There had been a third episode that formed yet another painful memory. Within a year after their return to Tokyo, Oyone became pregnant again. Her health after the move being far from robust, Sōsuke, not to mention Oyone, was extremely concerned. Yet they summoned up their hopes—This time for sure! they both thought—

and were increasingly buoyed with each uneventful month that passed by. But then, at the beginning of the fifth month, Oyone committed a surprising blunder. Since the municipal water supply had not yet been put through to their district, the maid constantly had to scurry back and forth to draw water at the well, where she also did the laundry. One day, needing to speak with the maid while the latter was still at the well, Oyone went out herself and, while talking, stepped over a basin near the faucet, whereupon she slipped and fell on the mossy wet planks there, landing on her buttocks. Fearing that she had ruined things again, she was too ashamed of her carelessness to tell Sōsuke about the mishap and maintained a rigorous silence. The days passed, however, without any ill effect on the quickening fetus or any palpable injury to herself; only then did she finally, and with much relief, make a clean breast of the matter to her husband, long after the fact. Not disposed from the start to reproach his wife, Sōsuke let the incident pass with only a mild admonition. "You must avoid doing anything risky or you'll run into trouble," he said.

In due course, then, the pregnancy approached full term. Oyone had now reached the stage where the baby could come any day, and Sōsuke could think of nothing but his wife, even while at the office. On his way home he would dwell incessantly on whether or not she had given birth during his absence, and pause outside the lattice-work door to his own house in anticipation. On a couple of occasions, on not hearing the half-expected newborn cries, he leapt to the conclusion that something had gone awry and charged headlong into the house, only to feel mortified at the awkward figure he must have cut.

Fortunately, Oyone went into labor late one evening, a time when Sōsuke, being at home and having no other business, could stay by her side and help. In this respect, at least, it was a propitious beginning. The midwife was sent for without any great haste; gauze and such were all laid out and at the ready. The delivery itself took place with unexpected ease. Sadly, however, the infant emerged from the confines of the womb into the world without taking so much as a single breath of air. Wielding a tubular glass instrument, the midwife repeatedly forced her own breath into the tiny mouth, but to no avail. What had come into this world was an inert lump of flesh—clearly etched, they could see, with a pair of eyes, a nose, and a mouth. But from its throat there issued nary a cry for them to hear.

The midwife had paid Oyone a house call just a week earlier and examined the fetus, even auscultating its heart, and pronounced it to be in excellent condition. Even supposing for the moment that the midwife's examination were faulty, if fetal development had in fact ceased at some point prior to the delivery, surely Oyone would have suffered ill effects, unless, of course, the fetus were aborted. Sōsuke's subsequent wider search for an explanation yielded a startling, and horrifying, discovery: that the fetus must have been perfectly normal up to the final moments of the delivery, only to be strangled by a prolapsed umbilical cord that became wrapped around its neck. In the event of this abnormal occurrence, the only possible remedy lies in the hands of a skilled midwife, who on detecting the obstruction as she reaches in, will disentangle the cord and pull it out of the way. This much the midwife whom Sōsuke had engaged, being well on in years, clearly understood. In this case, however, as sometimes happens, the prolapsed cord had ringed the tiny throat not once but twice; as the midwife probed the constricted area with her fingers she missed one coil, which pressed hard against the infant's windpipe until it choked to death.

The midwife was partly at fault, to be sure, but the greater blame lay with Oyone's mishap. When, in her fifth month, she fell over backwards and landed hard on the ground beside the well, she had created the conditions for a prolapsed umbilical cord. When Oyone listened to this explanation as she lay on her sickbed, she nodded feebly and said nothing. Her eyes, noticeably sunken from fatigue, misted over behind her long, constantly fluttering lashes. Murmuring consolations, Sōsuke wiped the tears from her cheeks with his handkerchief.

Such was the couple's history where children of their own were concerned. Having suffered the anguish of losing a child three times over, they were not disposed to speak about children much at all. Nevertheless, however unspoken, these memories suffused the most private part of their life together with a sadness that showed no sign of dissipating. At times, even in the midst of laughing together over some little thing, they would both experience intimations of these shadows from their past. Even at the moment of her outburst, then, Oyone had no intention of going over with Sōsuke again the details of this shared experience. Nor could he have seen any reason to sit there and listen had his wife simply dredged up those same sad, familiar events.

What Oyone had now begun to unburden herself about had nothing to do with the facts of their common past. Learning from her husband of the chain of circumstances that had led to the loss of her third child, she had come to see herself as a mother of monstrous cruelty. Although she had not committed the deed with her own hands, she concluded that she might as well have laid in wait on the shadowy path connecting the darkness with the light in order to wring the breath from the very one to whom she herself had given life. Having reached this conclusion, Oyone could not help viewing herself as a criminal guilty of the most horrendous of acts. Thereafter, unbeknownst to anyone, she had been subjected to hitherto unimagined torments of conscience. And there was not a soul in all the world with whom she could suffer some portion of these torments. She did not divulge her feelings even to her husband.

After this last episode, Oyone went through with the same three weeks' bed rest she would have undergone after a normal childbirth. Physically, this interval brought her much-needed repose. Emotionally, however, the three weeks became a daunting test of her endurance. Sōsuke made a small coffin for the infant's body and conducted a funeral unwitnessed by anyone. After that he made a small wooden tablet inscribed in black lacquer with the posthumously bestowed Buddhist name of the deceased. Although the infant thus commemorated bore a sanctified name, what this small soul might have been called in everyday life, neither parent could say. At first Sōsuke kept the tablet on top of the chest of drawers in the sitting room, where in the evening, on returning from the office, he would without fail burn incense before it. The scent occasionally reached Oyone's nostrils. Confined to the six-mat room, she was lying at some remove, yet her senses were keen enough for it to register. After a period of time something prompted him to take down the small tablet and place it in the bottom drawer of the chest. In this same drawer were carefully stored, wrapped separately in cotton cloth, the memorial tablets of the child who had died in Fukuoka and of Sōsuke's father, who had ended his days in Tokyo. When the Tokyo home had been disposed of, Sōsuke had not wanted to be burdened with ancestral tablets as he wandered about the country; he deposited all of them at the family temple[49] and took with him only the newly made tablet of his late father.

While confined to her bed, Oyone's eyes and ears kept her acutely aware of each and every step Sōsuke took in the house. Lying faceup on her futon, in her mind's eye she tied together the miniature tablets of her two dead offspring with the long, invisible thread of her own sad destiny. Following the thread still farther, she saw it dangling down on a wraithlike shadow—the aborted fetus, which never assumed a human form and for which no tablet had been made. Each and every one of the recollected episodes—in Hiroshima, Fukuoka, and Tokyo—was bound by the same immutable fate, whose solemn reign she felt compelled to acknowledge; once she had done so, and once she had realized that she had been molded by this fate into a mother who, over the months and years, was mysteriously doomed to relive the same misfortune again and again, she detected to her dismay a curse being whispered in her ear. Even as her body, lying there on the futon, eagerly submitted to the biological imperative of three weeks' rest, she was conscious every moment of this whispered curse reverberating on her eardrums. And so it was that this three-week period of repose in fact turned into a protracted, excruciating test of Oyone's spirit.

After passing the first two weeks of this confinement with her gaze fixed inward, she reached the point where just lying there stoically became impossible. The day after the visiting nurse departed,

Oyone stole out of bed and walked around a bit. But she was not easily distracted from the anxiety that continually gnawed at her. However much she forced her body to move about, her mind refused to budge. Discouraged yet again, she burrowed back under the covers so recently cast aside. At times she shut her eyes very tight, as if to keep the human world at bay.

Oyone completed the full three weeks of bed rest. When the time was up, her body naturally felt reinvigorated. After removing all traces of her sickbed, she peered into the mirror and detected signs of renewed life about the eyebrows. This was the season for the traditional changing of clothes.[50] Even the forlorn Oyone was by no means insensible to the Japanese predilection for marking the shift from spring to summer with bold, bright adornments. But the momentary stimulation it afforded only served to stir things up deep inside her until they floated to the surface, where they were exposed to the glare of the busy, festive world. This renewed encounter with the outside world incited in her a feeling of inquisitiveness about her own dark past.

One supernally fine morning, immediately after seeing her husband off to work as usual, Oyone went out. It was already the season for women to carry parasols. As she walked along briskly in the sunlight a few beads of sweat gathered on her forehead. Earlier, when changing into her clothes, her hand had accidentally touched the newest memorial tablet as she opened the bottom drawer of the chest; she now dwelled with each step on that unexpected sensation, until at length she passed through the gate of a certain *I Ching* divinator.[51]

Ever since childhood Oyone had entertained the same kinds of superstitions as are found in a majority of otherwise enlightened citizens. At the same time, as is the general rule with such people, on those occasions when she openly invoked one superstitious practice or another it was done in a playful, mocking fashion. It was unprecedented, then, for this sort of belief to have impinged on an innermost part of her being. Seated now face-to-face with the divinator, it was in all seriousness that she tried to ascertain whether Heaven had decreed that she was to bear a child, and if so, whether the child would survive to maturity. The divinator, who looked no different from other fortune-tellers who peddled their services on the street for a coin or two, lined up his six blocks this way and that, shuffled his fifty long sticks, keeping count all the while, then finally, after stroking his goatee portentously and pondering for a moment, studied Oyone's face closely and pronounced with complete equanimity: "You cannot have any children."

Oyone remained silent as she digested these words, considering them from every possible angle. Then, raising her head again, she replied with another question: "Why can't I?"

She had assumed that the man would deliberate again before responding, but without hesitating he looked her straight in the eye and replied unequivocally: "You will recall that you behaved unforgivably toward someone in the past. Your sinful behavior has become a curse that will prevent you from ever bringing a child into this world."

These words were a stab to her heart. All the way home her head drooped limply, and she had barely been able to raise it that night in front of her husband.

It was this judgment rendered by the divinator that Oyone had refrained from divulging. When, on this still night, with the dim glow from the lamp he had placed in the alcove about to dissolve in darkness, Sōsuke first heard of this incident from Oyone's lips, he could not help being perturbed.

"Really—to concoct such an idiotic errand when your nerves were so shattered to begin with! What was the point of spending good money to hear that sort of nonsense? Did you go back again after that?"

"Oh, no, never! It's too frightening."

"Well, I'm glad of that, at least. It's nothing but foolishness," Sōsuke pronounced as magnanimously as he could, and went to sleep.

14

Sōsuke and Oyone were without question a loving couple. In the six long years they had been together they had not spent so much as half a day feeling strained by the other's presence, and they had never once engaged in a truly acrimonious quarrel. They went to the draper to buy cloth for their kimonos and to the rice dealer for their rice, but they had very few expectations of the wider world beyond that. Indeed, apart from provisioning their household with everyday necessities, they did little else that acknowledged the existence of society at large. The only absolute need to be fulfilled for each of them was the need for each other; this was not only a necessary but also a sufficient condition for life. They dwelled in the city as though living deep in the mountains.

In due course their lives began to turn monotonous. In their effort to avoid the stress that comes with living in a complex society, they eventually cut themselves off from access to diverse experiences that such a society affords, and in so doing came to forfeit, in effect, the prerogatives regularly enjoyed by civilized people. Intermittently they themselves recognized that their daily lives lacked variety. While neither felt the slightest hint of dissatisfaction or inadequacy with regard to the other, within the confines of the inner lives that they had created for themselves lurked a muffled protest against something stultifying, something lodged there that would not admit new stimuli. That they nonetheless lived out each and every day with the same stoical spirit was not because they had from the outset lost all interest in the wider world. Rather, it was because the wider world, after having isolated the two of them from all else, persisted in turning a cold shoulder. Blocked from extending themselves outward, they began developing more deeply within themselves. What their life together had lost in breadth it gained in depth. For these six years, instead of engaging in casual interactions with the outside world, they had explored the recesses of each other's hearts. To the world they continued to appear to be two people. But in their minds they had become part of a single organism that it would be criminal to split apart. Their identities were so merged that the slenderest nerve endings in one of them were entangled with those of the other. They were like two droplets of oil on the surface of a large basinful of water. They had joined not through having repelled the surrounding water but rather through having been propelled by water into converging courses that brought them together in a single sphere.

United in this fashion, they experienced a harmony and a mutual fulfillment rarely attained in marriage—and concomitantly, a sense of tedium as well. Yet even when under the sway of such languor, they were cognizant of their good fortune. At times this tedium affected their consciousness like a scrim of oblivion, obscuring their love for a spell in a distracted haze. Still and all, no lacerating doubts arose to unsettle their equanimity. For they continued to be just as intimately joined to each other as they were estranged from the society around them.

Even as they sustained this remarkably close bond from one day to the next, year after year, they acted in each other's company as though unaware of anything out of the ordinary about their relationship. From time to time, however, they both made a point of reaffirming the love they felt for each other. This process invariably involved going back to a time prior to their life together—to the inescapable memory of how much, in order to unite themselves in marriage, they had been forced to sacrifice. Such recollections caused them to bow and tremble before the terrible retribution that Nature had proceeded to inflict on them. At the same time they never failed to pay homage to the power of Love. They walked along through life together on the path toward death, lashed by fate each step of the way. Yet the lash's tip, they realized, had been dipped in a honey-like balm that healed all wounds.

In his student days, as the scion of a Tokyo family of considerable means, Sōsuke had freely and fully indulged the flamboyant tastes common to his class. In his dress, his mannerisms, and his opinions, he exuded the aura of a bright young man of the modern age, and with head held high sauntered about wherever he pleased. Like his starched white collar, his well-turned cuffs, and the patterned cashmere stockings that showed just below his cuffed trousers, his mind was exquisitely socialized.

By nature quick-witted, Sōsuke was little inclined to study. Viewing academic pursuits merely as a means of social advancement, he scarcely ever entertained the notion of a scholarly career, which requires something of a retreat from society. In the manner of other ordinary students he simply attended classes and blackened with ink large numbers of notebooks. But once the notebooks had been deposited somewhere at home, he rarely looked them over or made any further notations; even the gaps created by absences from class for the most part went unfilled. Leaving the notebooks piled up neatly on his desk, he would vacate his impeccably tidy study and go out for a stroll. Not a few of his friends envied him this air of a man of leisure. Sōsuke himself took pride in it. His future as reflected in his own eyes shimmered like a rainbow.

Back then, unlike the present, he had many friends. The plain truth of it was that in his cheerfully callow view all people appeared, more or less interchangeably, as friends. He lightly traversed his youth with optimism intact and without ever managing to learn the true meaning of the word "enemy."

"So long as you don't show up looking glum," Sōsuke would say to his classmate Yasui, "you'll be welcome just about anywhere." And in fact he had never managed to look serious enough to offend anyone.

"That's easy for *you* to say—you're always so healthy," Yasui, who was always suffering from one ailment or another, would reply enviously.

Though originally from the province of Echizen,[52] Yasui had lived in Yokohama so long that his accent and general appearance conformed to those of someone born and bred in Tokyo. He lavished care on his clothes and affected long hair parted straight down the middle. While he and Sōsuke had attended different secondary schools, at the university they often found themselves sitting side by side at lectures, and from time to time would ask each other about material they had missed. Before long these classroom chats grew into a friendship. For Sōsuke, who was still a stranger in Kyoto, it was a boon to have made such a friend at the beginning of the academic year. With Yasui as his guide he drank in like warm saké all the impressions offered by his new surroundings. The two of them made almost nightly forays into the livelier neighborhoods, such as those clustered along the avenues of Sanjō and Shijō. Occasionally they wandered through the Kyōgoku quarter. Standing in the middle of a bridge, they would gaze down at the waters of the Kamo River and look up at the moon silently rising over the hills of Higashiyama. The Kyoto moon struck Sōsuke as rounder and larger than the moon of Tokyo.

When they grew weary of city streets and the crowds they would avail themselves of weekends to visit the outlying areas. Sōsuke delighted in the dense concentrations of brilliant greenery presented by the thickets of great bamboo dotting the landscape, and he marveled at the elegant rows of pines, their trunks, when reflecting the sunlight, seemingly dyed red. One day the two of them climbed up to the Pavilion of Compassion at Senkōji.[53] As they gazed up at a large plaque inscribed by the monk Sokuhi,[54] they heard the splashing of oars plying the stream in the valley floor. It so resembled the call of wild geese that they had to smile. Another time they trekked as far as the Heihachi Teahouse Inn[55] and spent the night there. They ordered from the hostess some unappetizing grilled river fish on skewers and downed them with saké. The hostess wore a light cotton towel around her head in the country style and old-fashioned baggy blue trousers.

For a while, immersed in these new sensations, Sōsuke managed to assuage his appetite for life. But in the course of roaming around the old capital and inhaling its venerable scent, at some point it began to seem stale. As the novel effect initially produced on him by the lovely mountains and sparkling waters wore off, he grew dissatisfied. With the warm blood of youth still coursing through his veins, he was unable to discover a verdant oasis that might quench its heat. Nor had he found any sphere of action in which his natural ardor could flare up and consume itself. His racing pulse only caused his whole body to tingle with nervous energy. Languishing there in the inn, arms folded against his chest, Sōsuke surveyed the mountains that stretched out in all directions. "I'm tired of these boring old places," he said presently.

With a chuckle, Yasui launched into an anecdote about a friend of his who hailed from a truly remote locale—just to keep things in perspective. The place was Tsuchiyama—the one where "the rain keeps coming down," as it says in the ballad[56]—and it had been a well-known post station on the old Tokaido Road. From morning to night, according to Yasui's friend, you could see nothing but mountains all around: It was like living at the bottom of a cone-shaped mortar bowl. As a child, he recalled, whenever the spring rains poured down he had panicked at the prospect of the family's inn being submerged, seemingly any minute, beneath the water flowing down from the surrounding mountains. It struck Sōsuke that there could be no crueler fate than to live out one's life stuck at the bottom of this mortar bowl.

"How can people possibly survive in such a place?" he exclaimed with a look of incredulity.

With another chuckle, Yasui related a story that this same friend had told him about the most prodigious native son that Tsuchiyama had given to the world: a fellow who had long ago swindled someone out of a strongbox and been crucified for his trouble.[57] Chafing as he was at the constraints of Kyoto life, Sōsuke allowed as how such events were indispensable, perhaps once in a century, to break the monotony.

At this stage of his life, Sōsuke's gaze was riveted to the world of the new. Once he had taken in the full cycle of local beauty spots that nature had to offer through the four seasons, he felt no need to visit blossoms here, autumn leaves there, simply for the sake of renewing memories of yesteryear. In his quest to establish a demonstrable record of a life lived to the full, his overwhelming priorities were the present in which he was now engaged and the future that was in the process of unfolding; the receding past was but an illusion, of as little value to him as a vanished dream. He began to cringe at the thought of viewing countless peeling shrines and weathered temples—indeed, at the very prospect of focusing his bright young eyes on history's faded relics. His sensibility was not yet so desiccated as to lure him down the sleepy byways of antiquity.

At the end of the school year, Sōsuke and Yasui took leave of each other with promises to meet again soon. Yasui's plan was first to return to his original home in Fukui Prefecture, then go on to Yokohama; if he were to send Sōsuke a letter to let him know when he had arrived, ideally they could later take the train back to Kyoto, stopping, if time permitted, at Okitsu, where they could make a leisurely tour of Seikenji, the Zen temple, the pine grove on Miho strand, perhaps even Mount Kunō.[58] Pronouncing this an excellent plan, Sōsuke anticipated the pleasure of receiving Yasui's note from Yokohama.

When Sōsuke had then returned to Tokyo, his father was still in the best of health and Koroku was but a child. After a year's absence, it actually thrilled him to breathe again the scorching, sooty air of the capital. Gazing down from some eminence on the congeries of roof tiles stretching out for miles in all directions under the blazing sun, he had almost exclaimed aloud: *This* is Tokyo! At this period in his life, each and every detail of this dizzying panorama assailed his senses with a force that drummed into his head the word "Mag-nif-i-cent!"

His future was like a tightly closed bud waiting to blossom into a flower as yet unknown to others, whose ultimate form was indeed far from clear even to him. What he could intuit clearly was that "boundless" was the best way to describe what lay ahead. Even in the

summer heat, he did not neglect to lay plans for his life after graduation. Although he had not yet decided whether to pursue a career in
the civil service or in business, he realized that in either case it would
be to his advantage to lay as much groundwork as possible now. His
father introduced him personally to some of his acquaintances and
provided indirect introductions to others. Sōsuke selected those
who might carry particular weight in the future and went to visit
these men. One of them had already left the city, ostensibly for a
summer resort. Another was simply not at home. Still another man
on his list told him to visit his office, saying he was too busy to meet
with him at home. Sōsuke arrived at seven in the morning, with the
sun still low in the sky, and took the elevator up to the third floor of
a red-brick building, only to be confronted to his amazement by the
spectacle of seven or eight others waiting there to see the very same
man. And yet it somehow excited him to visit new places like this
and encounter novel situations that, whether or not his errand
proved successful, made him feel as though he were adding to his
mental file a type of experience about which he had previously been
ignorant.

Similarly, in this phase of his life he considered the role assigned
to him by his father in the annual airing of the family heirlooms a
particularly fascinating opportunity. Seated on a damp rock in front
of the storehouse, feeling the cool breeze that blew through the
building, he pored with great curiosity over illustrated maps of famous places in Edo and a gazetteer entitled *The Fine-Grained Sands
of Edo*[59] that had passed through several generations of his family.
Then, sitting cross-legged in the middle of the parlor, where even the
mats were hot, he would pack the camphor crystals[60] brought to him
by the maid into little paper cones of the sort doctors use to dispense
medicinal powders. From childhood Sōsuke had a fixed set of associations linking the strong aroma of camphor with the sweaty dog
days of summer, earthenware moxa burners, and long-winged, fork-
tailed kites lazily circling overhead in a clear blue sky.

While thus caught up in one thing or another, Sōsuke was over-
taken by the approach of autumn.[61] Leading up to the traditional

watershed mark, the two hundred and tenth day in the old calendar,[62] the winds blew and rains fell. Clouds looking like splotches of thin black ink moved ceaselessly across the sky. In the space of two or three days the temperature fell precipitously. The time had come for Sōsuke to bind up his wicker trunk with strong hemp rope and prepare to return to Kyoto.

In the meantime, however, he had not forgotten the travel plans agreed to with Yasui. When he arrived in Tokyo two months earlier he had at first simply bided his time, but as the departure date approached and there was still no word from Yasui, he became concerned. Since they had parted ways in Kyoto, Sōsuke had not received so much as a postcard. He sent off a letter to Yasui's old home in Fukui; there was no reply. He then thought of making inquiries in Yokohama, only to realize he had neglected to ask Yasui for his address there. And so his hands were tied.

On the eve of Sōsuke's departure his father took him aside and, after handing him a sum of money that included, as his son had requested, something extra for the side trip on the way back to Kyoto, counseled him, "Now, be sure to watch your spending." Sōsuke had listened to this well-worn piece of parental advice in the fashion typical of young sons. "I won't be seeing you until you come home again next year," his father added. "Take very good care of yourself."

But when the time for him to return came around the next year, it was no longer possible for Sōsuke to go home. And the next time he did return to Tokyo his father already lay cold in death. Even now, Sōsuke could not recall the scene of their final parting without feeling a stab of remorse.

At the very last moment before he left for Kyoto, he had received a proper, sealed letter from Yasui, who wrote to the effect that while he had fully intended to stick to their plan of traveling together, something had come up that required him to return right away. He concluded with the hope that they could get together again in a leisurely fashion back in Kyoto. Sticking the letter into his suit pocket, Sōsuke boarded the train.

When he reached Okitsu, where the two friends were to have

stopped together, Sōsuke exited the station and walked alone straight down the town's single thoroughfare toward Seikenji. Now that it was September and the summer season over, the flow of vacationers had ebbed, leaving the inn relatively tranquil. Sōsuke stretched out prone in a room with a view of the sea and wrote a few lines on a postcard to Yasui, which included the words: "Since you did not join me, here I am all by myself in this place."

The following day, still sticking to their original plan, he went, again by himself, to view the pines of Miho and to visit Ryūgeji, a temple associated with the Tokugawa family, making an effort all the while to store up impressions that could later be revived in conversation with Yasui. Perhaps it was the weather, or perhaps it was the absence of the companion he had counted on, but Sōsuke found little pleasure in viewing the pine-covered beaches or making the ascent to the temple. Lounging about at the inn was even more tedious. Stripping off the yukata provided by the inn and draping it along with the short sash over a railing, he quickly left Okitsu.

On his first day back in Kyoto, Sōsuke, tired from the overnight train trip and busy with tidying up afterward, did not so much as step into the sunlit streets. When, on the following day, he got around to visiting the campus, he found the faculty not much in evidence and the students still few and far between. Strangest of all, Yasui, after so emphatically announcing his intent to return to Kyoto on a date that fell some days earlier, was nowhere to be seen. Perplexed, Sōsuke made a detour on his way home to Yasui's lodgings, which were located next to the well-wooded and well-watered precincts of Kamo Shrine. Before the vacation, in resorting to this out-of-the-way retreat, which might as well have been a country village, Yasui had stressed the need for some quiet backwater where he could properly study. The house he had chosen was flanked on two sides by weathered earthen walls that lent it an old-fashioned aura. The owner, Sōsuke learned from Yasui, had been a cleric on the staff of Kamo Shrine. His wife, a forty-year-old woman who wielded the Kyoto dialect quite expressively, saw to Yasui's needs.

"'Seeing to my needs' consists in her dropping off a lousy meal three times a day," Yasui had complained to Sōsuke shortly after moving in. Sōsuke was already acquainted from previous visits with the landlady responsible for the so-called lousy meals, and she, for her part, remembered who he was. No sooner had she caught sight of him than, after an elaborate greeting in her mellifluous Kyoto idiom, she took the words out of his mouth by asking him about Yasui's whereabouts. Evidently she had heard nothing from him since he left for home at the beginning of summer. Sōsuke mulled over this surprise all the way back to his lodging.

For the next week or so, on every visit to campus, he felt a presentiment as he entered the lecture hall: Would he catch sight of Yasui's face today? Would he chance to hear his voice? Each day he returned home with the same vague but palpable sense of dissatisfaction. Indeed, by the third or fourth day, viewing himself as having some responsibility concerning such things, since it was to him Yasui had clearly communicated his intention to return early, Sōsuke began to worry about his safety. He made inquiries about Yasui's movements, asking every classmate who had been at all friendly with him, but no one knew a thing. One of them did say that just the night before, in the midst of the crowds around Shijō, he had seen a man wearing a yukata who looked a lot like Yasui. Sōsuke did not consider it likely that it was, in fact, his friend. The very day after Sōsuke gleaned this bit of information, however, that is, an entire week after he had arrived back in Kyoto, Yasui himself burst in on him at his lodging dressed just as the classmate had described.

As Sōsuke gazed for the first time in a long while at the figure of his friend, not yet dressed for school and with straw hat in hand, he had the sensation that something new had been superimposed on this face since he had last seen it before vacation. His black hair had been slicked down with pomade and parted down the middle with ostentatious precision. In fact, Yasui announced, by way of an explanation for showing up out of the blue, he had just come from a barbershop.

That evening the two of them spent more than an hour engrossed in conversation. The peculiar mannerisms in Yasui's speech remained unchanged: a certain gravity in his enunciation; a reserved tone, as if holding back from expressing himself too freely in deference to Sōsuke; the verbal tic of "never-the-less..." which he overused as before. And yet in the course of their conversation he said not a word about why he had left Yokohama ahead of Sōsuke, nor explained where he had stopped en route, thus arriving in Kyoto later than his friend. He did mention that it was only three or four days ago that he had finally returned, and that he had yet to settle in again at the lodging he had moved into before the summer break.

"Where *are* you staying, then?" Sōsuke asked. Yasui named an inn in the Sanjō district. It was a third-rate establishment. Sōsuke knew of it.

"What are you doing in a place like that?" Sōsuke pressed him further. "Are you going to stay there much longer?"

At first Yasui replied vaguely that circumstances made it convenient to stay there for the time being. But then he announced a new development to his astonished friend: "I'm thinking of getting away from boardinghouse life... maybe I'll rent a small house."

Within the week, as good as his word, Yasui was the master of a house in a tranquil locale close to the university. In addition to the gloomy darkness common to all Kyoto houses, this cramped rental had pillars and latticework painted a darkish red color seemingly calculated to intensify the fusty look of the place. Near the front gate was a single willow tree; on whose property it stood was hard to say. Sōsuke observed its long branches whipping about in the breeze, practically touching the eaves of Yasui's house. The garden, unlike those of Tokyo, was laid out with some order. Befitting a region where rocks were easy to come by, a good-size boulder had been set in the garden directly opposite the parlor. Around its base spread a cool, luxurious carpet of moss. Behind the house stood an empty toolshed, its threshold rotted out, and beyond that, the neighbor's bamboo thicket, all of which was visible to anyone visiting the toilet.

Sōsuke first visited the house at the beginning of the term, just a few days shy of October. As he could recall to this day, it had still been so hot that he was carrying a black umbrella around as a parasol.

Peering through the lattice door as he closed his umbrella, he had caught sight of the fleeting outline of a woman dressed in a broad-striped yukata. The ground-level area inside, made of hard-packed earth, extended to the rear of the house; from the entranceway, one could dimly see all the way back. Sōsuke stood there until the retreating figure in the yukata vanished through the back door. Then he slid open the lattice. Yasui himself appeared at the entrance to greet him.

The two went into the parlor, where they sat talking for a while, but at no point did the woman Sōsuke had spied so much as look in on them. She did not speak, nor make any kind of noise. The house was not at all large, so she must have been in an adjoining room, yet it had been quite as if there were no one there besides the two of them. This silent wraith of a woman was Oyone.

Yasui chatted volubly about his native region, about Tokyo, and about his courses this term. About Oyone, however, he spoke not a word. For his part, Sōsuke lacked the nerve to ask. And so the subject went unmentioned that day.

When the two met the next day, the woman was still very much on Sōsuke's mind. Yasui, meanwhile, said not a word about her, and acted as if there were nothing out of the ordinary. For all the unrestrained conversations these two fast friends had entered into, with the easy, trusting candor of youth, Yasui kept the door shut on this one topic. And for all Sōsuke's curiosity, it was not strong enough for him to try forcing it open. Thus a whole week went by in which the never-mentioned woman remained a barrier lodged between the consciousnesses of the two friends.

That Sunday Sōsuke called on Yasui again. Prompted by some business connected with an organization they both belonged to and having nothing to do with the woman, the visit was intended to be brief. No sooner had Sōsuke been seated in the same spot in the parlor, however, and begun gazing out at the small plum tree next to the garden hedge, were the same sensations he had experienced on his previous visit vividly evoked. Today, too, the house around him was perfectly silent. He could not help imagining the dim figure of the young woman hidden within this silence. At the same time he felt

no presentiment that she might actually reveal her presence, something that seemed just as unlikely as before.

In the midst of these ruminations Sōsuke suddenly found himself being introduced to Oyone. In contrast to the bold-striped yukata worn last time, her attire today, when she came in from the next
room, suggested that she was either on her way out to or just back
from an errand. This had taken Sōsuke by surprise. But there was
nothing eye-catching in the woman's dress, either in the color of her
kimono or the sheen of her obi, as might turn his surprise into astonishment. Moreover, on this first meeting Oyone showed little of
the alluring shyness common among young women. Indeed, she appeared to be a most ordinary person, albeit more tranquil and taci-
turn than the average. This woman was so composed, Sōsuke could
see, that it would make no difference in her behavior whether she
was off somewhere by herself or in the company of others, and he
concluded it was not necessarily out of shyness that she avoided mingling with people.

Yasui introduced Oyone with the words: "This is my little sister."
As she sat directly across from Sōsuke and took part in a desultory
conversation for a few minutes, he could not detect even a hint of
provincial speech.

"Have you been in Fukui until recently?" he asked, but before she
could reply Yasui broke in, "No, in Yokohama, for a long time now."

It soon became apparent that Yasui and Oyone planned to go
shopping in the city center that day, which was why Oyone had
changed out of her everyday clothes and, in spite of the heat, wore a
fresh pair of white socks. Sōsuke felt embarrassed at having intruded
on them at the moment they were about to leave the house.

"We've only just moved in, you see, and we find something else
we need every single day," Yasui said with an apologetic laugh. "We
have to go into town a couple of times a week."

"I'll walk out to the street with you," said Sōsuke, immediately
getting to his feet. Then, at Yasui's suggestion, he took a moment to
look around the house. After taking in the likes of a square charcoal
brazier with a tin ash pan, a cheap-looking brass tea kettle in the

next room, and an oddly brand-new wooden bucket next to the ancient sink in the kitchen, he made his way back through the house and out to the front gate. Yasui padlocked the gate and ran off to entrust the key to a neighbor. While Sōsuke and Oyone were waiting they exchanged pleasantries.

Years later, he could still recall the words that had been exchanged during those three or four minutes. These amounted to no more than the simple words of greeting any man might utter to any woman in an effort to be sociable—words that, if one were to describe them, might be said to be like water: pale and shallow. Sōsuke could not even have guessed the number of times he had uttered phrases of just this sort to complete strangers and passersby on the paths of everyday life.

Each time he recalled this exceedingly brief conversation word for word, he had to admit to himself how insipid, how virtually devoid of all color it had been. He could only marvel, then, at how those first, colorless murmurings had led to a future for the both of them dyed with the brightest of reds. All these years later, their lives no longer glowed with such a vivid color; in the natural course of things, the passion that had inflamed them had subsided into darker embers. Whenever he looked back on those early days, he cherished his memory of the brilliant history that had been launched by those innocuous words; at the same time he trembled at the power that fate could wield by transforming so casual an encounter into such a dramatic event.

Sōsuke recalled how, as the two of them stood before a mud wall outside the gate, the upper half of their shadows had been cast at an exaggerated angle against the surface. He recalled Oyone's shadow there on the wall, topped off by an irregularly shaped cone where her parasol had obscured her head. He recalled how mercilessly the early-autumn sun, already beginning its decline, had beat down on them. He recalled, too, that when Oyone, parasol in hand, moved into the not very cool shade of the willow tree, he had stepped back in order to frame with his gaze both the purple of her parasol with its fringe of white and the only slightly faded green of the willow branches.

Now, whenever he thought back on that day, everything remained clear to him. Nothing extraordinary had happened. They waited until Yasui reappeared from behind the wall, then the three of them headed toward town. The two men walked shoulder to shoulder while Oyone, who was wearing loose-fitting sandals, fell slightly behind. The conversation was more or less confined to the men, and was in any case cut short when a bit farther on Sōsuke parted ways with the pair and returned home.

Yet the impressions made on him that day stayed with him for a long while. At home again, in the bath, then later, when seated by the lamp, the image of Yasui and Oyone, like figures in a flat, brightly colored print, repeatedly flashed before his mind's eye. That was not all; when he bedded down for the night he began to wonder if Oyone was in fact, as she had been introduced, Yasui's sister. Although, short of putting the question directly to Yasui, there was no way to resolve these doubts, he wasted no time jumping to his own conclusion. Reflecting as he lay there on the way that the two interacted, there was plenty of room for such a conclusion, he decided, and smiled to himself. Then he sensed how absurd it was to prolong his idle speculation on the matter. Finally he got up and blew out the lamp, which he had left burning.

Sōsuke was far too friendly with Yasui to let so much time pass between meetings that his memories could gradually fade away until they left no trace. Besides being together every day on campus, they continued to visit each other, as they had before the vacation. When Sōsuke visited Yasui it did not always happen, however, that Oyone came out to greet him. On roughly one out of three visits she would not appear, reverting instead to the totally silent presence she had maintained on his first visit. But this did not ultimately prevent them from becoming quite friendly; before long they were on good enough terms to joke with each other.

Soon it was fall. Although Sōsuke had little interest in sightseeing in Kyoto, as he had done the previous autumn, when invited by Yasui and Oyone to gather mushrooms, he discovered a fresh aroma in the bright, crisp air. He also accompanied the two of them on an outing to enjoy the autumn foliage. As they made their way from Saga toward Takao, cutting across the flanks of the mountains, Oyone used her parasol as a walking stick and hiked up her kimono in a manner that left her underskirt showing around her ankles. As the sun shone down on a stream more than three hundred feet below their high vantage point, revealing clearly, even from this distance, the streambed beneath the translucent flow, Oyone looked over at the two men and said, "Kyoto is lovely, isn't it?" Still gazing down on this scene, Sōsuke exclaimed to himself that Yes, Kyoto was lovely indeed.

Outings of this sort, the three of them together, were not uncommon. More often, though, they would get together at Yasui's house. Once, when Sōsuke stopped by for one of his regular visits, he found Yasui to be out and Oyone sitting alone in the house as if abandoned in the midst of autumn's desolation. After a few words of sympathy he ensconced himself in the parlor, where, as they warmed their hands over the brazier that stood between them, Sōsuke lost himself in an unexpectedly lengthy conversation before returning home. Another time, he was sitting idly at his desk in his lodging room, uncharacteristically at loose ends, when all of a sudden Oyone turned up at his door. She had been shopping nearby and was just dropping in for a moment, she said. At Sōsuke's urging she stayed for some tea and sweets, and left only after a long, leisurely chat.

Amid these various comings and goings, the leaves had fallen from the trees. Then, one morning, the high mountain peaks were capped with white snow. The dry riverbed was scoured by winds, and thin, long shadows of people moved across the bridge. The Kyoto winter that year was utterly merciless, inflicting its piercing cold silently yet relentlessly. Yasui was hard hit by the harsh weather and contracted a severe case of influenza. He alarmed Oyone by running a fever a good deal higher than those brought on by an ordinary flu. Before long, however, his temperature went down. He seemed to be coming out of it, but his symptoms lingered and he was never able to make a full recovery. Thereafter Yasui would suffer the ups and downs of a slight fever for days on end.

The doctor said that the respiratory tract appeared to have been affected and urged a rest cure away from the city. Yasui reluctantly packed his wicker trunk; Oyone, her carryall. Sōsuke accompanied them to Shichijō station and saw them to their compartment, keeping up a cheerful conversation until it was time for the train to depart.

"Come visit us sometime," said Yasui from the compartment window after Sōsuke had alighted from the train.

"Yes, please do," Oyone chimed in.

The train slowly slipped by Sōsuke, who stood on the platform glowing with good health; then, with a sudden acceleration and a belch of steam, it headed for Kobe.

The convalescing Yasui welcomed the New Year in his new surroundings. From the first day of his arrival on he sent Sōsuke a picture postcard more or less every day, in none of which was omitted an invitation to come visit them anytime. Each card also included without fail a couple of lines in Oyone's hand. Sōsuke made a special stack of these cards on his desk so that whenever he came home they were the first thing to catch his eye. From time to time he went back over them all in order, reading some through again, glancing at others. Finally another card arrived in which Yasui had written that he was completely well now and would be coming home. But here they'd come all this way and had yet to receive a visit from Sōsuke, so as soon as he got this card he should leave immediately, even if he would only be able to stay a brief while. These few words supplied a sufficient goad to Sōsuke, who abhorred above all the tedium of an uninterrupted routine. He boarded a train and arrived at Yasui's inn that very night.

As the three of them, now happily reunited, sat facing one another in the bright lamplight, the first thing Sōsuke noticed was the lustrous color that the recently ailing Yasui had regained. If anything, he looked healthier than ever. Yasui himself announced that yes, he was feeling very well indeed, and as if to prove the point rolled up his shirt sleeve and stroked a pulsing blue vein. Oyone's eyes sparkled with delight. Sōsuke took particular note of their sheer liveliness.

Heretofore his dominant impression of Oyone had been one of utter composure, even in the midst of riotous noise or scenes of disorder. Now it became obvious to him that this image had been largely conveyed through the steady gaze that she seldom allowed to be diverted.

The next morning the three of them went out in front of the inn and gazed at the sea's dark currents flowing far offshore. They breathed air redolent of pitch oozing from the pine trees. The winter sun unabashedly ran its short course across the sky and sank into the west. As it receded from sight it dyed the low-hanging clouds yellow and red, like cooking-stove flames. Even when night fell no wind blew; only the occasional passing breeze bestirred the pines. The warm, sunny weather lasted through the entire three days of Sōsuke's stay.

Sōsuke said he wanted to stay on awhile before returning. Oyone said they should indeed enjoy themselves a little longer. Yasui said they owed the fine weather to Sōsuke's arrival. But at last the three of them packed up their wicker trunks and carryalls and returned to Kyoto. The rest of the winter had proved mild, with the north winds deflected back to the cold lands from whence they came. The patches of snow that clearly marked the mountaintops here and there gradually melted away, and then, all at once, green buds burst forth everywhere.

Whenever Sōsuke thought back on those months, it struck him that had the progression of the seasons been arrested then and there, and had he and Oyone been turned into stone on the spot, they would have been spared much pain. The drama commenced at winter's end, when the faint signs of spring were just emerging, and reached its climax when the cherry blossoms scattered, giving way to fresh green leaves. It had been a life-and-death struggle. Their agony could be likened to that of raw, green bamboo being roasted over a hot flame until the oil came out. The unwary couple had been suddenly knocked over by a furious wind. By the time they got back on their feet, their entire world was covered with grit. They found themselves likewise encrusted, yet they had no inkling of when the storm wind had blown them over.

The world had heaped on the couple unmitigated censure for their moral failings. At first they were taken aback, but before they could accept the censure of their own consciences, they felt obliged to establish their own sanity. To their astonishment, what they discerned was not a pair of shameful sinners but rather two senseless people who had defied all logic. There was no excuse, no reason whatsoever for their actions. Therein lay their unspeakable anguish. They were left to contemplate ruefully how this cruel fate had lashed out against them so suddenly, as if on a whim, and, in a perversely playful way, ensnared two innocent mortals in its trap.

By the time the couple's conduct had been fully exposed to the glaring scrutiny of others, they were themselves beyond any tortured moral equivocation. Submissively offering their pale foreheads, they were branded with the mark of burning flames. Henceforward they found themselves bound together by invisible chains and were constrained to walk lockstep, hand in hand, wherever they might go. They abandoned their parents. They abandoned their other relatives. They abandoned their friends. More generally, they abandoned society. Or they were abandoned by all of them. Sōsuke naturally faced expulsion from the university. He chose, for the sake of appearances, to withdraw formally, thus managing to salvage some shred of human dignity.

Such was the past shared by Sōsuke and Oyone.

15

BURDENED with such a past, the couple had gone off to Hiroshima, where they continued to suffer. Then they went on to Fukuoka. There, too, they suffered. Returning to Tokyo, they remained weighed down by the crushing burden of their past. It had proved impossible for them to enter into close relations with the Saekis. After Sōsuke's uncle died, the attitude of his survivors, the aunt and Yasunosuke, grew ever more distant, such as to preclude for a lifetime a relationship based on full mutual trust. This year Sōsuke and Oyone had not even gone to pay them their annual year-end visit, nor had the Saekis come to visit them. Even Koroku, whom they had recently taken in, did not at heart respect his brother. When the couple first returned to Tokyo, Koroku had openly detested Oyone, and with a childlike forthrightness—a sentiment not lost either on her or on her husband. Under the sun the couple presented smiles to the world; under the moon they were lost in thought: And so they had quietly passed the years. Now another year had consumed itself and was about to end.

In the waning days of December all of the shops along the area's main street were festooned with straw roping and paper amulets. Dozens of ornamental bamboo stalks flanked the busy street, reaching up to the shop eaves and rustling in the cold wind. Sōsuke had bought a slender pine bough, slightly over two feet long, and nailed it to a pillar on their gate. Then he placed a large, yellowish orange[63] on top of the New Year's rice cakes and put them on a stand in the alcove. On the wall in back of this offering hung a black-ink sketch of doubtful quality, depicting a plum tree from which protruded a clamshell-shaped moon. Sōsuke himself was at a loss as to why the orange and rice cakes should be set before this peculiar scroll.

"What on earth is all this supposed to mean?" he asked Oyone as he studied his own handiwork.

Oyone had no idea, either, what was signified by this perennial decoration. "I really don't know. But you should just leave them," she said, turning toward the kitchen.

"So we can eat them later, I suppose..." Sōsuke ventured, tilting his head quizzically as he fussed a bit more over the cakes and orange.

The preparation of the New Year's dumplings was left until the evening, when the sticky rice dough and a cutting board were brought into the sitting room so that everyone could take part. There were not enough knives to go around, however, and Sōsuke sat through the proceedings without lifting a finger. Koroku, by dint of brute strength, carved out the most dumplings; by the same token he produced the largest number of lopsided duds, some of them truly grotesque. Every time he came up with a particularly odd shape, Kiyo burst out laughing. With a wet dish towel to protect his hand, Koroku pushed the knife hard against the crusty edge of the dough. "The shape doesn't matter so long as we can still eat them," he said, his whole face flushed from exertion.

All that remained to welcome in the New Year was to roast the anchovies and fill the stacks of serving boxes with assorted vegetables boiled in soy. As the darkness gathered on this last night of the old year, Sōsuke, rent money in hand, went up to the Sakais to pay his respects. Intending to make his visit as unobtrusive as possible, he went around to the kitchen door, where bright lights blazed beyond the frosted glass and a great commotion could be heard. A shop boy clutching an account book, evidently come to settle some outstanding balance, rose from his perch on the raised threshold and greeted Sōsuke.

The master of the house and his wife were both in the sitting room. In one corner sat a tradesman in a liveried jacket who appeared to be well-acquainted with the household, his head bent over an ample pile of small straw wreaths, for which he was now assembling various attachments.[64] Beside him were strewn the necessary materials: sprigs of *yuzuriha* and *urajiro*,[65] sheets of calligraphic paper, and scissors. A young housemaid sat in front of Mrs. Sakai on the tatami, spreading out bills and coins that appeared to be change from some payment.

"Thanks for coming by," Sakai said, looking over at Sōsuke. "Now that we're down to the wire you must be very busy. You can see the mess things are around here. Please have a seat. Well, I'm sure you're as fed up with this New Year's business as I am. No matter how much fun something may be, after it's rolled around more than forty times it gets pretty stale."

Sakai spoke as though the New Year's observances were a great nuisance, yet in his demeanor there was not a trace of exasperation. Belying his tone were lively words, a glowing face, and cheeks still tinged, it seemed, from the strength of the libations poured out at the dinner table. Sōsuke chatted for twenty or thirty minutes, smoking the cigarettes that were proffered, before taking his leave.

At home, Oyone was waiting, soap and towel in hand, to go out to the baths. She had planned to take Kiyo with her, it seemed, and so could not have left in her husband's absence.

"Did something keep you up there? You've been gone quite a while."

Oyone glanced at the clock. It was getting on toward ten. Besides the bath, Sōsuke was informed, Kiyo was supposed to have her hair done afterward. Even in a quiet, modest household like theirs such little crises could arise on New Year's Eve.

Still standing, Sōsuke asked Oyone if all the year-end bills had been paid. Only one remained, she answered, for firewood. "If the man turns up, please pay him," she said, removing from her breast pocket a soiled billfold of the sort men carry around, along with a change purse, which she handed to her husband.

Pocketing these, he asked, "Where is Koroku?"

"Oh, he went out. He said he wanted to take in the city lights on New Year's Eve. In this frigid weather, no less! He certainly is putting himself out." Oyone's reply elicited giggles from Kiyo, who followed close on her heels.

"Well, he's still young," said Kiyo by way of justification, after she stopped laughing. Then she stepped down to the kitchen door and set out Oyone's clogs for her.

"What lights did he hope to take in?" Sōsuke asked.

"Oh, he said something about the main avenue from Ginza to Nihombashi."

Oyone had already stepped down into the well of the kitchen doorway. The sound of the back door being slid open reached Sōsuke's ears soon after that. Sitting alone beside the brazier he gazed into the glowing charcoal until it was reduced to ashes. He could already imagine the Rising Suns that would be flying tomorrow, the sheen of silk top hats on the heads of men making their New Year's rounds. He could hear the sounds of sabers rattling, horses neighing, and shuttlecocks being struck.[66] In just a few hours he would be obliged to observe those seasonal rituals supposedly designed, more than any others on the calendar, to bring about a sense of spiritual renewal.

Many scenes of apparent gaiety and conviviality thus flashed through his mind, but none caught his imagination and swept him up in the spirit of the season. He felt like an outsider at a banquet who, not having been invited, had no right to become intoxicated. But he was, by the same token, spared from getting drunk. No expectations for the future arose other than to continue his life with Oyone and to weather the ordinary vicissitudes of each passing year. It was a fitting emblem, then, of his everyday life for him to be sitting here alone on this tumultuous eve of the New Year, quietly minding the house.

It was well after ten when Oyone returned. In the lamplight her cheeks radiated an unusually healthy glow. Still warm from the bathhouse, she wore her kimono open at the neck, revealing her undergarment and the full length of her nape.

"It was absolutely mobbed," she said, breathing a sigh of relief. "It was hard to find a bucket or a faucet that was free."

Kiyo did not return until after eleven. Thrusting her head out from behind the shoji, her hair neatly arranged, she apologized for being so late: She had been made to wait, she explained, while the hairdresser finished with a couple of other customers.

This left only Koroku, who was still out somewhere. When the clock struck midnight, Sōsuke suggested that they retire. Oyone, feeling that on this night of all nights in the year it would be odd not to wait up for Koroku, tried to keep their conversation going as best she could. Fortunately, it was not long before he turned up. He had strolled from Nihombashi to Ginza, he explained, but by the time he circled back toward Suitengū,[67] the outbound streetcars were packed and he'd had to let a number of them go by before he could board one.

Koroku had stopped at the Hakubotan in hopes of winning the gold watch that was one of the luck-of-the-draw prizes the shop was giving away to lure customers. Having to buy something in order to qualify even as there was nothing he wanted, he settled on a box of little beanbags with bells on them. He had then seized one of the hundreds of numbered balloons that were being spit out by a machine. His number did not get him the gold watch, but it did win something else, he said, producing a packet: the store's brand of powdered soap.

"Please take it," he said, setting it down in front of Oyone. "It's for you." Next, he plunked down in front of Sōsuke the bell-studded beanbags, which had been sewed in the shape of plum blossoms, saying, "Please pass these on to the Sakai daughters."

Thus concluded the small household's meager celebration of New Year's Eve.

16

THE SECOND day of the new year brought a snowfall that coated the capital and its festive straw-and-paper garlands with white. Before the roof became visible again, the couple was startled more than once by the sound of snow cascading down the tin flashing on the eaves. The loud thuds in the middle of the night were especially alarming. The mud that covered their lane as the snow melted, unlike the mud created in the wake of rain, refused to dry out in just a day or two. Every time Sōsuke went out he returned with his shoes in a complete mess, and as soon as he stepped into the house and caught sight of Oyone he would say, "This simply won't do."

Sōsuke's manner suggested that his wife was at fault for the state of the lane outside their house. Finally she made as if to apologize. "Well, I beg your pardon, I am most dreadfully sorry!" she said, and burst out laughing. Sōsuke was at a loss for a suitably sharp quip.

"You know, Oyone," he resumed, "in this area it looks for all the world as though you can't get anywhere without wearing high clogs. But in the flatlands downtown, it's another story. Every street there is so dry that the air is full of dust, and if you're wearing high clogs you feel like such a fool you don't want to go anywhere. I swear, living way out here, we're about a century behind the times."

His complaint notwithstanding, Sōsuke did not look the slightest bit vexed. For her part, Oyone simply heard him out with about the same mild interest she might show in watching the cigarette smoke that hovered below his nostrils.

"You should tell that to Sakai-san," she taunted him gently.

"Oh, right, and then I'll get him to lower the rent!" he said, without, however, showing any inclination to visit the landlord.

The previous day, New Year's Day, he had gone by the Sakais' house early in the morning and, simply dropping off his calling card at the door, hastily retreated back through the gate before the master of the house could appear. On this second day, amidst the falling snow, there was no coming and going anywhere. On the third day, a maid came down around sunset with a message from the Sakais to the effect that they would be delighted if Mr. and Mrs. Nonaka, and "the young master, too," were free to come spend the evening.

After the maid had left, Sōsuke asked suspiciously, "What do you suppose they have planned?"

"I'm sure it'll be poem-cards,[68] with all those children," said Oyone. "You should go."

"It's kind of them to ask: *You* should go. I haven't played that game for ages . . . I'd be hopeless."

"Neither have I. I wouldn't be any better at it," she said.

The couple showed no sign of reaching an agreement on who should accept this invitation. In the end they decided to make Koroku fulfill this obligation for all of them.

"Off you go, 'young master,'" Sōsuke said to Koroku, who smiled thinly as he got to his feet. Sōsuke and Oyone were much amused by the conferral of this title on Koroku, and burst out laughing at the sight of the reaction it elicited when invoked by them. Leaving the holiday air of his home behind, after a transit of but a hundred yards, Koroku found himself seated in the lamplight of another festive household.

In the course of his visit Koroku removed from his sleeve pocket the beanbags shaped like plum blossoms that he had brought home the other night and, emphasizing that they came from his brother, presented them as gifts to the Sakai daughters. In exchange, he arrived back home with a small, unadorned doll (another end-of-the-year premium) stuffed into the same pocket. The doll's forehead was slightly chipped, and on that spot a simple daub of black ink had been applied. In a thoroughly earnest manner Koroku announced that the doll, as he had understood, represented the Sodehagi character in the play by Chikamatsu.[69] The couple failed to grasp the resemblance between this doll and Sodehagi. Koroku himself had not, of course, had the faintest idea when first presented with the doll by Mrs. Sakai, who had then launched into a detailed explanation. When he still did not get the point, she had her husband write on a piece of paper, side by side, a line from the play and, in parentheses, the punning parody that was meant to be embodied by the doll: "Ah, this narrow hedge, like an iron block . . . (Ah, this callow wench, from crying pocked . . .)."

Sōsuke and Oyone again broke into lighthearted laughter that befitted the New Year. "Such a clever gag," said Sōsuke. "I wonder, who thought this up?"

"How would I know?" replied Koroku sullenly before leaving the doll on the floor and retreating to his room.

A few days later—it must have been the seventh—the same maid as before came in the evening bearing a message from the Sakais, which she faithfully recited to Kiyo just as she had been instructed: "If Mr. Nonaka should be at his leisure, he is kindly invited to come by for a chat." Sōsuke and Oyone had lit the lamp and were just sitting down to dinner when Kiyo delivered this message. Sōsuke, rice bowl in hand, was commenting to Oyone about the New Year's celebrations finally coming to an end. On hearing the message from the Sakais, Oyone looked at her husband and smiled.

"Yet another one of their gatherings?" Sōsuke wondered aloud. His eyebrows contracted peevishly as he set down his bowl. But on further questioning of the maid, who was waiting at the door, it emerged that no other guests had been invited; she also volunteered that Mrs. Sakai and the children would not be at home, having gone away to visit some relatives.

"Well, then, I guess I'll drop by," said Sōsuke, and left the house.

Sōsuke hated socializing. He was not one to turn up at any gathering, unless it was absolutely unavoidable. He did not cultivate personal friendships, either. He had no time for paying visits here and there. To this general rule Sakai was the sole exception. Sōsuke had even gone up to see him several times with no particular purpose in mind, simply to pass the time—with this man who, by contrast, was the most social person in the world. Even to Oyone, that the exceedingly gregarious Sakai and her reclusive husband should get together and converse freely seemed an astonishing phenomenon.

When Sōsuke arrived, Sakai said, "Let's chat over here," and led him across the sitting room, then down a corridor to a doorway that opened onto a small study. Hanging in the alcove was a scroll inscribed with only five characters, characters so large and intimidating, however, that they might have been written with a brush made of palm fronds. Below it on the alcove shelf stood an arrangement consisting of a single, magnificent white peony. The only other furnishings were a desk and some cushions, all laid out very neatly.

Standing just inside the darkened doorway, Sakai twisted a switch somewhere and, as soon as the electric light came on, invited Sōsuke in. "Just a moment," he then said, as he lit the gas heater with a match. The heater was quite small for a room of this size. These preliminaries finished, Sakai offered his guest a cushion. "This is my private grotto," he said. "When things start to get on my nerves, I take refuge here."

Atop his thick, quilted cushion, Sōsuke himself felt a certain tranquillity. As the gas fire burned, all but inaudibly, a palpable warmth enfolded him from behind.

"In this room I am freed from all social contact: I can truly relax. Please stay here with me as long as you like. When you come down to it, this New Year's business has gotten to be more trouble than it's worth. Up until yesterday afternoon I was completely stretched. There just seemed to be no end to it. Finally, around noon today, I turned my back on the busy, everyday world. I felt sick and took to my bed—slept like a baby. I only woke up a short while ago, had a bath, ate something, smoked a cigarette... Then it suddenly dawned on me that my wife had gone off with the children to her relatives, and I was all alone. No wonder it's so quiet, I said to myself. But then, all of a sudden I felt bored. What moody creatures we are!

Still, no matter how bored I was, I couldn't be bothered to go out to watch or listen to any more festivities, and the very thought of gulping down another New Year's spread was frightening. Anyway, I felt like spending some time with someone very un-festive—no, that sounds rude...someone who has few connections with society...oh, that sounds even worse! Well, in a word, somebody like yourself who is above the world. And that's why I sent the maid to invite you over."

Sakai spouted all this in his usual smooth and voluble manner. Once in the company of this inveterate optimist, Sōsuke often forgot about his own past. At certain moments it had even crossed his mind that if he had stuck to the conventional path, he might have turned out to be a fellow rather like this.

Just then the maid slid open the narrow door; after offering Sōsuke a second, more formal welcome, she set before him a dessert plate that looked to be made of wood. Then she placed an identical plate in front of Sakai and withdrew without a word. On each plate sat one large steamed bean-jam-filled bun, the size of a child's rubber ball, and beside it a toothpick about twice the normal size. Prompted by his host not to let the bun get cold, Sōsuke noticed that in fact it had been freshly steamed, and admired the yellowish skin of this rare treat sitting on his plate.

"But they're not really fresh, you know," Sakai explained. "Actually, they gave me a few to take home at this place I went to last night, after I'd said, half joking, how delicious they were. At least they were nice and hot. These I just had warmed up so you could have a taste."

Using his oversize toothpick, Sakai made a hash of his bun and began to munch on the shreds. Like the sycophantic women who aped in vain the alluring frown of Xi Shi,[70] Sōsuke dug into his own bun with the same abandon as his host.

While they were eating, Sakai brought up the subject of a peculiar geisha he had met at the restaurant the night before. Evidently, she was very fond of the *Analects* and carried a pocket edition[71] around with her all the time: on the train, out on the town, everywhere.

"Anyway," he continued, "she told me about this one disciple,

Shiro,[72] who is her very favorite. When I asked her why, she said it's because he was honest almost to a fault. Whenever he learned something from the Master, he'd worry that he might be taught something new before he was able to put the first thing he learned to use.[73] Now I myself don't know much about Shiro, and I wasn't sure what to say, but I asked her if this wasn't like falling in love with someone and then, before you could marry the person, worrying about falling in love with someone else just as nice."

Sakai delivered himself of such anecdotes without a second thought. Judging from the casual tone he adopted in telling these tales, it appeared that, having frequented the demimonde more or less continuously all his adult life, he had long since become inured to the stimuli afforded by this milieu. Still, out of force of habit, he went on visiting his old haunts several times a month. When probed a little further on the subject, he replied that even he, who took most everything in stride, occasionally felt inured to physical pleasure and had to seek a balm for his spirit by retreating to his study.

Sōsuke, himself no stranger to the demimonde, did not have to feign interest in such stories; he responded, rather, in an undemonstrative, man-about-town fashion. It was this very nonchalance that piqued the curiosity of Sakai, who made as if to read into his guest's very ordinary remarks traces of some possibly far from ordinary past. But the moment Sōsuke betrayed a hint of resistance to having his past explored further, Sakai changed the subject. He clearly did so not as some delaying tactic but out of deference to his guest's reticence, such that Sōsuke took no offense at all.

In the course of the conversation Koroku's name came up. Sakai turned out to have several novel observations to make about the young man, of a sort that would escape notice by an older brother. Expressing neither assent nor dissent, Sōsuke heard out Sakai's characterization with considerable interest. Eventually Sakai formulated a question about Koroku: While the young man clearly had a head for complicated if impractical matters, was he not also rather naïve for his age, so like a child in the unselfconscious way he revealed his emotions? Sōsuke immediately concurred in this assessment. And yet, he went on to add, this was perhaps a quality that, regardless of age, clings to those whose education has been of the formal, academic variety, devoid of any socialization.

"I see your point," Sakai said. "But then, take the opposite case. People who are well versed in the ways of the world but don't have a head for books may seem more sophisticated, but they never really grow up. They're the ones who cause more trouble."

Sakai paused for a moment, then continued. "What about letting Koroku live with us as a *shosei*?[74] I suppose that might contribute to his socialization." Sakai'd had no one in his employ ever since his previous *shosei* passed his physical for the draft and got himself sent to boot camp, about a month before the family's pet dog was taken sick to the veterinarian's, leaving the position vacant ever since.

Sōsuke was overjoyed at this fortuitous solution to the problem of what to do about Koroku—a solution that had spontaneously materialized, without any solicitation on his part, here at the beginning of this New Year. At the same time, not having dared for a long time to entertain any real expectations of goodwill and kind favors from the world, he was momentarily shocked into indecisiveness by Sakai's sudden offer. But then, he judiciously realized, if he were able to place Koroku in this position very soon, with the money they would save on his keep, plus a modest contribution from Yasunosuke, he could fulfill his brother's hopes for a university education. When Sōsuke revealed this plan to his host, holding back nothing, Sakai nodded as he listened, and then responded offhandedly, "Sounds just fine to me." And so the matter was settled then and there.

Sōsuke should have called it an evening at this point. And in fact he did try to leave. But his host prevailed on him to stay for a while longer. The evening is young, he said, showing Sōsuke his watch to prove it. Sakai seemed very much at a loss for something to do. For Sōsuke's part, if he were to leave now it would only be to go straight to bed. Sakai, settling back down again, lit up another strong cigarette. Eventually Sōsuke followed his host's example and assumed a less formal posture on his soft cushion.

Returning to the subject of Koroku, Sakai observed, "Younger brothers can be a real bother. I've been saddled with one who's nothing but trouble, so I know what I'm talking about." He proceeded to describe how extravagant his brother had been in his college years, in contrast to his own simple, austere life as a student. Sōsuke inquired about the subsequent progress of this flamboyant younger brother, partly in the expectation of gaining another glimpse of the vindictive workings of fate.

"Adventurer!" This was the single word that exploded from Sakai's mouth.

After graduation, Sakai went on, his brother had been hired on his recommendation by a certain bank, but all he did was complain that he wasn't making enough money. After the Russo-Japanese War was over, ignoring Sakai's efforts to dissuade him, he had gone off to Manchuria, declaring his intention to do something really big. Once there he got himself involved in—of all things!—some colossal scheme to transport soybean mash down the Liao River, a venture that went bust practically overnight. He was not a principal investor, but when all the accounts had been reckoned he emerged with a large debt. Not only could he not continue with this venture; its collapse inevitably spelled his personal ruin.

"What became of him at this juncture, I really didn't know at the time," Sakai continued. "But when I did finally hear from him again—well, I was in for a shock. This time he was off to Mongolia, wandering all over the place. As you can imagine I was worried about further trouble—after all, he seems to have an unlimited capacity for speculation. Still, so long as he was over there and I was over here, I could go on assuming that he'd get by somehow, and didn't need to concern myself too much. He sent me the occasional letter, but all it would be about was how arid Mongolia is, so that when it gets hot they have to wet down the dusty roads with water from the open sewers, and when that runs out, they resort to horse piss, and so the whole place has this terrible stink—you know, that kind of thing. Oh yes, he did bring up money, but so what? With me in Tokyo and him in Mongolia, all I had to do was ignore his requests. As long as he stayed away there was no problem. But then, all of a sudden, who should turn up here in Tokyo, just before New Year's!"

As though he had just recalled something, Sakai interrupted himself here and took down from the alcove pillar a decorative object from which dangled a handsome tassel. It was a short sword, one foot in length, wrapped in a silk brocade bag. The scabbard was fashioned from a green, mica-like material of exotic appearance and was encircled in three places by bands of silver. The blade was only seven inches long, and its cutting edge proportionately narrow. By contrast, the scabbard was very thick and took the shape of a hexagonal oaken club. Closer inspection revealed two slender sticks inserted through the hilt and running parallel to the scabbard; they were secured to the latter by the silver bands.

"This is what he brought me as a souvenir—a Mongolian sword," said Sakai, swiftly unsheathing the blade. From the handle he then pulled out the two sticks, which appeared to be made of ivory. "These are actually chopsticks. Evidently Mongolians wear their swords at all times, so whenever they chance upon a meal all they need to do is whip them out, slice the meat, then dig in with these chopsticks." Sakai performed a spirited demonstration, sword in one hand, chopsticks in the other. Sōsuke studied the articles' fine craftsmanship.

"He also gave me some of the felt they use to make their tents— it's a lot like the pressed wool that antique rugs are made of."

Sakai proceeded to describe the skill of Mongolian horsemen; the resemblance between the thin, rangy Mongolian dogs and Western greyhounds; and the steady encroachment on Mongolian territory by the Chinese—in short, everything he had heard from his brother on his recent return from that country. This was all quite new to Sōsuke, who took in each piece of information with genuine interest. As he listened his curiosity was piqued as to what Sakai's brother was doing in Mongolia in the first place.

"Adventurer!" Sakai exclaimed again, with equal vehemence. Then he went on: "I have no idea what he's doing there. He tells me he's raising some kind of livestock—and that it's been a great success, but there's absolutely no reason to believe him. I've been taken in too many times by his empty boasts. As for the item of business that's brought him to Tokyo, it sounds utterly preposterous. He claims he needs to borrow twenty thousand yen for 'King' something-or-other of Mongolia. And so he's rushing around telling people that he'll lose his standing over there if we don't lend him the money. Needless to say, I was the first person he asked. Okay, say it really *is* the King of Mongolia, or he *does* put up vast tracts of land as collateral—how is anyone here in Tokyo supposed to collect the debt way over there if he doesn't pay up? So I say no, and the next thing, my brother comes sneaking in to see my wife behind my back, and has the gall to tell her that with my attitude I'd never make it big."

With a snort of amusement, Sakai turned to Sōsuke, whose face wore an oddly tense expression. "What do you say?" Sakai asked, "Would you like to meet him just this once? He goes around draped in baggy clothes trimmed with fur and all, and might be worth a laugh or two. I'll be happy to introduce you. In fact, he's coming to dinner the day after tomorrow. But you mustn't let yourself get suckered into anything. If you just let him do all the talking and say nothing, you'll be perfectly safe. It would be a lark." Sakai was persistent in his invitation.

"Would it be just your brother who's coming to dinner?" asked Sōsuke, weakening some.

"No, there's some other fellow who came back with him from over there—he's supposed to come too. His name is Yasui, I think. I haven't met him yet, but my brother's been very keen on introducing him, so that's why I planned this dinner."

Sōsuke went out Sakai's gate that night with an ashen face.

17

THE UNION between Sōsuke and Oyone had dyed their existence a somber hue and reduced their presence, they felt, to mere wraiths that barely cast a shadow on the world. From one year to the next each lived with the sensation of harboring deep inside a frightening moral contagion, though neither one of them ever acknowledged this feeling to the other.

Early on, what weighed most heavily on their minds was the havoc their transgression wreaked on Yasui's future. By the time their emotions had cooled down somewhat, the news reached them that Yasui, too, had withdrawn from the university. They naturally felt responsible for this damage to his prospects. Next a rumor reached them that he had returned to his native province; then a report that he was sick and confined to his bed. Each new tiding sent sharp pangs into their already burdened breasts. Finally, they received word that Yasui had gone to Manchuria. At the time, Sōsuke wondered to himself whether he had in fact recovered from his illness or whether this talk of his having gone to Manchuria was not simply a fabrication: The Yasui he knew was both constitutionally and temperamentally unsuited to places like Manchuria or Taiwan. Sōsuke did everything he could to find out the truth, casting his net of inquiry as widely as possible. Through certain channels he was able to ascertain that Yasui was indeed in Mukden and that, moreover, he was in vigorous health and very active in his business ventures. At this news, the couple turned toward each other and breathed a sigh of relief.

"Well, it's for the best," said Sōsuke.

"It's certainly better than being sick," said Oyone.

From then on they avoided all mention of Yasui's name. They could not even bring themselves to think about him. For it was because of them that Yasui had dropped out of school, returned to the provinces, and fallen ill; it was perhaps even because of them that he had fled to Manchuria. And yet no matter how painful their cumulative remorse, they were in no position to make amends for the wrongs they had done him.

At one point Sōsuke had asked Oyone, "Tell me, has any kind of religious faith ever touched you?"

After a simple reply in the affirmative, she turned the question back on him: "And you?"

Smiling dismissively, Sōsuke did not reply. Nor did he interrogate her about the particulars of her faith, which was just as well as far as she was concerned. Under the loose rubric of faith there were no elements that had coalesced and settled into any definite pattern for her.

In any case, the two of them had come this far without either sitting in a church pew or passing through a temple gate. At length they had found peace through that simple blessing of nature: the balm of time. Even as they continued to suffer pangs of conscience on occasion, these increasingly seemed to come from somewhere far away, too faint, too weak, and too disconnected from flesh-and-blood passions to qualify as either terrifying or excruciating. Finally, then, not having found God or encountered the Buddha, they focused their faith on each other. Their spirits locked together in an embrace, they began to form a protective circle around themselves. It was in this state of isolation that they had managed to find peace. Their lonely peace was complemented by a certain sweet sense of pathos. As much as they came to revel in their pathos, they were far enough removed from the realms of philosophers and poets to harbor any self-conscious need to proclaim aloud their good fortune in having achieved it. Their experience was therefore unalloyed in comparison to that of the writers and thinkers who must strive to describe states of this nature. Such had been the couple's inner life up until the seventh day of this New Year, when Sōsuke was invited to the Sakais' and heard the news about Yasui.

As soon as he returned home and was face-to-face with Oyone, who had been waiting for him beside the brazier, he startled her by saying, "I'm not feeling too well and I'm going straight to bed."

"What is the matter?" She raised her eyes to meet his gaze. Sōsuke just stood there, stock-still. His behavior was so unusual that Oyone could not recall his ever having been in such a state. She suddenly stood up, looking as though assailed by some nameless dread, and almost mechanically proceeded to take bedding out of the closet and lay it out according to her husband's wishes. While the bed was being made up, Sōsuke remained standing to one side with his hands thrust into his sleeves. The moment Oyone was finished, he threw off his clothes and burrowed under the covers. Oyone did not move from his bedside.

"What is the matter?"

"I don't know. I just don't feel very well. But if I stay put for a while I'm sure I'll feel better."

Sōsuke's response came from under the covers. At the sound of his muffled voice a look of helpless pity came over Oyone's face. She remained seated there, motionless.

"Go on back to the other room—I'll call if I need you," he said.

At length Oyone returned to the sitting room.

Alone, with his head still under the covers, Sōsuke lay there stiffly with his eyes shut. In the darkness he turned over and over again in his mind what he had heard from Sakai. Until the very moment it happened he could never have imagined that he would hear news of Yasui in Manchuria from the mouth of his landlord. Nor would it have occurred to him in his wildest dreams, prior to the conclusion of his evening with Sakai, that fate was on the brink of placing him side by side with Yasui, or perhaps face-to-face, at the table of this same host. As he lay there thinking back over the past few hours he was astounded, not to mention saddened, by the suddenness, the utter unpredictability, of this turn of events. Sōsuke had never claimed to be the kind of strong man who could be felled only by an abrupt, totally unforeseeable event such as this. He had no doubt that far gentler methods would have been sufficient to dispose of a weakling like himself.

From his brother, Koroku, to Sakai's brother, on to Manchuria and Mongolia, then the return to Tokyo and Yasui—as he went back over and over again the flow of the evening's conversation, Sōsuke was astonished by the sheer weight of chance. He made an anguished calculation of the odds of someone encountering such a rare, random event so perfectly designed to revive the most excruciating regrets from the past: one in so many hundreds—or thousands? His anger rose and his breath turned hot in the darkness under the covers.

The wound that had finally started to heal over the past few years began, suddenly, to throb to the point of burning. It seemed about to split open again, letting the poisonous air around him infect it without quarter. Perhaps he should tell Oyone everything so that she could share his misery. Yes, he would.

"Oyone, Oyone," he called out.

She raced to his bedside and peered down intently at his face. He had poked his head out from under the covers. Her own face was illuminated in profile by the light from the next room.

"I want a glass of hot water," Sōsuke dissembled, losing his nerve at the last moment.

The next day he got up at the usual time and ate his customary breakfast. As Oyone served him he noted, with a mixture of pleasure and pity, the look of relief on her face.

"You gave me quite a shock last night," she said. "I thought there was something really wrong with you ..."

Sōsuke quietly sipped the tea in his cup and did not look up. He could find no words for a suitable reply.

From early that morning a dry, cold wind had been raging, snatching up many hats along with clouds of dust. Having ignored Oyone's admonition to avert a fever by staying home all day, he boarded the usual streetcar; amidst the heightened roar of the moving carriage and the driving wind outside, he tucked in his chin and kept his gaze fixed narrowly straight ahead. On alighting at his stop, he traced a persistent whining sound to the wires overhead. Looking skyward he found a stolid sun shining more brightly than ever amidst this ferocious display of Nature's power. The wind whipped coldly between his legs. To Sōsuke's eyes the columns of swirling dust advancing toward the palace moat appeared as distinct as slanted sheets of rain when driven before the wind.

At the office he could not apply himself to his work. With a writing brush in one hand and his chin propped up with the other, he lost himself in unbidden thoughts. From time to time he idly scraped at the ink stone; he smoked with abandon; then, as if recalling something, he would look out the window. Wherever he looked the world still belonged to the wind. Sōsuke could think of nothing but going home as soon as possible.

When at last he arrived, Oyone studied his face anxiously.

"Did things go all right today?" she asked.

He had no choice but to say all was well, except that he felt a bit tired. He wasted no time in sitting down and warming his legs in the *kotatsu*, not budging until dinner was served. Meanwhile the wind died out, just as the sun set. In contrast to the daytime, the world now seemed completely still.

"My, what a relief that wind has stopped. The way it was blowing earlier in the day, it frightened me just to sit here like this." Oyone spoke of the fierce wind as if it were an evil spirit and something to fear.

Sōsuke responded with composure, "It's quite warm tonight, isn't it? What a nice gentle start for the New Year." Having finished dinner, he was smoking a cigarette when he said out of the blue, "Oyone, what do you say we take in a show at the theater?"[75] He rarely made such invitations to his wife, and she naturally found no reason to decline. Entrusting the care of the house to Koroku, who said he would rather toast some rice cakes than hear some old-style ballad-singing, the couple went out.

They arrived somewhat late and the theater was full. Room was made for them at the very back, where, in the absence of cushions, they sat as best they could, half kneeling. "What a mob!" "Well, it's still New Year's." Whispering to each other, they surveyed the large hall packed closely with row upon row of bobbing heads. Those closest to the podium were shrouded in a fog of tobacco smoke. In Sōsuke's eyes these serried rows of black-haired heads belonged to so many creatures of leisure, whose lives allowed them to frequent such places of entertainment where they would while away half the night. Each and every face he glimpsed aroused envy.

His gaze refocused on the podium, he tried to give all his attention to the *jōruri* ballad, but to no avail: It did not interest him. He stole a few glances at Oyone, who kept her eyes unwaveringly trained on the podium, seemingly oblivious to her husband. Sōsuke had to count her then among all these people who had aroused his envy.

At the entr'acte he turned to her and said, "Well, shall we leave?"

Surprised by such abruptness, Oyone asked, "You don't like it?" When he made no reply, she said, in what sounded like an effort to appease him, "Well, I don't really care one way or the other." This solicitous response in turn renewed Sōsuke's sympathy for his wife, whom he had been so determined to have join him for a night out. In the end he sat through the rest of the performance.

On their return they found Koroku sitting cross-legged next to the brazier reading a book, holding it from the top and against the light with no concern for the spine. The iron kettle had been left off the brazier long enough for the water to turn tepid. On a wicker tray remained three or four pieces of toasted rice cakes. Some soy sauce had found its way from the wire grating used for toasting to the dish on which it sat.

Getting to his feet, Koroku asked, "Did you have a good time?" The couple warmed themselves at the *kotatsu* for ten minutes and went to bed.

The next day brought Sōsuke scarcely any more peace. After work he boarded the usual streetcar, but once inside, he summoned up an image of Yasui and himself arriving at the entrance to the Sakais' at more or less the same time, and he had to ask himself what sense it made to be traveling homeward so swiftly, as if to hasten the moment of this encounter. At the same time he wondered how Yasui had changed over the years, and even wished that he might, unobserved, simply catch a glimpse of the man.

Two nights earlier, Sakai had characterized his brother with the single word "adventurer." The utterance now reverberated loudly in Sōsuke's mind. Sōsuke enumerated various traits that might fall under this rubric: desperation and abandon; discontent and loathing; licentiousness and depravity; recklessness and ferocious determination. Then he tried to imagine to what degree such traits might pertain not only to someone like Sakai's brother—who doubtless possessed one or another of them in some measure—but also to Yasui, who, as part of some joint enterprise, had joined the brother for the trip back from Manchuria. The "adventurer" that took shape in Sōsuke's imagination was naturally cast in the most lurid colors possible within the range of connotations allowed by the term.

Having arrived at this distorted image of "adventurer" in which depravity was emphasized to the extreme, Sōsuke felt himself obliged to accept complete responsibility for Yasui's deplorable transformation. He wanted to catch a single glimpse of the man as he approached the landlord's house in order to form a general impression, however hazy, of his present character. He also wanted to console himself with the discovery that Yasui had not become as depraved as he feared.

Sōsuke searched his memory for a safe spot close to the Sakais' house from which he could peer out at others without their being aware, but unfortunately could not think of one. Were Yasui to arrive after sundown, the same darkness that rendered Sōsuke invisible would also render unrecognizable the faces of those who approached the house.

In the meantime the streetcar had reached Kanda. Sōsuke was pained by the prospect of changing cars here and proceeding toward his destination. His nerves balked at so much as a single step in the direction of the place where Yasui was due to arrive. As he stood at the stop, his voyeuristic impulse to steal a glimpse of the man, which had not been strong to begin with, was thoroughly suppressed. He walked through the cold streets along with many other people; unlike them, he had no clear destination in mind. Lamps in the shops began to light up. The streetcars lit up as well. He entered a small restaurant that specialized in beef dishes and began to drink. He tossed back his first small bottle of saké in a daze. The second, he forced down his throat. Even a third failed to make him drunk. Nevertheless Sōsuke went on sitting there, leaning back against the wall and staring off into space with the look of one who was in fact drunk.

It was the dinner hour, and customers streamed in and out. Most of them consumed their meals in a perfunctory manner, quickly paid their bills, and left. As Sōsuke continued to sit in silence amidst this hustle and bustle he eventually came to realize that he had spent twice or three times as long there as anybody else; finally, unable to stay in his seat any longer, he got up and left.

Out in front of the restaurant both sides of the street received sufficient illumination from the shop lights for him to distinguish clearly the hats and clothing of each passerby beneath the eaves. But the light was too weak to brighten up the frigid expanse beyond. Oblivious to the glow of gas and electric lamps at each shop entrance, the night appeared as dark and vast as ever. Wrapped in a greatcoat dark enough to merge into this realm, Sōsuke walked on. He imagined that the very air he breathed turned gray as it made its way into his lungs.

With a constant clanging of bells, streetcars busily passed to and fro in front of his eyes; yet this evening the thought of boarding one of them did not so much as cross his mind. He had forgotten how to stride forward with a steady gait, in step with all those around him who moved purposefully along the street. He was a man without roots, he reflected, someone who resembled a manikin being jerked this way and that. He began to wonder, with a sense of mounting dread, about his future, what would become of him if this state of affairs persisted. From all his previous experiences in life he had taken one maxim most deeply to heart: Time heals all wounds. But the night before last that maxim, which he had made into his personal motto, had been completely shattered.

As he walked through the dark night he was overwhelmed by an urge to escape from his present mental state. Thoroughly weak, agitated, unstable, anxious; seriously wanting in courage and bereft of any largeness of spirit—this was how he came to see himself. Oppressed by something that weighed down heavily on his breast, all he could think about was what practical course he might adopt that would deliver him from his current predicament, the causes of which—his own sins of commission and omission—were at the moment quite detached in his mind from the delayed effect they had produced. For now he had no capacity to think about others, consumed as he was by concern for himself alone. Up until now he had made his way in a spirit of sheer forbearance. The time had now come for him to forge a new, active approach to life. Any kind of approach that could be glibly stated or passively absorbed simply would not do. It would have to be a way of life that would shore up the core of his being.

As he walked along he kept muttering over and over to himself the word "religion." But with each repetition the word no sooner rang out than it died away, without any reverberation. This "religion" was an ephemeral word: It left no more trace than would smoke cupped in his hands once he had spread them open.

By association with religion Sōsuke was reminded of an episode long ago that had to do with *zazen*.[76] When he was in Kyoto, a classmate of his used to go to Shōkokuji[77] to sit in meditation. At the time he had laughed at such frivolity—so out of touch with the times, he thought to himself. That this classmate's everyday conduct did not appear to differ much from Sōsuke's struck him as further proof of the absurdity of such pursuits.

Now, all these years later, it came to him that his classmate may well have had a reason not to begrudge the time spent on these sessions that was quite different from any of the frivolous ones Sōsuke had imputed to him. On realizing how callow his judgment had been, he felt deeply ashamed. If it were possible, through the power of *zazen*, to attain to the state that had long been described in terms such as "at peace with oneself," "confirmed in one's destiny," and the like, then he would gladly take off from work for ten or twenty days and give it a try. When it came to matters such as this, however, he was a rank layman and quite unable to form any clear idea of what achieving such a state might entail.

After finally wending his way home and seeing the familiar figures of Oyone and Koroku, within the usual setting of sitting room and parlor, the lamp here, the chest of drawers there, Sōsuke became acutely aware of how thoroughly strange his experience over the past four or five hours had been. A small earthenware pot rested on the brazier, steam rising from the narrow gap below the lid. Beside the brazier his regular cushion had been set out in his customary place, and in front of it his tray table.

Staring at the circular base of his rice bowl, which had been carefully turned upside down in his absence, and at the chopsticks he had grown so thoroughly used to holding in his hand every day and evening for several years, Sōsuke said, "I won't be eating anything now."

"Oh well, it did seem late," Oyone said, obviously disappointed. "I supposed that you'd probably stopped by somewhere for supper. 'But then, if he hasn't eaten, that would be too bad,' I said to myself." Using a tea towel, she picked up the pot by the handles and placed it on the tea-kettle pad, then called Kiyo to remove the tray table.

It was Sōsuke's habit, whenever something caused him to make a detour after work and delay his return, to give Oyone a general account of what had happened as soon as he was settled back home. For her part, until she had heard his account Oyone felt somehow remiss herself. This evening, however, for the first time Sōsuke balked at explanations; he said nothing about getting off the streetcar at Kanda or about stopping by the restaurant and forcing drinks down his throat. Left in the dark, Oyone appeared keen to ply her husband with questions about this and that in her typically innocent way.

"Look, there really isn't any particular reason why I'm late . . . I just felt like having some beef at one of those restaurants down there."

"And after that, for the sake of your digestion, you walked all the way home?"

"Well, yes."

Visibly amused, Oyone laughed out loud. Sōsuke, though, was in pain.

"While I was out, did Sakai send someone down to ask me over?"

"No. Why?"

"Well, the night before last he said something about having me up for dinner."

"Again?" said Oyone, looking somewhat exasperated.

Letting the matter drop, Sōsuke went to bed. But his mind buzzed with commotion. From time to time he opened his eyes and saw the lamp flickering dimly, as always, in the alcove. Oyone appeared to be sleeping soundly. Up until recently he had been the one who slept well while Oyone was often troubled by insomnia. Eyes shut, he felt his frayed nerves further assailed by the clear, inescapable sound of the pendulum clock in the next room. At first it struck many times in a row. Later it struck only once. For a while the low, muffled tone reverberated down to his earlobes, tapering off like a comet's tail. The next time it struck twice, with an inexpressibly mournful gong. In the interval the only decision Sōsuke was able to come to was that he must find a way to attain serenity in life. When the clock struck three, he barely heard it at all. Of the chimes at four, five, and six o'clock he was quite oblivious. He was aware only that the world was swelling, the heavens expanding and contracting in great waves. Like a ball dangling from a string, the earth swung to and fro in space, describing a wide arc. It was a dream orchestrated by demons. He awoke from it with a start, at seven in the morning. There was Oyone bending over him with her usual smile. The bright sun had immediately banished that dark world to some faraway place.

18

WITH A letter of introduction tucked in his breast pocket, Sōsuke passed through the temple compound's main gate. He had obtained the letter from the friend of a colleague at work. This colleague would slip a copy of *Maxims for Life*[78] out of his jacket pocket and read it on the streetcar on his way to and from the office. One day when the two of them were sitting next to each other on the streetcar, Sōsuke, who was ignorant of this text, never having had the slightest interest in such writings, had asked his colleague what he was reading. The man held up the small, yellow-bound volume for Sōsuke to see and replied that it was an odd sort of book. Sōsuke inquired further about the content. Apparently struggling to find the right words for a succinct reply, the colleague had remarked, in a curiously offhand fashion, that it had something to do with the study of Zen. This remark had stuck in Sōsuke's mind.

Several days prior to securing the letter of introduction, he had gone over to his colleague's desk and asked him out of the blue, "Do you practice Zen yourself?"

Alarmed at the look of severe tension on Sōsuke's face, the man responded evasively, "No, no, I just read a few things in my spare time." Sōsuke's jaw sagged with disappointment as he went back to his desk.

That very day on the way home, he again found himself on the streetcar with this same colleague. It appeared to have dawned on the man after his glimpse of Sōsuke's earlier disappointment that this morning's question had been prompted by something deeper than a wish to make conversation, and so he renewed the topic in a more sympathetic manner. He confessed that he had never actually practiced Zen himself, but said that if Sōsuke wanted to learn more, he fortunately had an acquaintance who frequently visited a temple in Kamakura, and he could arrange an introduction. Right there on the streetcar, Sōsuke wrote the acquaintance's name and address in his date book. The very next day, carrying a note from his colleague, he made a considerable detour in order to call on the man, who was kind enough to compose on the spot the letter of introduction now lodged in his pocket.

At the office Sōsuke had asked for ten days' sick leave. Even with Oyone he maintained the pretext of actually being sick.

"My nerves are really out of sorts," he told her. "I've asked for a week or so off from work so I can go somewhere and take it easy."

Having recently come to suspect that all was not well with her husband, she had quietly but constantly worried about him, and was privately very pleased by this uncharacteristic show of decisiveness by the normally temporizing Sōsuke. Still, she was astonished by the abruptness of it all.

"And where do you plan to go and 'take it easy'?" she asked, wide-eyed with curiosity.

"Actually, I was thinking of Kamakura," he replied placidly.

There being virtually no common ground between her retiring husband and the fashionable seaside town, this sudden juxtaposition of the two struck Oyone as comical, and she could not suppress a smile. "My, aren't you the dandy," she said. "I think you should take me with you."

Sōsuke felt too beleaguered to appreciate his beloved wife's humor.

"I'm not going anywhere fancy," he said defensively. "There's a Zen temple where they'll put me up—I'll stay there for a week or ten days just taking it easy and giving my mind some rest. I don't know if this will make me feel better or not, but they say if you spend some time in a place with fresh air it can work wonders for your nerves."

"That's absolutely true. And you should definitely go. What I said before—I was only joking."

Oyone felt a pang of genuine remorse for having made light of her husband's plan. The next day, bearing his letter of introduction to the temple, he boarded the train at Shimbashi terminal.

On the envelope was written "To the Reverend Brother Gidō."

When Sōsuke's colleague's friend finished writing his letter, he had made a point of explaining: "Until recently this monk served as an acolyte to the head priest, but I've heard that he has restored a retreat in one of the sub-temples and is now living in it. I'm not quite sure which one—when you arrive you can ask somebody—but I think that it's called the Issōan."

Sōsuke had thanked him, put the letter away, and then, before taking his leave, listened to the man's explanations of such unfamiliar terms as "acolyte" and "retreat."

Just inside the main gate, tall cryptomeria trees rose up on both sides, cutting off the open sky and abruptly casting the path into deep shadow. The moment Sōsuke entered into this gloomy atmosphere he was struck by the temple's apartness from the everyday world. Standing there, at the entrance to the temple precincts, he felt a chill come on, not unlike that which announces the onset of a cold.

Initially he proceeded straight along the path. Buildings were scattered about on either side and ahead of him, some looking like assembly halls, others like cloisters. He saw no one coming or going. All was scoured by age and desolate in the extreme. Stopping in his tracks in the middle of the deserted path, Sōsuke cast his gaze in all directions, wondering which way to turn and whom to ask about the whereabouts of the Reverend Gidō.

The temple compound stood in a clearing that extended some one or two hundred yards up the mountain slope and was hemmed in from behind by a wall of dark green trees. The terrain to either side of him likewise sloped sharply upward into steep hillsides, such that there was little level ground. Sōsuke spotted two or three auxiliary temples, each with its own impressive gate, rising up from stone stairways and perched at higher elevations. A good many more similar edifices, each enclosed by a hedge, were scattered across the more level portion of the compound. Sōsuke approached some of the buildings and noted, hanging from the tiled roof of each gate, a plaque bearing the name of the particular cloister or retreat.

As he walked along, stopping to read a couple of the old plaques, now stripped of their gilding, it occurred to him that it would be more efficient to concentrate on looking for the Issōan, and then, if Gidō were not to be found at this retreat, to move farther into the compound and make inquiries. Retracing his steps, he inspected each and every building and eventually came upon the Issōan at the top of a long flight of stone steps that led up to the right from just inside the main gate. The retreat, its exposed front blessed with full sun and its rear tucked cozily into a hollow at the base of the mountain that rose up behind it, appeared well designed to keep winter at bay. Entering the retreat, Sōsuke stepped into the earthen-floored kitchen, approached the shoji leading into the building proper, and called out two or three times to announce himself. No one appeared to greet him. He stood there for a while peering at the shoji, trying to make out some sign of life inside. He waited still longer, but to no avail; there was no sign, no hint of anyone. Baffled, he went back through the kitchen and out toward the gate. Just then he saw a monk climbing the stone steps, his freshly shaven head aglow with a bluish hue. His pale face was that of a young man, perhaps twenty-five years old at most. Sōsuke waited at one of the open portals of the gate and asked, "Does the Reverend Gidō reside here?"

"I am Gidō," the young monk replied.

Sōsuke was pleasantly surprised. He removed the letter of introduction from his breast pocket and handed it to Gidō, who read it on the spot. After folding the letter up and putting it back in the envelope, he welcomed Sōsuke warmly and without further ado led him into the retreat. They deposited their clogs on the kitchen floor, opened the shoji, and stepped inside. There was a large square hearth sunk into the floor. Gidō removed the coarse, thin surplice he wore over his gray robe and hung it on a hook.

"You must be very cold," he said, raking up pieces of hot charcoal from under a thick layer of ashes.

The monk spoke with an ease that was rare in someone so young. The quick smile that punctuated his well-modulated utterances struck Sōsuke as distinctly feminine. Wondering what fateful episode had led the man to shave his head, Sōsuke felt a twinge of pity for this monk who comported himself with such gentility.

"It seems very quiet today," he said. "Has everyone gone out?"

"No, it's like this every day. I am the only one here. I don't even bother locking up when I have an errand to do. I just leave the place open. I was out on an errand just now. That's why I was regrettably not here to greet you when you arrived. Do please forgive me."

Thus did Gidō offer his guest formal apology for his absence. Sōsuke realized that his arrival could only add to the considerable burden on this monk, charged as he was with looking after the large retreat all by himself, and his face betrayed some embarrassment.

"Oh, but you mustn't be concerned on my account. It is all for the sake of the Way."

Gidō's words conveyed much grace. He went on to explain that at present, besides Sōsuke, there was one other layman in residence whom he had been looking after. Evidently, it had already been two years since the man first arrived at the compound. When, two or three days later, Sōsuke first encountered this layman, he turned out to be an easygoing fellow with the face of a playful arhat. At that moment he was dangling a bunch of daikon, which he presented as a special treat. He had Gidō boil and serve the large white radishes at a meal for the three of them. This layman had such a monkish look about him that, as Gidō laughingly related, he managed to insinuate himself from time to time into the clerical ranks at the ceremonial feasts offered up in the town by the faithful.

Sōsuke heard a good deal about other laymen who came to the temple for training. Among them was a seller of writing brushes and ink who, for three or four weeks at a stretch, would make his rounds on foot with a load of goods strapped on his back; when he had sold nearly all of his stock, he would return to the temple and resume his life of meditation. In due time, when the wherewithal to buy his meals was depleted, he would pack up a new supply of brushes and ink and go back on the road. These two facets of his life alternated with a certain mathematical inevitability, apparently without his ever finding it monotonous.

When Sōsuke compared the everyday lives of these people, seemingly so free from petty obsessions, with the present state of his own inner life, he was dismayed by the glaring disparity. Were they able to practice *zazen* in this way because they led such carefree lives? Or had their minds become carefree as a result of their practice? He could not tell which.

"It's certainly not a matter of being carefree," said Gidō. "If it could all be done as a kind of pleasant pastime, we wouldn't have all these devoted monks suffering through twenty or thirty years of wandering from one temple to another."

The monk proceeded to offer him some basic guidelines for *zazen*, followed by a general description of what it was like to rack one's brains morning, noon, and night over a koan posed by the Master, all of which was deeply unsettling for Sōsuke. Gidō then stood up and said, "Let me show you to your room."

The monk led Sōsuke away from the hearth, across the sanctuary, and then along the veranda a few steps to some shoji that gave onto a six-mat room. At that moment Sōsuke felt for the first time how far from home his solitary journey had taken him. Yet his mind was still more agitated than it had been in the city, perhaps because of the very tranquillity of his surroundings.

After what seemed like an hour or more, he heard Gidō's footsteps reverberating again from the direction of the sanctuary.

Kneeling deferentially at the threshold to Sōsuke's room, the monk said, "I believe the Master is prepared to conduct an interview. Let us go now, if it's convenient for you."

Leaving the retreat vacant, they set out together. Proceeding up the main path a hundred yards or so farther into the compound, they came to a lotus pond on the left-hand side. With nothing growing at this chilly season the stagnant pond was murky and devoid of anything that might have conveyed a sense of purity and enlightenment. But across the pond, a glimpse of a pavilion, ringed by a railed veranda and backing into a rocky cliff, presented a rustic scene of the sort depicted in paintings of the literati style.

"That is where the Master resides," said Gidō, pointing up at the edifice, which appeared to be of relatively recent construction. Skirting the shore of the pond, the two of them climbed five or six flights of stone steps. At the top, with the structure's massive roof towering directly above them, they made a sharp turn to the left. As they approached the entranceway, Gidō excused himself and made his way to the rear entrance. Presently he reemerged through the front door, ushered Sōsuke in, and led him to the room where the Master was seated.

The Master looked to be around fifty years old. His ruddy face had a healthy glow. His smooth skin and taut muscles, without a wrinkle or sag, suggested a bronze statue and made a deep impression on Sōsuke. Only his lips, which were exceedingly thick, revealed a hint of slackness. But this small detail was obliterated by a vibrancy that flashed from the Master's eyes, the likes of which were not to be seen in any ordinary man. Encountering this look for the first time was for Sōsuke to glimpse a naked blade glinting in the dark.

"Well, it's really all the same, wherever you begin," said the Master as he turned toward Sōsuke. "'Your original face prior to your parents' birth—what is that?'[79] Why not mull this one over a bit?"

Sōsuke was not at all sure about the "prior to your parents' birth" part, but concluded that, at any rate, the idea was to try to grasp the essence of what, finally, this thing called the self is. He was too ignorant of Zen even to ask for further clarification. Along with Gidō he withdrew in silence and returned to the Issōan.

Over dinner Gidō explained to Sōsuke that consultations with the Master took place once in the morning and once in the evening, and that at noon there were sessions known as the Exposition of Principles.[80]

"It may turn out that you won't have reached a proper understanding by the consultation time tonight," he added solicitously, "and so perhaps I could take you to the Master tomorrow morning, or even in the evening." Gidō then advised him that, since it would initially be difficult to remain sitting in meditation for a long stretch, it might be a good idea for Sōsuke to light an incense stick in his room, as a sort of timer to signal moments in which to take little breaks between his meditation sessions.

Incense in hand, Sōsuke passed by the sanctuary, entered the six-mat room assigned to him, and sat down on the tatami in something of a daze. He was overwhelmed by a sense of how utterly removed these so-called koan were from the reality of his present life. "Suppose I was suffering at this moment from a stomachache," he put it to himself. "So I go off somewhere in search of relief from the pain and I'm presented with, of all things, a difficult mathematical problem, and I'm told, 'Oh, here's something for you to mull over.'" The situation he faced now was no different from this. Mull it over? All right, he could certainly do that, but to do it before his stomachache had let up was asking entirely too much.

Nevertheless, he'd taken a leave of absence and come all this way. And even if only out of consideration for the man who had written him the introduction, and now for this Gidō who was doing so much to look after him, he could not act rashly. He resolved to summon up whatever courage he could in his present state and face the koan head on. Sōsuke himself had absolutely no idea where such efforts might lead him or what effects they might produce deep within. Beguiled by the enticing word "satori," he had embarked with uncharacteristic boldness on a most challenging venture. Even now he clung to the tenuous hope that his venture would succeed, that he just might be delivered from the weakness, instability, and anxiety that assailed him.

He propped up a slender incense stick in the cold ashes inside the brazier and set it to smoldering, then sat on a cushion and folded his legs, as he had been taught, into a half-lotus position. After the sun set, his room, which had not seemed particularly cold by day, suddenly turned frigid. The temperature fell low enough to send shivers up and down his spine as he sat.

Sōsuke pondered. But it was all so nebulous that he did not know whether to begin by considering the general approach to take in his thoughts or proceed directly to the concrete problem assigned to him. He began to wonder if he had not come on a wild-goose chase. He felt like someone who, having set out to lend a hand to a friend whose house has burned down, instead of consulting a map and traveling by the most direct route, gets caught up in some totally irrelevant diversion.

All manner of things drifted through his head. Some of them were clearly visible in his mind's eye; others, amorphous, passed by like so many clouds. It was impossible to determine whence they had arisen or where they were headed. Some would fade away only to be replaced by others. This process repeated itself endlessly. The traffic coursing through the space inside his head was boundless, incalculable, inexhaustible; no command from Sōsuke could possibly put a stop to it, or even momentarily arrest it. The harder he tried to shut it off, the more copiously it poured forth.

In a panic he recalled his everyday self and looked around the room, which was lit only by a dim lamp. The incense stick propped up amid the ashes had burned down only halfway. He became aware as never before how terrifyingly time prolonged itself.

Once again Sōsuke pondered. Immediately, objects of all shapes and colors began to pass through his mind. They moved along like an army of ants, which, having passed by, was promptly followed by another. Only Sōsuke's body remained still. His conscious being was forever on the move: an excruciating, unremitting, almost unbearable motion.

His body, rigid from the meditating, began to ache, starting with his kneecaps. His spine, which he had kept ramrod straight, began to bend forward. Sōsuke took hold of his left foot with both hands at the instep and lowered it. He got to his feet and stood aimlessly in the middle of the room. He felt the urge to open the shoji, step outside, and simply walk about in front of the gate. The night was still. It did not seem possible that anyone else was around, asleep or awake. He lost the courage to go outside. Yet the prospect of just sitting there and being tormented by demonic phantasms was terrifying.

Resolutely he propped up another stick of incense and proceeded to repeat more or less the same sequence he had gone through before. In the end he reasoned that if the main point of this was to ponder the koan in question, it could not make much difference whether he pondered while sitting or while lying down. Taking the soiled futon from where it lay folded in the corner he spread it out and burrowed under the covers. At this, worn out from his exertions, without a moment's pause in which to ponder anything, he fell into a deep sleep.

When Sōsuke awoke the shoji near his pillow were already light, hinting at the sun's bright rays that would soon be cast on the white paper. Naturally, at this mountain temple where by day everything was left deserted and unlocked, he had not heard any sound of the retreat being shuttered the night before. The very instant he became aware that he was not lying in his dark room at the base of the embankment below Sakai, he got up and went out to the veranda, where a giant cactus growing up to the eaves loomed before his eyes. From there he retraced yesterday's steps, past the altar in the sanctuary and back to the anteroom with the sunken hearth, where he had first entered upon his arrival. Gidō's surplice was hanging from the same hook as before. The monk himself was in the kitchen, crouched down in front of a stove in which he was building a fire.

"Good morning," Gidō greeted Sōsuke cordially as soon as he saw him. "I was going to invite you along earlier, but you seemed to be sleeping so peacefully that I took the liberty of going without you."

Sōsuke learned that the young monk had completed the first *za-zen* session by dawn and then returned to the retreat in order to prepare rice.

On closer inspection he noted that Gidō, as he fed kindling into the fire with his left hand, was holding up with his right a book with black binding to which he redirected his attention at every available moment. The book bore the imposing title of *Hekiganroku*.[81] Sōsuke wondered to himself if, instead of getting trapped in his own random thoughts, as he had the previous night, and overtaxing his mind, it would not be a lot simpler to borrow some standard texts used in this denomination and get the gist of it by reading. But when he suggested this course to Gidō, the monk rejected it out of hand.

"Reading over texts is no good at all," he said. "In fact, to be honest, there is no greater obstacle to the true spiritual practice than reading. Even people like me who have gotten to a certain stage—we may read *Hekiganroku*, but as soon as the text goes beyond our level, we don't have a clue. And once you get into the habit of jumping to conclusions on the basis of something you've read, it becomes a real stumbling block when you sit down to meditate. You start imagining realms beyond the one where you belong, you eagerly wait for enlightenment, and just when you should be forging ahead with all deliberate speed, you run up against a wall. Reading things is a snare and a delusion—you really should just forget about it. If you feel you absolutely must read something, then I'd suggest a work like *Incentives to Breaking Zen Barriers*.[82] It will inspire you to greater commitment. Still, it's something you read only for the sake of reinforcing that commitment, without imagining it has anything to do with the Way."

Sōsuke did not really understand what Gidō meant. But he was aware that standing here in front of this youthful monk with the bluish bald head made him feel like a dim-witted child. His once overweening pride had long ago been ground down into nothing— ever since the events in Kyoto. From that time on, until this day, he had accepted his ordinary lot and lived accordingly. All thought of achieving worldly distinction had been expunged from his heart. He stood before Gidō simply as the person he was. He was forced to recognize, moreover, that in this place he was no better than an infant, far weaker, still more witless, than in his ordinary life. This came as a revelation to him, one that eradicated the last vestige of his self-respect.

While Gidō extinguished the flames in the stove and waited for the rice to finish steaming, Sōsuke stepped out from the kitchen into the temple grounds and washed his face at the well. Directly ahead of him rose a tree-covered hill. At its base a small plot had been leveled for a vegetable garden. His face still dripping in the cold wind, Sōsuke made a detour to inspect the garden. Once there, he saw that a large grotto had been carved out of the bottom of the cliff. He stood there for a spell peering into its dark recesses. When he returned to the anteroom a warm fire burned in the sunken hearth and the iron kettle was on the boil.

"I prepare things on my own, you see, and breakfast tends to be late, but I'll bring you your tray in a moment," Gidō said apologetically. "And being way out here, I'm afraid it's pretty poor fare we can offer you. I'll try to make up for it by treating you to a proper bath—tomorrow, hopefully." Sōsuke gratefully took a seat on the other side of the hearth.

Presently, breakfast over, he found himself back in his room with his attention riveted on the singular question that confronted him: What was his original face before his parents were born? Since the problem defied rational thought, however, it was impossible to begin by extrapolating from what had been given; no matter how hard he pondered he could not get a handle on it. He soon tired of pondering. It occurred to him that he really should write to Oyone to let her know he had arrived safely. With palpable delight at this ordinary task to be done, he hastened to remove a roll of writing paper and an envelope from his satchel and began a letter to his wife. As he proceeded to write about one thing and another—how quiet it was here, to start with; how much warmer it was than in Tokyo, perhaps because the sea was so close; how fresh the air was and how nice the monk, the one he had the introduction to; how unappetizing the food; how rudimentary the bedding—he had before he knew it used up more than three feet of writing paper, at which point he lay down his brush. But of his struggle with the koan, of the pain in his knee joints from sitting in meditation, of his sense that his nervous disorder was only being made worse by all this pondering, he wrote not a single word. On the pretext of having to get the letter stamped and posted, he immediately left the temple compound. After wandering around the town some, haunted all the while by thoughts of his original face, of Oyone, and of Yasui, he returned to the retreat.

At the noon meal Sōsuke met the lay practitioner Gidō had spoken of. Every time the man passed his bowl to Gidō for more rice, he refrained from making any deferential requests and instead simply pressed his palms together in thanks and expressed his other needs with hand gestures. To receive one's meal silently in this fashion, it was explained to Sōsuke, was in keeping with the dharma. The guiding principle here, apparently, was that to speak or make any more noise than necessary would interfere with the process of meditation. Witnessing such exemplary seriousness, he felt rather ashamed of the way he had been conducting himself since the previous evening.

After lunch, the three of them sat talking awhile. The lay practitioner told him that once, while engaged in meditation, he had fallen asleep unawares; the moment he regained consciousness he had rejoiced at his sudden enlightenment, only to realize on opening his eyes that, alas, he was his same old self. Sōsuke had to laugh. He was relieved to see that one could also approach Zen with light-heartedness of this sort. But as the three of them parted to return to their respective quarters, Gidō simply urged him on: "I'll let you know when it's time for dinner. Please apply yourself to your meditation until then."

At this, Sōsuke felt a renewed sense of obligation. He returned to his room with a queasy feeling, as though he had swallowed a hard dumpling that now lodged undigested in his stomach. Again he lit a stick of incense and began his sitting. Distracted by the nagging thought that he had to equip himself with some sort of response to the koan, no matter what it was, he eventually lost all concentration and ended up simply wishing for Gidō's early approach from the sanctuary to summon him to dinner.

Amidst all his anguish and fatigue the sun sank low in the sky. As the light reflected on the shoji slowly faded away, the air inside the temple turned chilly, from the floor upward. From early in the day no breeze had stirred in the branches. Sōsuke went out on the veranda and gazed up at the high eaves. Beyond the long row of black tiles, their front edges perfectly aligned, he watched the tranquil sky enfold the pale blue light within its depths, until both sky and light faded away.

19

"PLEASE watch your step." Gidō led the way down the stone steps in the dark, with Sōsuke following a pace behind. Here, away from city lights, the footing by night was uncertain, and the monk carried a lantern to illuminate their one-hundred-yard passage through the compound. They reached level ground at the bottom of the stone steps, where tall trees thrust out their branches from left and right, blocking out the sky and seemingly close to grazing the tops of their heads. Dark as it was, the green of the leaves was still visible. It all but soaked into the weave of their clothing and sent a chill through Sōsuke. The lantern itself seemed to emit the same color of light and, in contrast to the mighty tree trunks that it managed to bring into outline, looked exceedingly small. The faint light it cast on the ground was no more than a few feet in diameter, a small pale gray disk bobbing along with them in the dark.

Past the lotus pond, they turned left and climbed up toward the Master's residence; there the going became rough for Sōsuke, who was making the trek for the first time at night. At a couple of points the front edge of his clogs struck against the exposed surface of buried rocks. Gidō knew of a shortcut that, before reaching the pond, led straight to the residence, but the ground there was still rougher, and on Sōsuke's account he had chosen the more roundabout path.

Once inside the entryway Sōsuke detected a good many clogs strewn about the dimly lit earthen floor. Bending low, he proceeded to thread his way through the footwear and stepped up into an eight-mat room. Alongside one wall six or seven men had seated themselves deferentially at right angles to the corridor leading from the entrance to the Master's quarters. A few of them had the gleaming bald heads and black robes of monks. Most of the others were dressed as laymen, though in formal *hakama*. Not a word was spoken. Sōsuke stole a glance at the men only to be arrested by the severity of their faces. Their mouths were hard-set, their eyebrows closely knit in concentration. They appeared heedless of whoever was next to them and oblivious to anyone entering from the outside, no matter what manner of man he might be. With the bearing of living statues they sat utterly still in this room to which no fire brought warmth. To Sōsuke's mind these figures added an even greater austerity to the already frigid atmosphere of the mountain temple.

After a while the sound of footsteps filtered into the desolate silence. At first a faint echo, the tread of feet on the wooden floor grew steadily heavier as they approached the area where Sōsuke was sitting. Then, all of a sudden, the figure of a solitary monk loomed in the doorway leading to the corridor. The monk moved past Sōsuke and, without a word, exited the temple into the darkness. Just then a small bell tinkled from somewhere deep inside.

At this, one of the laymen wearing a *hakama* of sturdy Kokura cloth stood up from the row of men seated solemnly with Sōsuke alongside the wall; he crossed over silently to the corner of the room and sat down again, directly in front of the open doorway to the corridor. Next to where he sat, within a wooden frame about two feet tall and one foot wide, there hung a gong-shaped metal object that was, however, too thick and heavy to be an ordinary gong. It glowed a midnight blue in the scant light. The man in the *hakama* picked up the wooden hammer from a stand and struck the center of the gong-shaped bell twice. Then he stood up, passed through the doorway, and advanced down the corridor. Now, in a reverse of the previous pattern, as the footsteps moved deeper into the temple's interior they grew fainter and fainter, and ultimately died out. Still seated firmly in his place, Sōsuke was inwardly shaken. He tried to picture to himself what momentous things might be happening to the man in the *hakama* right now. But throughout the temple confines, complete silence prevailed. Among those who sat in a row with him no one moved even a single facial muscle. Only Sōsuke's mind stirred, with imaginings of what might be occurring in the temple's inner recesses. All of a sudden the handbell rang again in his ears, accompanied by the sound of approaching footsteps along the length of the corridor. The man in the *hakama* appeared in the doorway, crossed over to the entrance without a word, and vanished into the frosty air. The man whose turn was next stood up, struck the gong-like bell as before, and marched off down the corridor. Hands planted formally on his knees, Sōsuke waited his turn.

Shortly after the second-to-last man in line before Sōsuke had gone to take his turn, a loud shout resounded from down the corridor. Because of the distance, the sound was not so loud as to strike Sōsuke's eardrums with any great force, but it reverberated enough to bespeak a mighty upwelling of righteous indignation. The tone was so distinctive that there was only one person from whose throat it could have issued. As the very last man in front of him stood up, Sōsuke, gripped by the consciousness that his turn was next, lost most of what little composure he had left.

He had prepared a kind of response to the koan he had been assigned the other day, the best he could come up with. Still, it was exceedingly tentative and flimsy: nothing more, really, than an empty phrase concocted for the occasion, composed of words meant to convey a semblance of assurance where there was in fact none, in order to demonstrate some capacity for discernment when he found himself in the Master's presence. Not that it occurred to Sōsuke in his wildest dreams that he would be so lucky as to escape his predicament with this pathetic, rehearsed response. Nor, of course, did he have any intention of putting something over on the Master. By this point he had become a good deal more earnest than when he first arrived. He felt quite mortified to find himself in the false position of appearing before the Master simply out of a sense of obligation, with nothing to offer but vague words that had popped into his head, as if serving someone a sketch of a rice cake instead of the real thing.

As Sōsuke struck the gong-bell in the same fashion as those before him, he was fully aware that he was not qualified to wield the same hammer as the others. He was filled with self-loathing at how he had simply gone ahead and mimicked them like a tame monkey.

Dreading in his heart his own weak self, he went through the doorway and started down the corridor. It was a long way. The rooms to his right were dark; after turning two corners, he saw lamplight coming through a shoji at the very end of the corridor. He advanced to the threshold of that room and came to a halt.

The protocol for such audiences was a triple kowtow to the Master before entering. The supplicant bowed as he would in the course of an ordinary greeting, with his forehead nearly touching the tatami, while at the same time placing his hands, palms up, at either side of the head—and then raising them a bit, up to ear level, as if reverently presenting an offering. Kneeling at the threshold, Sōsuke performed the first kowtow according to the prescribed form. From within the room came the command: "Once will suffice." Dispensing with further protocol, he entered the room.

The only light came from a single dim lamp, so dim that one could not have read even relatively large characters by it. Sōsuke could not recall having ever seen anyone function at night with the sole aid of such paltry lamplight. Although naturally stronger than moonlight and not of such a bluish hue, it did have the lunar quality of looking as though it might vanish behind murky clouds at any moment.

In this indistinct light, four or five feet straight ahead of him, Sōsuke could make out the figure of the one whom Gidō called "Rōshi."[83] His face had the same cast-in-metal impassiveness and color as before. His entire body was wrapped in vestments the color of tannin or persimmon or tea. His hands and feet were out of view. He appeared in the flesh only from the neck up. His countenance, which possessed an utmost solemnity and tension that conveyed imperviousness to time, was riveting. And his head was perfectly smooth-shaven.

Seated in front of this face, the spiritless Sōsuke exhausted what he had to say in a single phrase.

The response was immediate: "You'll have to come up with something sharper than that!" the voice boomed. "Anybody with even a bit of learning could blurt out what you just did."

Sōsuke withdrew from the room like a dog from a house in mourning.[84] From behind him reverberated a vehement ringing of the handbell.

20

FROM THE other side of the shoji a voice called out: "Nonaka-san, Nonaka-san." Still half asleep, Sōsuke was sure he had answered this call; yet before uttering a response, he had in fact lost consciousness and fallen back into a deep sleep.

Later, when he awakened for a second time, he leapt to his feet in consternation. Going out on the veranda, he found Gidō clad in a gray robe, with the sleeves tied up to free his hands, energetically wiping down the floor. As he squeezed out a wet rag in his benumbed red hands, the monk said good morning to Sōsuke with his customary gentle smile. Again this morning, the first meditation long since over, he had been busy attending to his chores around the retreat. Reflecting on his indolence, staying in bed even after attempts had been made to wake him, Sōsuke felt utterly ashamed.

"I'm sorry I overslept again today," he said, as he sidled away from the kitchen door toward the well. He drew some cold water and washed his face as quickly as possible. His beard had grown out enough for his cheeks to feel prickly to the touch, but he had no room in his head to bother about such things. He brooded ceaselessly over the contrast between Gidō and himself.

The day Sōsuke had received his letter of introduction he had been told not only what a decent man this monk was but also how advanced he was in the practice of the discipline. And yet Gidō had turned out to be as self-deprecating as some unlettered lackey. To see him like this, sleeves rolled up, scrubbing away, surely no one could imagine that he was the master of his own retreat. He looked more like some sort of temple bookkeeper or at most a postulant.

Prior to this dwarfish young man's ordination, while still a lay practitioner, he had evidently sat in the lotus position for seven days straight without moving a muscle. The pain in his legs was such that he could hardly stand up; eventually he could only make his way to the privy by leaning against the wall. At the time he was working as a sculptor. On the day he was enlightened into the True Nature,[85] he had dashed up the hill behind the temple in an excess of joy and shouted out in a loud voice, "Everything on earth, plants and trees, mountains and streams, without exception they enter into Buddhahood."[86] It was only then that he shaved his head.

Gidō told Sōsuke that it had been two years since he had been entrusted with this retreat but that he had yet to sleep in a proper bed with his legs stretched out comfortably. Even in winter, he said, he slept sitting up, fully clothed, leaning back against the wall. When he was still an acolyte, he added, he had even had to wash the Master's loincloth. In those days, whenever he managed to steal some time from his chores to sit and meditate, someone would sneak up behind him and play some nasty trick, and people were always saying vicious things about him, such that during his novitiate he often found himself reproaching the ill fate that had landed him in a monastery.

"It's only lately that things have gotten a little easier," he said. "But I still have a long road ahead. Sticking to the practice is a tough business. If there were an easier way to go about it, I wouldn't be so foolish as to keep slaving away like this for ten or twenty years."

Gidō's account left Sōsuke in a demoralized fog. Besides the frustration over his own lack of commitment and spiritual resources, there was the obvious but unanswerable question of why, if success in this arena required so much time, he had come to the temple in the first place.

"You mustn't think that what you're doing is a waste of time," said Gidō. "Ten minutes of meditation yields ten minutes worth of achievement, of course, and twenty minutes of meditation doubles the merit you accrue. And once you've made the initial breakthrough, you can continue your practice without having to keep coming back here all the time."

Sōsuke felt duty-bound to return to his room and meditate again.

He was greatly relieved when, while he was thus engaged, Gidō came to announce that it was time for the Exposition of Principles. There was nothing but misery in sitting here rooted to the spot, agonizing over a conundrum that was as hard to grasp as a bald man was by the hair. Rather than this, any sort of active, physical exertion was preferable, no matter how much energy it might require. He simply wanted to move about.

The location for this event was about as far from the retreat as was the Master's temple, some one hundred yards away. They reached it by once again passing the lotus pond, then, instead of turning left, following the path straight ahead to where the building stood, its majestic roof tiles soaring among the pines high above. Gidō carried a black-bound book in his breast pocket. Sōsuke naturally had nothing to bring. He had not even known until he came here that "exposition of principles" meant something like what in school would be called a lecture.

The high-ceilinged hall was surprisingly spacious and very cold. The faded tatami blended with the ancient columns in a manner redolent of the distant past. The people seated here all appeared appropriately subdued. Although everyone had sat down wherever he pleased, in no particular order, there was no noisy conversation and not so much as a chuckle to be heard. The monks, wearing vestments of navy-blue hemp, sat in two rows facing one another, arrayed on either side of the barrel-backed officiant's chair that was placed front and center. The chair was painted vermilion.

Presently the Master appeared. Sōsuke, who had been staring down at the tatami, had no idea when he had come in or what path he had taken to cross the room. He only noticed the Master when his impressive figure was already perched, utterly serene, in the officiant's chair. He then watched as a young monk standing close to the chair undid a purple silk wrapping and produced a book, which he proceeded to set down reverently on a table. Sōsuke followed the monk with his eyes as he made a deep bow and retreated.

At this point all of the monks in the congregation pressed their palms together and began to recite from *The Testamentary Admonitions of Musō Kokushi*.[87] The lay congregants who were scattered about near Sōsuke all joined in at the same droning pitch. The recitation had a melody-like rhythm to it and sounded somewhere in between sutra-chanting and normal speech: "Among my students there are three grades: those who can be said to have gone the limit, who have cast off all bonds with others and have single-mindedly examined themselves—they are known as the highest grade; those whose practice of the discipline is not pure, who indulge in eclectic studies—they are termed the middle grade..." The passage was not very long. Sōsuke had at first not known who Musō Kokushi was, but he learned from Gidō that Musō and Daitō Kokushi[88] were the patriarchs responsible for the resurgence of the Zen school. Gidō went on to tell him about how Daitō had been lame in one leg and unable through the years to sit in the lotus position. He was so exasperated by this failing that, shortly before he died, determined to force his body to do his bidding, he wrenched his leg until it broke and finally assumed the full lotus position, spilling enough blood in the process to soak his robe.

Presently the recitation proper began. Gidō removed the black-bound volume from his pocket, opened it, and slid it over the tatami to where Sōsuke could see the first page. The work was entitled *On the Inextinguishable Light of Our School*.[89] Gidō had explained to Sōsuke when he first inquired about the book that it was an especially suitable work for him. According to the monk, it had been compiled by a disciple of the Abbot Hakuin,[90] an eminent priest named Tōrei or the like, with the purpose of presenting in proper order the various stages of Zen training, from the most basic to the most advanced, along with the psychological states that accompanied each stage.

Sōsuke's visit to the temple had come in the middle of this recitation series, and he found it difficult to absorb everything that was said. The speaker was articulate, however, and Sōsuke, as he listened in passive silence, found many things of interest. Clearly with the aim of spurring on earnest novices, the recitations regularly included anecdotes about Zen adepts who had struggled mightily along the way, thus lending some spice to these expositions.

Today's session had proceeded in this fashion up to a certain point when, changing his tone abruptly, the Master launched into a denunciation of those who manifested a lack of sincere commitment in the course of his individual interviews.

"Just recently," he said, "there was someone who actually complained in my presence that even now, in this place, he was under the sway of illusion."

Sōsuke shuddered in spite of himself. For he in fact was the one who had made such a complaint during his interview.

An hour later, as they returned together side by side, Gidō said to him, "The Master often interrupts the recitations with cutting remarks about the novices' indiscretions during their interviews."

Sōsuke said nothing in reply.

21

THERE amid the temple grounds the days came and went, one after another. During that time two longish letters arrived from Oyone. Naturally neither of them contained anything untoward or unsettling. Deeply as he cared for his wife, Sōsuke procrastinated over answering her letters. Were he to decide to leave the temple without having resolved the riddle that had been posed to him, his journey would have been for naught, and he would be unable to look Gidō in the face. Every waking moment the indescribable burden of these worries weighed on him relentlessly. The more times he saw the sun rise and set over the temple compound, the more anxious he became, like a quarry closely pursued from behind. Yet he could think of no solution to the riddle other than the one he had first proposed. And no matter how thoroughly he considered other possibilities, he remained convinced that this was the only one. Still, he had arrived at this conclusion through simple ratiocination, and it hardly seemed fitting. When he tried to erase this one sure solution from the picture in order to see what compelling alternative might present itself, however, nothing whatsoever came to mind.

He pondered alone in his room. When he grew tired, he went out through the kitchen to the vegetable garden. Then he entered the grotto that had been carved out of the base of the cliff and stood there absolutely motionless. Gidō had told him that he mustn't allow himself to be distracted. Rather, what he must do was to focus his attention ever more closely until his concentration was rigidly fixed and he himself became like a rod of iron. The more Sōsuke listened to exhortations like this, the more impossible it seemed to him that he would ever reach such a state.

"Your problem," Gidō said another time, "is that your head is already full of the notion of getting it over and done with, and that won't work." His words paralyzed Sōsuke even further. Suddenly he began to think again about the return of Yasui. If he were to become a constant visitor at the Sakais' and not go back to Manchuria for some time, the most prudent course for the couple would be to vacate their rented house immediately and move somewhere else. He could not help asking himself if, instead of idling his time away here, it wouldn't make more sense for him to return to Tokyo right away and prepare to relocate if necessary. If it were to happen that, while he was steeling himself here at the temple, news of Yasui's return reached Oyone, this would, he realized, greatly aggravate matters.

With the air of a man at the end of his tether, he sought out Gidō and said, "It doesn't seem remotely possible that enlightenment will come to someone like me." This declaration was made two or three days before Sōsuke in fact went home.

"No, that's not true," the monk replied without a moment's hesitation. "Anyone with true conviction can be enlightened. You should try approaching it with the same rigid fixation as those drum-beating Nichirenites.[91] When you have been totally permeated by the koan, from the crown of your skull to the tips of your toes, a new cosmos will manifest itself in a flash before your eyes."

With a deep sadness Sōsuke acknowledged to himself that neither his circumstances in life nor his temperament would permit him to act with such blind ferocity—never in his entire life, let alone in the few days that remained to him at the temple. It had been his firm intention to excise from his life the net of complications that had enmeshed him of late, but this wandering off to a mountain temple had turned out to be nothing but a fool's errand.

This was the conclusion he came to privately, but it was not in him to reveal this to Gidō. His heart was too full of admiration for this young Zen monk: for his courage and passion, his dedication and kindness.

"There's a saying: 'The Way is near yet we must seek it from afar,' and it's true," said Gidō ruefully. "It's right in front of our nose and yet we just can't see it."

Sōsuke withdrew to his room and set up more sticks of incense.

Regrettably this state of things prevailed until it was time for him to leave the temple. No new life opened up for him. On the day of his departure, Sōsuke, freely and without reserve, gave up any lingering hope of realizing his goal.

"You have been a great help to me through all of this," he said to Gidō as he bade him farewell. "It's really too bad, but things could not have turned out any other way. I doubt I'll have a chance to see you anytime soon. I wish you all the best, then."

"I've been hardly any help at all!" Gidō said, his tone most consoling. "Everything just rough and ready, you know. You must have been very uncomfortable. I assure you, though, even the amount of meditating you've managed to do this time makes a difference. And your having resolved to come here was a worthy accomplishment in itself."

Nevertheless, Sōsuke keenly felt that he had merely wasted a lot of time. The monk's efforts to put the best construction possible on it only served as a further reminder of his own weakness and, though saying nothing, he felt deeply ashamed.

"The time it takes to reach enlightenment depends on the individual's temperament," said Gidō. "Whether you get there quickly or get there slowly has no bearing on the quality of the experience. There are those who break through with no trouble at all only to be blocked after that from developing further; and there are others who take a long time getting through the initial steps but, once they do, experience lasting joy. You absolutely must not give up hope. The main thing is to stay passionately committed. Look at someone like the late Abbot Kōsen.[92] He was a Confucian scholar and already middle-aged when he began to practice Zen. After he'd spent three whole years as a monk without getting past the first precept, he said,

'It is because my sins are heavy that I have not been enlightened,' and went so far as to bow down humbly to the outhouse every day. But see what a wise man he turned out to be. This is one of various encouraging examples I could mention."

It was apparent that the telling of such anecdotes was Gidō's way of trying to fortify Sōsuke against renouncing all further pursuit of this path as soon as he was back in Tokyo. He heard the monk out respectfully, but inwardly felt that this great opportunity had already more or less slipped away from him. He had come here expecting the gate to be opened for him. But when he knocked, the gatekeeper, wherever he stood behind the high portals, had not so much as showed his face. Only a disembodied voice could be heard: "It does no good to knock. Open the gate for yourself and enter."

But how, he wondered, could he unbar the gate from the outside? Mentally he devised a scheme involving various measures and steps. But when it came to it he found himself unable to summon the strength to put his scheme into effect. He was standing in the very same place he had stood before even beginning to ponder the problem. As before, he found himself stranded, without resources or recourse, in front of the closed portals. He had been living from day to day in accordance with his own capacity for reason. Now to his chagrin he could see that this capacity had become a curse. At one extreme, he had come to envy the obstinate single-mindedness of simpletons for whom the possibility of discriminating among several options did not arise. At the other end of the spectrum, he viewed with awe the advanced spiritual self-discipline of those lay believers, both men and women, who abandoned conventional wisdom and did away with the distractions of analytical thought. It appeared to Sōsuke that from the moment of his birth it was his fate to remain standing indefinitely outside the gate. This was an indisputable fact. Yet if it were true that, no matter what, he was never meant to pass through this gate, there was something quite absurd about his having approached it in the first place. He looked back. He saw that he lacked the courage to retrace his steps. He looked ahead. The way was forever blocked by firmly closed portals. He was someone destined neither to pass through the gate nor to be satisfied with never having passed through it. He was one of those unfortunate souls fated to stand in the gate's shadow, frozen in his tracks, until the day was done.

Just before his departure, Sōsuke, accompanied by Gidō, paid a brief visit to the Master to take his leave. The Master took them out onto the railed veranda of a room overlooking the lotus pond. Gidō went to the connecting room and returned with tea.

"It will still be cold in Tokyo," the Master said. "When people leave after they've started to get the hang of it, they find that things go easier for them back home. But . . . well, it's too bad."

After politely thanking the Master for these parting words, Sōsuke exited the temple's main gate, the one by which he had entered ten days earlier. The dense growth of cryptomeria, still locked in winter's embrace, bore down on its tiles and towered darkly behind him.

22

REINSTALLED within the four walls of his house, Sōsuke cut a pitiful figure, even in his own eyes. For the past ten days he had simply doused his hair with cold water every morning and not so much as passed a comb through it. His face, of course, remained unshaven. Thanks to Gidō's kindness, he'd had properly hulled rice to eat at every meal, but the side dishes had been limited to boiled greens, boiled daikon, and the like. His face had taken on a distinct pallor and was markedly more emaciated than before his departure.

At the temple he had become accustomed to endless pondering, and indeed felt something like a hen brooding her eggs. His thoughts no longer flowed in their normal, spontaneous fashion. There was, however, one subject to which his thoughts would quickly revert, that of the Sakai household. He was not so much concerned with Sakai as with his brother—the "adventurer," as Sakai had memorably branded him—and with Yasui, now this brother's friend, news of whom had caused him so much agitation before his departure. But Sōsuke lacked the courage to march up to his landlord's house and take up the matter with him directly. He was even more loath to rely on Oyone in order to inform himself indirectly. During his retreat at the temple not a day had gone by without his praying that no word of Yasui's presence would reach her.

Seated in the parlor of the house that had been his home for several years now, he said, "Maybe it's just me, but it seems that train trips, even short ones, can be wearing...Did anything come up while I was away?" The expression on his face bore witness to the fact that even a short train trip was indeed too much for him.

For once Oyone was unable to produce the smile that she otherwise unfailingly showed her husband. At the same time, she could hardly tell him the honest truth—it would be cruel—that at this moment, just back from a place where he'd gone for the sake of his health, he actually looked worse than before.

"Well, even when the purpose is a rest cure, train trips will take it out of you," she said, aiming for a brisk, light tone. "So when you're finally home again you feel the fatigue. But just look at you, you've gone and let yourself go like some old codger! For goodness' sake, go straight to the bathhouse and get a shave and haircut." To drive her point home, she took a small mirror from the desk drawer as she spoke and held it up in front of him.

Listening to Oyone, Sōsuke felt as though a fresh breeze were blowing away the air of the Issōan. Now that he had left the temple behind and was home at last, he was once again his normal self.

"Has there been any message from Sakai-san?" he asked.

"No, nothing."

"Not even a word about Koroku?"

"No."

Koroku himself was not there, having gone to the library. Soap and towel in hand, Sōsuke went out.

When he showed up at the office the next day everyone inquired about his health. There were also a few comments to the effect that he looked a bit thinner, which to Sōsuke sounded like sarcasm slipping unwittingly out of his colleagues' mouths. The one who toted around *Maxims for Life* asked only if things had gone well. Even this simple question caused Sōsuke a few pangs of conscience.

That evening he was grilled again about the details of his sojourn, with Oyone and Koroku taking turns.

"It sounds like quite a happy-go-lucky place," said Oyone. "Imagine just popping out any time without having someone keep an eye on things."

"How much do they charge per day?" asked Koroku. "It might be fun to take a gun there and do some hunting."

It was Oyone's turn again: "Still, it must get boring, if the place is as deserted as all that. I mean, you can't just sleep all day, can you."

"And the food there doesn't sound very healthy—they really ought to serve something more nutritious," offered Koroku.

As he lay in bed that night, Sōsuke resolved that tomorrow he would go up to the Sakais' and in a roundabout fashion find out what he could about Yasui. If it turned out that the latter was still in Tokyo and could be expected to continue his visits up there, they would simply have to move somewhere far away.

The next day the sun rose to cast an unremarkable light on Sōsuke's head; then set without incident in the west. At nightfall, he announced that he was off to Sakai's for a while and went out the gate. He made his way up the slope without the benefit of moonlight. By the time he crunched over the gravel path, lit by gas lamps, and opened the back gate, he had built up his courage, telling himself how unlikely it was that he would run into Yasui right here, this very night. All the same, he went around to the kitchen door and did not neglect to ask the maid if her master had any guests with him at the moment.

"How nice to see you! It's still cold, isn't it?" said Sakai, in his usual high spirits. Sōsuke then noticed that there was a full complement of children in attendance, one of whom Sakai now called out to repeatedly as they continued their game of rock-paper-scissors. His opponent was a little girl who looked to be about five years old; on top of her head, perched like a butterfly, was a large red bow. She clenched her small hand in a fist that she thrust out with a competitive ferocity equal to her father's. The look of total determination on her face, along with the contrast between her tiny fist and her father's comparatively monstrous one, was a source of general merriment among the onlookers. Mrs. Sakai sat watching from the other side of the brazier.

"Look, everyone! For once Yukiko's beat him," she said, smiling with delight and revealing her spotless teeth. In front of the seated children was spread out an extensive array of glass marbles—white, red, and deep blue.

"Yes, I've been vanquished at last," said Sakai, sliding off his cushion as he turned to face Sōsuke. "Well, shall we retreat to the grotto once again?" he said, getting to his feet.

The Mongolian sword wrapped in silk brocade hung as before from the alcove pillar in the study. In a vase stood stalks of golden rape flowers that could not possibly have grown wild anywhere nearby. Fixing his gaze midway up the pillar, on the gorgeous colors of the brocade, Sōsuke said, "I see the sword is still here," then scrutinized his host's reaction with an intensity that he managed not to betray in his expression.

"Yes, I know it's absurdly exotic. And what am I to do with that damn brother of mine who thinks he can soften up his elders with such frivolous gifts?"

"And how is the young prince lately?," Sōsuke asked in an offhand manner.

"Oh, he finally went back a few days ago. Heaven knows, Mongolia is the perfect place for him. In fact, when I told him, 'A barbarian like you doesn't belong in Tokyo—you should get the hell out,' he replied, 'That's just what I've been thinking,' and off he went. No doubt about it, a character like him belongs out there beyond the Great Wall! Let him go digging around for diamonds in the sands of the Gobi desert—that's just fine with me."

"And his companion?"

"You mean Yasui? Naturally he went back too. When people get to that stage, they just can't seem to settle down anywhere. And to think that, at least from what I heard, he was once at Kyoto University. I wonder how he could have changed so much."

Sweat dripped from Sōsuke's armpits. He had no desire at all to hear in what specific ways Yasui had changed or precisely how unsettled he might be. At the moment Sōsuke was busy congratulating himself on his miraculously good fortune in not ever having blurted out to Sakai that he had been at the same university. And yet the fact remained, Sakai had made one attempt to introduce him to both his brother and the brother's companion on the night they had been invited for dinner. While it now appeared that by getting out of this invitation he had at least spared himself the humiliation of any such direct encounter, it was not inconceivable that in the course of conversation that night the host had made some passing mention of his name. Here Sōsuke felt a new appreciation for the comfort that an alias must afford those with a shady past. He was itching to ask Sakai if he had happened to mention his name in Yasui's presence, but in the end he could not bring himself to go that far.

The maid appeared bearing a very peculiar dessert that rose up from a large flat plate. It consisted of a tinted gelatin mold the size of a standard tofu cake, sprinkled with sugar, with what looked like two goldfish suspended inside. The confection had been sliced and then carefully slid onto the plate in a manner that preserved the molded shape intact. Still brooding, Sōsuke glanced at it and simply noted to himself that the dish was a bit unusual.

"Do have a slice," said Sakai while serving himself first, as usual. "Actually, we were invited to a silver anniversary celebration yesterday and they gave this to us to take home, so it should be full of good fortune. Why not eat a little piece and share a mouthful of happiness?"

In the name of partaking of the anniversary couple's felicity, Sakai gobbled one slice after another of the treacly confection, his cheeks bulging out each time. Here was a man in vigorous health, enviably full of gusto, for whom it mattered not whether he guzzled tea or liquor, whether he devoured rice or sweets.

"Not that there's really all that much to celebrate about a couple's living together for twenty or thirty years—long enough to have turned into a mass of wrinkles. But everything's relative, isn't it?" Sakai proceeded to steer the conversation in an odd direction. "Some time ago, I had an astonishing experience when I was passing by Shimizudani Park."[93] He had the man-about-town's practiced way of delivering his monologues, in which he coaxed his interlocutors along without exasperating them.

He explained that at the beginning of spring large numbers of frogs evidently hatch in a narrow, ditch-like creek that flows from Shimizudani to Benkei Bridge. As the frogs grow, noisily contending for space, hundreds, or rather thousands of lusty matings ensue there in the ditch. The mating pairs fill the ditch from Shimizudani all the way to the bridge, crowded side by side virtually on top of one another and blissfully absorbed in their acts of love, only to have passersby, street urchins and grown men alike, throw stones at the couples with deliberate cruelty, causing immeasurable slaughter.

"A veritable 'mountain of corpses,'[94] as the saying goes. Since the casualties are all couples, it's really quite pathetic. So just think of what goes on among all the creatures living in this world, when so many tragedies can be witnessed while strolling a mere two or three hundred yards through the park. If we consider a spectacle like that, don't you think we can both feel fortunate? We certainly don't have to worry that we'll get stoned to death because somebody resents our having a spouse. And if, beyond that, we and our wives together make it safely to the twenty- or thirty-year mark, then we really should count that as a blessing. So you see, now, you really must take a slice of this for good luck." So saying, the host ostentatiously seized a piece of the sugary mold with a pair of chopsticks and thrust it in front of Sōsuke, who received it with a wan smile.

Sakai went on indefatigably in the same fairly glib vein, and Sōsuke, in spite of himself, was to a point caught up in this current of chatter. Inwardly, though, he shared none of his landlord's tendency to take such a sanguine view of things. When, having finally excused himself and left the house, Sōsuke looked up once more at the moonless sky, he discovered in the profound darkness an ineffable combination of pathos and horror.

He had come to Sakai's tonight with one purpose in mind: to be relieved of his burden, no matter what the consequences. To achieve this aim he had overcome all feelings of shame and distaste and goaded his magnanimous, bluff host into a one-sided chat. And yet he had failed to learn what he wished in anything like the detail he had been determined to. Nor had he mustered the courage to reveal to Sakai even a small corner of his flawed nature—indeed, he had not even gone so far as to admit to himself the need to do so.

Sōsuke, then, had emerged unharmed from beneath the storm

cloud that had hovered so close overhead. But he was left with an ill-defined presentiment that from now on he would have to experience anxious times like this over and over, to some degree or another. It was destiny's role to enforce this repetition; it was Sōsuke's lot to dodge the consequences.

23

THE NEW month brought a relaxation of winter's grip. And by the end of that month the rumored retrenchment in connection with the increase in civil servants' salaries was by and large completed, at both the section and department levels. During this period the names of fired colleagues, some familiar, some not, would reach Sōsuke's ears, and more than once he said to Oyone upon arriving home, "I could be next."

To Oyone this sounded like a joke, but also as though her husband actually meant what he said. Every so often she could not help construing such words as an ill omen of the hitherto veiled future. Even in the mind of Sōsuke, the one who had spoken them, their meaning kept shifting like fleeting clouds.

When the new month arrived and with it the announcement that the unsettling retrenchment at the office was more or less over, Sōsuke, reflecting on his having been spared by fate, considered the result to be on the whole a predictable outcome. Then again, he saw it as quite a stroke of luck. Getting up from the table he looked down at Oyone.

"Well, it seems as if I've escaped," he said, a dour expression on his face.

His deadpan manner, neither happy nor sad, stuck Oyone as hilarious.

A few days later, Sōsuke received a five-yen raise. "It's less than the twenty-five percent they originally proposed," he said, "but that's understandable, what with a lot of men out of a job and others whose salaries have been frozen." He displayed considerable satisfaction at the raise, as though he had made off with a reward greater than he deserved. Naturally Oyone did not have it in her to find cause for complaint.

The next day Sōsuke found himself gazing down at a whole fish set before him, head and all, its tail curving over the edge of the plate. He inhaled the aroma of cooked rice, ruddy with the adzuki beans that had been mixed in. Oyone had made sure to invite Koroku, to this end dispatching Kiyo to the Sakais' house, where he was now in residence.

"Well, well, what a treat," said Koroku as he entered through the kitchen.

By now, plum blossoms could be seen here and there. Those that had been the first to open were already faded and half scattered. Mist-like rain began to descend. When it cleared, waves of humid air rose from the ground and from the rooftops steaming in the sun, reviving memories of springs past. On balmy days puppies gamboled about the oil-paper umbrellas set out to dry at back doors; heat shimmered off the glistening bull's-eyes painted in their centers.

"Winter's over at last," Oyone said. "Next Saturday you really should go over to your aunt's and settle things for Koroku," she urged. "If you keep putting it off, Yasu-san will end up forgetting, you know."

"Yes, I'll definitely drop by then," said Sōsuke.

Now that the Sakais had generously taken in Koroku, Sōsuke himself had volunteered to his brother that if at all possible, he and Yasunosuke would share in paying all of his additional expenses. Not waiting for Sōsuke to bestir himself, Koroku had broached the matter directly with Yasunosuke. His cousin consented to the plan, provided that Sōsuke went through the motions of making a formal request. And so Koroku achieved the desired outcome on his own initiative.

Thus this couple who were averse to all change found themselves back in calm waters. One Sunday afternoon, in order to wash away a four-day accumulation of grime, Sōsuke paid a rare visit to the bathhouse in the nearby business district. Inside, a fiftyish man with the shaved head of a priest and a man in his thirties with the look of a merchant were chatting, each commenting to the other that it finally felt like spring. The younger man announced that he'd heard his first bush warbler just that morning. The priest replied that he'd heard one two or three days earlier.

"It was the bird's first try, and it really made a mess of things."

"Yes, I know what you mean. They haven't got the hang of it yet."

Back home, Sōsuke repeated this exchange about the bush warbler.

Gazing through the glass shoji at the sparkling sunlight, Oyone's face brightened. "What a sight for sore eyes. Spring at last!"

Sōsuke had stepped out on the veranda and was trimming his fingernails, which had grown quite long.

"True, but then it will be winter again before you know it," he said, head lowered, as he snipped away with the scissors.

NOTES

1   *Kin* is a common way to read the Chinese character that Sōsuke has forgotten, while the "Ō" of "Ōmi" (a place-name), which Oyone offers as a mnemonic, is a rare reading that not a few native speakers of Japanese might forget.

2   Another common reading for a very common character.

3   This is the largest species of bamboo to grow in Japan—sometimes to a height of more than sixty feet. Its name (Chinese: Meng Zong) derives from that of a character in popularized Confucian tales extolling filial piety, who is described as walking barefoot through the late-winter snow in order to detect the early bamboo shoots craved by his aged parents.

4   Sometimes translated as "high school" or "higher school," it was in fact far more exclusive, there being just one in Tokyo, and functioned as a kind of preparatory school for young men bound for university—in this case, Tokyo Imperial University, the nation's most prestigious.

5   A long, pleated trouser-like skirt, usually divided at the inner seam and worn over a kimono from waist to feet; part of a man's traditional formal wear, although also worn by women on some occasions.

6   Polite for "older sister," also used for "sister-in-law"; often spoken as a term of address.

7   In this period, the site of modern office buildings devoted to governmental agencies and large businesses such as banks.

8   In February 1910 a film entitled *The Snows of Siberia*, purportedly based on Tolstoy's *Resurrection* (produced by Pathé), showed at the Fujikan Theater in Asakusa.

9 Short for Bodaidaruma (Sanskrit: Bodhidharma), this refers to the traditional representation of the semilegendary founder of the Ch'an or Zen sect as a cartoonish, roly-poly figure, often made into a papier-mâché doll that when knocked down will always right itself.

10 In this period, in a middle-class household, even when there was a maid to do the serving, the sharing in a meal by the mistress of the house when her husband had been joined by adult males, even relatives, would still be unusual enough to attract notice.

11 Itō Hirobumi (1841–1909), a four-time prime minister and one of the main architects of the Meiji state as well as the resident-general of Korea prior to its outright annexation in 1910, was assassinated on October 26, 1909, in Harbin, Manchuria. His assassin was a member of the Korean independence movement.

12 Horatio Herbert Kitchener (1850–1916), a British commander in the South African War, visited Japan in 1909.

13 At this time there were still only two national (Imperial) universities in Japan: the one in Tokyo, established in 1886; and the one in Kyoto (1897). The campus in Sendai (Tōhoku University) was established in 1907, shortly before the narrative present. In prewar Japan, compulsory education consisted of six years of elementary schooling. A few male students (female students had a separate track) went on to middle school, which lasted five years. Fewer still advanced to secondary (higher) school, of which there were originally only five campuses in the entire country. Nearly all secondary-school graduates entered one of the Imperial universities or a private college.

14 Normally a younger sibling in a situation of this kind would address an older brother with this polite form of address, which corresponds to "Nee-san" when addressing one's older sister; its absence would be noticeable.

15 A small, shrub-size version of a banana tree widely grown in Japan for ornamental purposes.

16 Usually Tsukishima; a string of islands made from landfill in the late 1800s and early 1900s at the mouth of the Sumida River in Tokyo, used primarily for industry.

17 "Yellow Patrinia" (*Patrinia scabiosifolia*), a wild, umbelliferous perennial: one of the "seven autumn grasses" that are prized in painting and poetry as well as in horticulture.

18 Usually Ki'itsu; a pseudonym of Suzuki Motonaga (1796–1858), a student of the celebrated Hōitsu.

19 Sakai Hōitsu (1761–1858), one of the most influential painters of the late Edo period, who took as his point of departure the style of Ogata Kōrin.

20 Ganku (1749–1838), the founder of a branch of the Maruyama-Shijō school characterized by what were then considered idiosyncratic still lifes, which bore traces of recent Chinese influence; Gantai (1782–1865) was his son.

21 The First Higher School (Dai-ichi Kōtōgakkō), the secondary school that Koroku attended, was located in Hongō Ward (now part of Bunkyō Ward), adjacent to the Tokyo University campus.

22 The impression of a custom-made seal is, to this day, the legal equivalent of a signature in Japan and other East Asian countries.

23 Japanese is normally written with a combination of Chinese characters (*kanji*) and a phonetic syllabic script (*kana*). In Sōseki's time a higher ratio of *kanji* was used in most styles of writing, but lines of solid Chinese characters without any *kana* would have stood out as much as, say, a passage of italicized Latin inserted into an English text.

24 The *Analects* of Confucius, traditionally said to date from around 500 BCE. The most widely diffused text dates from the early Han dynasty (202 BCE–8 CE).

25 *Hiyodori*: sometimes loosely rendered as "Persian nightingale."

26 A round, hollow, wooden percussion instrument decorated with a fish pattern, struck during the chanting of Buddhist sutras to mark the rhythm.

27 A wooden frame placed around a container for hot coals (replaced in more recent times by an electric element) and covered with a quilt to provide an area for warming hands and feet. There are both portable and stationary types of *kotatsu* (here the narrator refers to the former).

28 *Hossu*: an implement composed of a short staff and the bundled hair of an animal (typically from the tail), carried by officiants at various Buddhist ceremonies.

29 A sturdy flat-woven silk, often made of thread remnants, used for making everyday kimonos and bedding.

30 *Nattō*: fermented soybeans; along with tofu and a few other staples of the traditional diet, it was widely sold in the neighborhoods of populous towns and cities by itinerant peddlers down to recent decades.

31 Historically the official translation of the Japanese term *tōkanfu*, the English rendering masks the near total degree of control over Korean domestic as well as foreign affairs that this institution exercised between 1905 and 1910, when Korea's nominal status as a protectorate ended with Japan's formal annexation of Korea, after which direct rule was administered by a governor-generalship.

32 Squares of cloth, normally silk or cotton, of varying sizes, used to wrap up items. Ordinarily, two opposite corners go around the item while the other two corners are tied into a single knot at the top for carrying.

33 So-called because it is thought to have originated in the province of Mino (present-day Gifu Prefecture), this especially strong type of traditionally made paper was long preferred for such purposes as official copies of documents, envelopes, and insertion into shoji panels.

34 There were ten rin in a sen and one hundred sen in a yen. The prices quoted correspond to the late 1880s, or about twenty years before the novelistic present.

35 Watanabe Kazan (1793–1841): a pioneering painter with a Westernized style, he was particularly adept at portraiture. As a member of the shogun's advisory board for naval matters, he and several colleagues were punished for expressing unwelcome opinions, and in the end Watanabe committed suicide in jail.

36 Under the Tokugawa some daimyo and so-called bannermen (*hatamoto*: direct vassals of the shogun) were given purely nominal titles, derived from the ancient *ritsu-ryō* hierarchy imported from China, of *kami* or "governor" of this or that province.

37 The present-day city of Shizuoka, it was the administrative seat of Suruga, the Tokugawa family's home province and the place to which family members and their supporters returned after the shogunate's collapse in 1867, prior to the Meiji Restoration in 1868.

38 All of these items are associated with the Girls' Festival (sometimes called the Festival of Dolls), celebrated annually on March 3; the musician dolls represent a selection of the vocal and instrumental accompanists for the Noh drama.

39 The Japanese word for stepmother is *mama-haha* (*mama* is a prefix of ancient origin denoting indirectness, and not cognate with any Indo-European words), hence the girl's confusion.

40 "Granny," though not the more common word, which would be *o-baasan*; also sometimes "nanny," depending on the age of the nurse-maid.

41 The editors of Sōseki's complete works are silent on any basis for the printing process described here that might have existed in reality at the time. Though certain general features mentioned may seem to anticipate electrophotographic (soon renamed xerographic) techniques of reproducing print, the essential theory for this technology does not appear to have been proposed until the 1930s. Yasunosuke's new speculative venture appears then to have been a product of the author's imagination.

42 Tōkyō Jogakkan: a private secondary school for young women from well-to-do families, some with aristocratic lineages, that is no longer in existence.

43 *Kankōba*: originating in 1877 as more permanent successors to the industry and trade exhibitions through which modern manufacturing techniques and their products had been introduced in the early Meiji period, by the turn of the century these covered rows of tightly packed stalls, found throughout Tokyo and other major cities, had become for the most part purveyors of cheap goods and refreshments, attracting as many casual strollers as interested shoppers.

44 *Hayauchikata*: an archaic word for what would appear to be an acute referred pain from angina pectoris.

45   Present-day Yamanashi Prefecture. Although the feudal domains
      (*han*) were replaced by prefectures (*ken*) under control of the central
      government in 1871, the old names of provinces (*kuni*), such as Kai,
      most of which were not coterminus with the *han* and dated back to a
      much earlier period, continued to be used in this period as historical-
      geographical referents, as to a lesser extent they do to this day.

46   *Chaya*: Sakai seems to invoke here a mildly ribald double entendre
      with a variety of teahouse for which the full word is *hikitejaya*: tradi-
      tionally, outposts of brothels in the licensed quarters where assigna-
      tions were arranged.

47   Observance of the lunar New Year was common even after the adop-
      tion of the Western solar calendar at the beginning of the Meiji pe-
      riod. It fell, with considerable variance, around the middle of February.
      According to well-established tradition in China, it also marked the
      beginning of spring, and as such was celebrated in ceremonial dress,
      poetic references, and the like, while of course for the Japanese, as for
      the northern Chinese, Koreans, etc., meteorologically, this springtime
      remained a fiction.

48   In transliterated Japanese, this word was already common in the early
      twentieth century; still in use, it is almost exclusively applied to
      women.

49   *Bodaiji*: the particular Buddhist temple with which a family main-
      tained some historical connection and where cremated remains of de-
      ceased members would sometimes be interred.

50   *Koromogae*: according to the reduced schedule for these semi-ritual
      seasonal changes of clothing that evolved in the Edo period out of
      more elaborate older practices, the day for changing into lighter gar-
      ments suitable for late spring and summer was the first day of the
      fourth month in the lunar calendar, i.e., roughly middle to late May in
      the solar calendar. With encouragement from the newly emergent de-
      partment stores, the observance of this custom, adjusted for the date
      change, continued into the modern era.

51   Fortune-telling based on the Chinese *Book of Changes* (*I Ching*) has
      been a common practice in Japan since early on in the centuries-long

process of Japanese importation and adaptation of Chinese philosophy, literature, and religion.

52   Roughly corresponding to the present-day Fukui Prefecture, north of Kyoto on the coast of the Sea of Japan, it was also not far from the city of Kanazawa, which boasted one of the country's few secondary schools.

53   Located on the flank of Arashiyama at the western edge of Kyoto, the Kannon hall of this temple is called the Daihikaku, rendered literally here as "the Pavilion of Compassion."

54   Sokuhi Nyoitsu (1616–1671) was a celebrated calligrapher and a monk of the Ōbaku branch of Zen (Chan) Buddhism; he founded a temple in the Ogura district of Kyoto and later became the abbot of a temple in Nagasaki.

55   A traditional accommodation dating from the sixteenth century, it is located in the Kawabata quarter of Sakyō-ku (northeast Kyoto), in a scenic area.

56   Of a type known as *mago-uta* (packhorsemen's songs), this ballad, popular in the Edo period (thanks in part to an excerpt included in a puppet play by Chikamatsu), tells of the ill-starred romance between Seki-no-Koman, a prostitute attached to one of the way-station inns, and a packhorseman named Tamba Yosaku. Tsuchiyama, located in present-day Mie Prefecture, was one of two way stations that flanked the Suzuka pass (the other was called Ōsaka).

57   The traditional mode of execution called *haritsuke*, though normally translated as "crucifixion," antedates by centuries any contact with the West. In the earlier recorded incidents (from the eleventh and twelfth centuries) the condemned was either tied to a wooden plank or stretched out on the ground then pierced with nails; in the Edo period, execution took the form of driving lances into the body of the condemned after it was bound to a wooden, cruciform frame.

58   All celebrated places in the vicinity of Shimizu in Shizuoka Prefecture. The last is the home of the original mausoleum for Ieyasu, the first Tokugawa shogun, before the one at Nikko was built.

59   *Edo sunago*: a celebrated, multivolume gazetteer compiled by Kikuoka Tenryō; containing maps and illustrations of locales throughout Edo accompanied by descriptive prose entries, citations of poems, etc., it was first published in 1732, followed by a revised, enlarged edition in 1772.

60   Extracted from the *Cinnamomum camphora* tree (*kusunoki*) native to Japan, in various forms this substance has been used in incense, medicine, and, in this case, as an insect repellent particularly effective against moths.

61   In the original, *risshū*: sometimes misleadingly rendered as "the beginning of autumn," the term refers to a traditional scheme of dividing the year (as defined by a lunar calendar) into twenty-four segments according to calculations of the sun's position in relation to the earth's orbit (originally, of course, thought to be the earth's position in relation to the "sun's orbit"). Transposed to the solar calendar, this date would fall sometime during the first half of August.

62   A day traditionally associated with rainy, windy weather—and the start of the typhoon season; in the solar calendar it falls sometime between the end of August and the second week of September.

63   *Dai-dai*: a type of orange bush imported from the Asian continent grown chiefly for the ornamental value of its leaves and bitter fruit, which ripens late in the year and remains on the branch into the New Year, hence this Japanese reading assigned to the Chinese character for this plant—literally, "from age to age."

64   *Wakazari*: a traditional New Year's decoration consisting of a small wreath made of straw to which is attached a kind of streamer woven from straw and various leaves and fronds, such as those mentioned next in the text.

65   *Yuzuriha* (*Daphniphyllum macropodum*): chosen in part for its shiny oval leaves, possibly also for the literal meaning of its name: "leaves that give way [i.e., to new ones]," apt for the New Year. *Urajiro*: an evergreen fern with leaves whose undersides are a pale grayish-white.

66   *Yarihago*: a game in which a shuttlecock is batted back and forth using small paddles (generally rendered as "battledore"), traditionally played by young girls at New Year's.

67 Located in the Ningyō-chō district of Nihombashi, at the traditional heart of Edo/Tokyo, the shrine is dedicated to various gods and historical figures associated with water (e.g., the boy emperor Antoku and his nurse Nii-no-ama, who drowned while fleeing the conquering Genji forces) and popularly thought to offer protection from such calamities as shipwrecks and death in childbirth.

68 A game played mainly around New Year's that involves the matching of cards bearing the first and second halves (consisting, respectively, of seventeen and fourteen syllables) of a hundred famous classical poems in the thirty-one-syllable *waka* form.

69 Sodehagi is the wife of the eleventh-century rebel Abe Sadatō, as portrayed in the eighteenth-century puppet play (*jōruri*) by Chikamatsu Hanji. A line from this character's star turn in the third act of this play, in which she laments her estrangement from her birth family, is parodied in the puns mentioned in the text.

70 A semilegendary beauty at the court of the Chinese state of Yue (fifth century BCE) who is said to have been sent to debauch the Prince of Wu in order to bring about his downfall. The anecdote about her envious cohorts' unsuccessful emulation of her brow, furrowed from an indisposition but in a manner that only enhanced her beauty, is related in *The Chuang-tzu*.

71 See note 24. Here, a colloquial translation with a chatty commentary; published in 1907 by Hakubunkan, it proved extremely popular.

72 Chinese: Zilu (widely referred to in Western writings as Tzu-lu, the Wade-Giles romanization).

73 *Analects*, chapter 5, number 14: "Whenever Zilu heard something new, until he had succeeded in carrying it out, he was constantly worried lest in the meantime he should learn of something else [to be accomplished]."

74 At times misleadingly rendered as "houseboy" or "student lodger," *shosei* denotes a distinctive arrangement that thrived mainly in the Meiji period whereby, typically, a secondary-school or university student would live in a household (mostly upper-middle class or higher) and, in exchange for room and board, perform a range of duties, from

tutoring the family's young children to errand-running and menial chores.

75 The "theater" here is a *yose*, a small, traditional-style theater with cushions on tatami mats rather than chairs and a small stage with a podium at the front. For much of the Edo period—also, with the exception of the last half of Meiji era, in the modern period, when the number of such theaters eventually shrank to a very few—*yose* had also been used informally to refer to the main forms of entertainment on view: comic monologues (*rakugo*) and intricate tales of adventure, often based on historical events (*kōdan*). The aforementioned exception in modern times, which applies to the performance that the couple attend here, was created by the enormous popularity of *jōruri* ballads, a form rooted in the late seventeenth century but given a new lease on life from the mid-1880s to the 1910s, through the reappearance of young women balladeers (*onna-gidayu*), who for much of the Edo era had been banned from the stage.

76 Literally, sitting in meditation, a practice included in some of the earliest forms of Buddhism introduced into Japan (including the orthodox synthesis of doctrines and practice embraced by the long-dominant Tendai sect), after the thirteenth-century importation from China of the Chan (Japanese: Zen) sect. With its central emphasis on this practice, *zazen* came to be more or less exclusively associated with the several independent branches of this denomination that evolved on Japanese soil.

77 A Zen (Rinzai sect) temple built in the fourteenth century under the auspices of the shogun Ashikaga Yoshimitsu; one of Kyoto's Five Mountains (*Gozan*), each a major center of learning and art during the Ashikaga period (fourteenth–sixteenth centuries) and beyond.

78 *Saikontan* (Chinese: *Caigentan*): a popular collection of pithy exhortations by Hong Yingming (1560–1615) that draws syncretically on Confucian, Taoist, and Buddhist principles.

79 The phrase "prior to the birth of one's father and mother" is used with some frequency in Buddhist discourse, especially of the Chan or Zen schools, to mean something like "time out of mind," and has been loosely glossed in metaphysical terms—at least by secular commenta-

tors—as the realm of absolute truth, beyond all contingencies of time and space.

80 *Teishō*: the constituent characters for this compound mean literally to raise (or "bring up") and to enunciate, suggesting a highly formulaic exposition that, in keeping with the historical aversion in Zen Buddhism to the analytical mode, is perhaps closer to a recitation than what is generally meant by a lecture.

81 A compilation of one hundred koan with commentaries, the original version of which is attributed to the Chan master Xuedou Zhongxian (Japanese: Setchō Juken; 980–1052). Sometimes translated as *The Blue Cliff Record*, here Sōseki actually gives the work a less common title, *Hekiganshū*.

82 *Zenkan sakushin*: compiled as a primer for neophytes in 1600 by the Chinese monk Chu-hung, this work achieved wide currency in Japanese Zen due to the high esteem in which it was held by Hakuin, the influential Zen reformist of the mid-Tokugawa era.

83 Although this word, which has been anglicized in recent decades, has been used throughout this section of the original to refer to the person hitherto called "Master" in the translation, the phrasing here suggests that to address him directly as "Rōshi"—i.e., in the vocative case— presupposes a closer degree of discipleship than the likes of Sōsuke could presume.

84 This is a literal rendering of the original, which is an established locution of classical Chinese origin. (There seems to be no agreement as to which ancient text it first occurred in.)

85 *Kenshō shita*: one of numerous Buddhist terms that tend to be flattened out into "enlightened" in English. It is defined in several nontechnical dictionaries as *daigo*, or a "great satori."

86 The Iwanami edition of *The Gate* attributes this quotation to the *Chūingyō*, a sutra translated early in the transmission of the Indian canon to China, in which the historical Buddha, after his own death, is presented as preaching the merits of the Great Vehicle (Mahayana) to the souls of all sentient beings who have recently died and are waiting to be reborn again. The authenticity of this particular passage, however,

which proclaims that now that the Buddha has attained to enlightenment, all sentient beings can immediately enter into the same state, has been questioned on the grounds that it cannot be found in the oldest extant texts outside Japan, and hence, some have alleged, must be a later Japanese embroidery (or "forgery," as at least one scholar has alleged).

87 A posthumously published work by Musō Soseki (1275–1351), a major figure in the furtherance of the prestige (and secular power) of Rinzai-sect Zen in the Muromachi period. Kokushi (roughly, "preceptor-general") was a government-conferred title given to prominent teacher-monks belonging to the three state-favored denominations in the medieval period (besides Rinzai Zen, the Ritsu and Jōdō sects).

88 Daitō Kokushi (1282–1337): another prominent Rinzai cleric and the founder of the Daitokuji in Kyoto.

89 *Shūmon mujintō ron*: by Tōrei Enji (1721–1792), a disciple of Hakuin and the abbot of the Ryūtakuji. (It has been translated into English as *Discourse on the Inexhaustible Lamp of the Zen School*.)

90 Hakuin Ekaku (1685–1768), the abbot of the Shōinji, who devoted special efforts to encouraging Zen practice among laymen, and through his writings and teachings effected a significant revival of the Rinzai sect in the mid-Edo period.

91 The objects of this back-handed compliment are the faithful of the Nichiren denomination, of which there is one main branch and several offshoots, both in Japan and in various other countries, all of them professing adherence to the distinctive emphases, doctrinal, liturgical, etc., formulated by the medieval Buddhist innovator Nichiren (1222–1282). A central devotional practice is the invocation of the title of the Lotus Sutra, accompanied by the rhythmic beating of a drum or a wooden block. (Nichiren, for his part, had routinely denounced the practices of Zen as the work of *temma*: "archfiends.")

92 Abbot Kōsen (1816–1892): in the Meiji period, as the abbot of the Engakuji (the model for the temple depicted in *The Gate*), he reached out to secondary-school and university students, even as they underwent rigorous education in the now heavily Westernized curricula, and thus contributed to an emergent, specifically intellectual, interest in Zen.

93 Still extant, the park is located about three hundred yards north of Benkei Bridge (which is on the outer palace moat near Akasaka Mitsuke Station), opposite what is now the Hotel New Otani in central Tokyo.

94 *Shishi-ruirui*: no such established locution is to be found in the standard reference works, though the meaning is clear from the individual components.

TITLES IN SERIES

For a complete list of titles, visit www.nyrb.com or write to:
Catalog Requests, NYRB, 435 Hudson Street, New York, NY 10014

* *Also available as an electronic book.*